# THE BROTHERS O'BRIEN
# THE LAW OF VIOLENCE

# THE BROTHERS O'BRIEN
# THE LAW OF VIOLENCE

## WILLIAM W. JOHNSTONE
### with J. A. Johnstone

**PINNACLE BOOKS**
Kensington Publishing Corp.
www.kensingtonbooks.com

PINNACLE BOOKS are published by

Kensington Publishing Corp.
119 West 40th Street
New York, NY 10018

PUBLISHER'S NOTE
Following the death of William W. Johnstone, the Johnstone family is working with a carefully selected writer to organize and complete Mr. Johnstone's outlines and many unfinished manuscripts to create additional novels in all of his series like The Last Gunfighter, Mountain Man, and Eagles, among others. This novel was inspired by Mr. Johnstone's superb storytelling.

All Kensington titles, imprints, and distributed lines are available at special quantity discounts for bulk purchases for sales promotions, premiums, fund-raising, educational, or institutional use. Special book excerpts or customized printings can also be created to fit specific needs. For details, write or phone the office of the Kensington special sales manager: Kensington Publishing Corp., 119 West 40th Street, New York, NY 10018, attn: Special Sales Department; phone 1-800-221-2647.

PINNACLE BOOKS and the Pinnacle logo are Reg. U.S. Pat. & TM Off.
The WWJ steer head logo is a trademark of Kensington Publishing Corp.

ISBN-13: 978-0-7860-3112-2
ISBN-10: 0-7860-3112-3

First printing: May 2013

10 9 8 7 6 5 4 3 2 1

Printed in the United States of America

First electronic edition: May 2013

ISBN-13: 978-0-7860-3113-9
ISBN-10: 0-7860-3113-1

# Chapter One

It was the opinion of Dr. John Henry Holliday that Chopin's Nocturne in C-sharp minor transformed a stinking, shadowed saloon at the ragged edge of nowhere into a place of beauty. The nocturne's clouded, dark atmosphere full of suspense and inner tension suited his mood perfectly. He sat back in his rickety chair, pulled the whiskey bottle closer and, eyes closed, listened.

The saloon gal at the piano had a depth of spirit that pleasantly surprised him. Through the genius of the composer, she seemed to wring from the keys the regret of a life ruined and half finished and the wistful, impossible hope of better days to come.

Blowsy, too blond, too wrinkled, too used up as she was, the woman's playing nonetheless touched Doc's soul and penetrated the carapace of distrust that surrounded him and the disease that had reduced him to a dangerous and terrible corpse.

The nocturne stopped abruptly.

And Doc opened his pale eyes.

A big man dressed like a puncher, a breed Doc detested, had grabbed the woman by the arm and hauled her to her feet. "Enough of that crap." The man was bearded, big in the shoulders and at least twice Doc's weight. "I want a knee-trembler."

"You're hurting me, Kyle," the woman said. "Let go of my arm."

The man called Kyle ignored her statement. "Get over there into the corner and stand against the wall, Rosie, and I'll come over for a little fun."

The woman hesitated, and Kyle said, "Now, or I'll give you the back of my hand."

A couple drovers who'd been sitting with the big man cheered and one of them said, "That's tellin' her, Kyle."

"Excuse me, sir, but I was enjoying the lady's playing." Doc's words dropped into the saloon like green apples dropping into a barrel.

Kyle's shaggy eyes brows crawled lower over his eyes like huge, hairy caterpillars. His mouth was wide, thick-lipped, brutal. He'd drunk too much and was on the prod. "You stay the hell out of this, pops."

Doc was thirty-six that fall, but, gray and skeletal, he could have been eighty. Or ninety. "You may indulge your baser instincts after the lady completes the nocturne. Not a moment before, you understand?"

Kyle pushed the blond woman away from him with such force she slammed into the bar and rattled the bottles on the shelf. "On your feet, pops." His eyes were yellow, shining like new coins. "And do it now."

"Why?" Doc said.

"There ain't no why. I'm just gonna slap you around a bit and teach you some manners."

"I'm a Southern gentleman, born and bred. I need no instruction on manners from the likes of you. And besides, I've imbibed so much whiskey tonight, I doubt very much that I can stand."

"Leave the old man alone, Kyle," the woman said. "He didn't mean nothing."

"You shut your trap, Rosie," Kyle said, grinning as he clenched and unclenched fists as big as Smithfield hams. "And get against the wall like I told you."

"Kyle, I've got a two-hundred dollar mirror behind the bar," the saloon owner said. He was small, neat and worried. "If you bust it, you'll pay for it."

One of the punchers at the table said, "Hell, Lou, don't fret it. Kyle's pa will pay for your damned mirror."

"Like he pays for everything else Kyle does," his companion said. "Ain't that right, Kyle?"

But the big man said nothing. Kyle, a bully who'd found a victim, was intent on Doc and was grinning in anticipation.

"Kyle, is that your name, son?" The voice behind the big man was soft, drawling, the accent from farther north, up Montana way.

"What's it to you?" Kyle said, turning.

The man at the end of the bar had shed his fur coat and revealed the threadbare, former finery of a frontier gambler who looked as though he was trying to outrun a losing streak and fading fast.

"Your name means nothing to me, boy." The gambler was a tall, thin man with calculating green eyes. "But if you'll take my advice, you'll step away from this." He smiled. "I mean, you'll step real fast and not look back."

"When I need advice from you, I'll ask for it," Kyle said. "This old man doesn't have the manners to carry guts to a bear and it's high time I taught him some."

"Your funeral," the man from Montana said, a shrug in his voice.

The gambler's name was Dave Chaney and he'd killed his man in the past. Aware of the ways of gunfighting men, he'd noticed the carpetbag at Doc's feet was open and had drawn his conclusions.

Kyle, a knuckle and skull fighter who'd beaten one man to death and crippled a few others, was not gunfighter savvy. The ways of men who lived by the Colt were foreign to him. That night, in a dismal saloon in a dismal settlement ten miles north of Santa Fe, he should've known better.

He again turned his attention to Doc. "On your feet and take your medicine for manners." He grinned and raised his huge, scarred fists. "We'll call these your manners medicine."

Doc gave Rosie credit for trying again.

The woman got between Kyle and Doc and said, "Let him alone, Kyle. Come on lover, we'll go into a corner and have us some fun."

But the big man roughly pushed the woman aside. "After I've finished with Methuselah here. Then I'll take care of you real good."

Doc sighed deeply. "When you've got your mind on a thing, you're not easily discouraged, are you

Kyle? Well, perhaps this will give you something else to think about."

Doc's long-barreled Colt blasted from under the table.

Later the saloon owner said, "Hell, it looked like Kyle Stuart's left knee exploded. I mean, there was blood and bone all over the place. It was a dreadful sight."

Doc fired only that one shot, but it was indeed devastating.

Kyle Stuart shrieked and went down like a felled redwood as his knee disintegrated.

The two ranch hands ran to the big man as Doc rose to his feet, his smoking revolver hanging loose in his right hand. "Better get him out of here. If he's to save that leg he needs a competent physician in a hurry."

One of the punchers, short, stocky and belligerent, made a move as though he was about to draw, but Dave Chaney stepped to his side. "Don't try it, cowboy. There's been enough gunplay for one night."

The puncher pointed a finger at Doc. "You're a dead man."

Doc smiled and nodded. "Of that, my friend, there is no doubt."

"Go. Get Kyle out of here," Chaney said. "Take him to a doctor if you can find one."

Cocooned in pain, Kyle was curled into a fetal position on the sawdust floor, blood pooled around him. When his punchers lifted the man upright he screamed, and Rosie, sharing the man's agony, echoed that terrible cry with one of her own.

Before he stepped outside, the whimpering Kyle's arm around his neck, the short puncher turned and said to Doc, "Remember the name Colonel James Stuart and remember it good because he'll be coming after you."

"I am," Doc said, "all a-tremble."

"Do I know you, sir?" Doc Holliday asked.

"No. The name is Dave Chaney, from up Montana way and other places."

"You're a gambling man, I'd say, Mr. Chaney."

Chaney nodded. "Hit a losing streak in Fort Worth and I can't seem to shake it."

"Fort Worth is a dung heap."

"I've got no arguments on that score."

"My name is John Henry Holliday, but most folks call me Doc."

"Ah, then you're a physician."

"No, dentist. Or at least I was about a hundred years ago."

Doc idly watched the black swamper mop Kyle's blood and bone off the floor and then motioned to his bottle. "Can I offer you a drink?"

Chaney shook his head. "No, Doc, I have to be moving on. If I bide too long in one place, my bad luck catches up with me, like the dust cloud that follows a stopped stage."

Doc smiled. "An apt metaphor and circumstances I understand. I'm somewhat low on the ready myself, but I can offer you a grubstake."

Chaney shook his head. "Thank you, but no. I'm

headed for Santa Fe where I hope to change my luck, if the cards fall as I hope they will."

"Then good luck to you, sir," Doc said.

Chaney looked uncomfortable. "Doc, a word of advice if I may," he said finally. "Come sunup put as much git as you can between you and the New Mexico Territory."

"You mean between me and Kyle's daddy?"

"Just that."

"It was my intention to head up Colorado way to a place called Glenwood Springs," Doc said. "I was told the waters there do wonders for lungers like me." He smiled. "The springs won't cure me of course, but they'll help me die a little slower. Or so I was reliably informed."

"Sorry to hear that, Doc," Chaney said. "It's a hard thing for a man to have a misery like that."

"Does Santa Fe have any snap?" Doc asked. "Denver is dead and so are most other places where gambling men like you and me are no longer welcome."

"Secondhand information again, Doc, but I hear the tinpans who come into town are high rollers and so are the local ranchers. I believe if a man plays his cards right, there's money to be made in Santa Fe."

"Then that's where I'll go," Doc said. He was breathing hard, his chest whistling.

"Maybe Glenwood Springs is the better option, Doc," Chaney said. "You don't look well."

Doc waved a white, blue-veined hand. "So, I lose a couple weeks off my miserable existence. Glenwood Springs can wait until after Santa Fe. I'll ride out with you at first light."

"Doc, I prefer to ride alone," Chaney said. "If it's all the same to you."

"I don't want to be alone on the trail," Doc said. "What if I have a coughing fit and fall off my horse, huh? I need someone to help me."

"Doc, don't hitch your star to mine. You'd be putting your money on the wrong hoss."

"Sometimes I feel the need to depend on a man, Mr. Chaney," Doc said. "Right now, all I've got is you."

Chaney could've said what he thought, that Doc Holliday was a leech, and a dangerous one at that.

But he didn't.

He nodded. "I'm going to stretch out in the livery stable. I'll see you at dawn."

Doc nodded. "Yes, please go now. I'm about to cough up some lung and it's not a pleasant thing to see."

# Chapter Two

"Luther, since you're the segundo of Dromore I want you in Albuquerque," Shamus O'Brien said. "Remember, you'll be greeting royalty so be on your best behavior."

"Colonel, I won't bend the knee to any belted earl," Ironside said. "Even if he is a friend of old Queen Vic."

"Of course you won't bend the knee, Luther. We stopped bowing and scraping to aristocrats a hundred years ago. I'm not talking about Sir James Lovell, I'm talking about Bonnie Prince Charlie."

Ironside nodded. "Well, that's different."

"Of course it's different. Sir James's letter said Charlie's the finest Aberdeen Angus bull in Britain, bar none. He's won more prizes and sired more calves than any other bull in Queen Vic's Balmoral herds and he'll improve our own stock, depend on it."

"If he survives the winter," Ironside said.

"Charlie will survive. Scottish winters are even worse than our own."

Outside the study window random flakes of snow tossed in a rising wind and the log fire in the grate hissed and sparked as a few found their way down the chimney.

"Take Shawn with you, Luther," Shamus said. "His knowledge of beef breeds like the Hereford and Aberdeen Angus is sadly lacking. In fact, his knowledge of cattle in general is sadly lacking."

"He's good with a gun, though. Real fast on the draw and shoot."

Suddenly Shamus was irritated. "That is hardly relevant, Luther. All you need do is take possession of the bull, say your farewells to Sir James after telling him that Colonel O'Brien of Dromore thanks her majesty for her magnificent gift. Then you bring Bonnie Prince Charlie home."

He laid his whiskey glass on the table beside him. "Guns and fast draws don't come into it, Luther."

"Yeah, and how many times have I heard that afore the shooting started?" Ironside muttered.

"What did you say, Luther?"

"Nothing. I didn't say nothing."

"I should hope not. The times are changing and men of violence like yourself must change with them. Peace is rarely denied to the peaceful, Luther. Remember that."

The door opened and Jacob O'Brien stepped inside, sparing Ironside from further lecturing.

"And talkin' of the peaceful," Ironside said, grinning. "How are you, Jake?"

Jacob's ragged mackinaw was dusted with snow and his scuffed boots were muddy. He hadn't shaved in several days and his untrimmed mustache was ragged. An angry graze above his left eye was red against his weather-beaten skin.

Shamus wanted a report on range conditions, but, always suspicious of his son's doings, he focused on the graze. "What happened to your face?"

Jacob's gloved hand strayed to his forehead. "I rode into a tree. A lightning-struck wild oak to be exact."

"How the hell did you manage that, Jake?" Ironside asked.

"Fell asleep in the saddle is how."

Shamus shook his head. "I can't imagine your brother Samuel doing that, or Patrick. They are both much more careful than you."

"Sam burned his hand on the red hot handle of the fry pan when he was cooking bacon and Pat twisted his ankle trying to get a close-up look at some cougar kittens." Jacob smiled. "It's dangerous out there on the range, Colonel, even for careful folks."

"Where are Samuel and Patrick now?"

"Getting bandaged up and their wounds kissed by Lorena."

Shamus sighed. "Get yourself a drink, Jacob, and then tell me about my cows and my grass."

* * *

Jacob delivered a range report that pleased Shamus greatly and then he said, "Shawn told me you and him are heading to Albuquerque to collect the Aberdeen Angus bull, Luther. I hear that a couple years back the XIT ranch down Texas way started to cross Angus bulls with their longhorns and are getting real good results. More prime beef on the hoof, they say."

"Shawn needs more education on the ways of cattle," Shamus said. "That's why he's going."

Jacob smiled. "My brother isn't much of a hand, but he's real good with the Colt's gun on the draw and shoot."

"Oh dear." Shamus sighed and shook his head, like a man lost in sadness. "You taught my sons very well, didn't you, Luther?"

So heavy with irony was that statement that the colonel's words seemed to clang around the room. But before Ironside could respond, Jacob said, "The Angus is worth five thousand dollars of anybody's money, Pa. Men will kill for a sight less. Having Shawn handy is a good idea."

Shamus poured himself bourbon and held up the glass to the waning afternoon light as though seeking inspiration in its amber glow and captured firelight. "Luther, tomorrow you and Shawn will leave at first light," he said finally. "Bring back Bonnie Prince Charlie and do your best to avoid Jacob's bad men."

Ironside nodded. "As you say, Colonel."

"It was real nice of old Queen Vic to send you the bull, Colonel," Jacob said.

"Well, we've done so much business in the past, I suppose she appreciates my custom." Shamus nodded to himself. "But as you say, Jacob, it was a nice gesture."

"What's next, Pa, a knighthood?" Jacob said, grinning.

"Sure, Victoria can tap her sword on my shoulder," Shamus said. "But only after she pulls her redcoats out of Ireland and her ironclads leave Dublin harbor forever."

"And when will that happen, Colonel?" Ironside asked.

"God only knows, Luther. Probably after you and I are dust. The English will blame the Irish for being what they are for many years to come."

From experience, Jacob realized his father could go on for hours about the chained Irish and he changed the subject quickly. "How do you plan to get the Prince home, Luther? You could ride the rails to Santa Fe and then drive him south."

"That's one way, Jake, but I reckon I'll take him along the Rio Grande to Las Huertas Creek then swing east toward Dromore. I figure eighty miles across country, more or less, is enough to get Shawn used to a cattle drive."

Jacob smiled. "He's going to love that. Bacon and beans and sleeping on rock isn't my brother's idea of a good time."

"Save him from getting soft," Shamus said. "And it will keep him away from the ladies for a few days."

"There will be no ladies on this trip," Ironside said, his unshaven jaw set. "And no bacon and beans, either. Shawn will eat what I eat on the trail, salt pork and pan bread. I'll make a man of that boy yet."

"I think you've done that already, Luther," Jacob said.

Shamus glared at his son but said nothing.

"Damn right I have, Jake," Ironside said, pleased.

# Chapter Three

After a few days, Dave Chaney moved on, but Santa Fe suited Doc Holliday just fine. Even though the high country tortured lungs that tuberculosis had turned to lace, he prospered at the poker tables and through steady, careful play had amassed a fairly large stake.

Some nights, a gray cadaver walking through the riotous red, blue, and yellow of the canopied streets, he enjoyed the smell of spices in the air and the passing parade of miners, cowboys, soldiers, and Mexicans, especially the beautiful, sloe-eyed senoritas who looked boldly at men, aware of their raw desires.

Doc drank only enough whiskey to keep him alive and shunned opium, though he now and then loitered outside the dens where Chinese girls in gowns covered with jade dragons glided back and forth in a haze of the creamy smoke that offered the promise that nothing, not even suffering, was real.

He loitered, but did not go inside.

Nor did Doc avail himself of saloon girls. Long since impotent, from even before the street fight in Tombstone, he led a celibate . . . existence . . . in which women no longer played a part.

At the gaming tables, he laid aside his long-barreled Colt, its bulk too apparent on his thin, almost transparent frame. But he hid an Iver Johnson Arms & Cycle Works stingy gun in a pocket and considered the .38 top-break all the protection he needed.

But one snow-flurried night in early October 1887, Doc Holliday discovered how wrong he was about that.

Tired and ill, he was bucking the tiger at the faro table in the Union Hotel when a tall, bearded man stepped beside his chair. Big in the belly and shoulders, the end of his nose sported a magnificent wart that sprouted coarse black hair.

When Doc glanced up at him, the man said, "You be Doc Holliday?"

"I be. And who might you be, my fine fellow?"

The big man pulled back his vest. Pinned to his cartridge belt, he revealed a star-in-a-circle badge cut from a silver peso. "I'm United States Deputy Marshal Reuben Gill. We need to talk in private on a matter of some urgency."

Doc nodded, his skinny neck poking out of a celluloid shirt collar that looked three sizes too big for him. "I'm always glad to accommodate the law. Damned dealing box is rigged anyway." He leaned forward in his chair and snarled to the startled dealer, "You're a robber."

"On your feet, Doc," Gill said. "I want no trouble here."

"No trouble," Doc said, rising. "But he's still a damned robber."

The marshal led the way to the hotel parlor, empty at the late hour except for two old maids in white lace dresses who alternately knitted and dozed by the fire. A pair of porcelain Pekinese guarded the mantle and scowled at Doc as he entered.

Gill chose a table away from the windows and Doc ordered whiskey, the marshal settling for a glass of buttermilk.

When the drinks were served, Doc said, "What can I do for you, Mr. Gill?" He smiled. "It's been a while since the law ran me out of town."

"I'm not running you out of town, Doc," Gill said. "But I'm advising you to leave for your own good. You can't see it, but right now there's a hangman's noose hanging above your head."

Doc managed to suppress a rattling laugh. "Who's after me, Marshal, Jack Ketch?"

"Worse, Doc, a man by the name of Colonel James Stuart. He owns the biggest spread around these parts and he cuts a wide path." Gill shook his head. "James is a Scotsman and he's wild and right now he wants your head."

"I've heard the gentleman's name mentioned," Doc said. "In a dreary saloon in a pissant settlement north of here."

"From what I've been told, after you shot Stuart's youngest son it wasn't dreary anymore."

"For heaven's sake, I shot a loudmouth in the knee," Doc said. "He didn't give me much choice."

"Yeah, everybody I talked with said it was self-defense and I didn't argue the point. But there is a complication. Kyle Stuart bled to death later that night."

"And now his father wants me dead."

"You catch on quick, Doc," Gill said. "James Stuart wants your head in a California collar."

"Hell, you can't hang a skinny little fellow like me, Marshal. I mean, it just can't be done."

"You'll kick fer a spell, that's for sure." Gill's open face revealed that he wasn't being cruel, just stating a fact. He doubted that Doc weighed ninety pounds.

Doc sat in silence, thinking.

Outside in the street, a brewer's dray creaked past and in one of the saloons a woman yelped, then laughed.

Somebody feeling her up, Doc thought. Aloud he said, "So what am I facing, Marshal?"

"James Stuart has another son as wild as his pa, and he makes Kyle look like a choirboy. The talk in the street is that the old man has covered his bets and declared his intentions. He's imported a fast gun out of Texas, a range detective and sometime bounty hunter by the name of Wolf Hartmann, and if he's the same Hartmann as I'm thinking about, he's a hundred different kinds of hell."

"He is," Doc said, his thin face bleak and haggard. Suddenly he looked old. "I was in Tombstone when Hartmann shot Nigger Harry Wilson on a five-hundred-dollar dodger for murder and rape. Nigger

Harry was fast with the iron himself, but he wasn't a patch on Hartmann."

"Then I've got more bad news. Wolf Hartmann may already be in the city. I haven't seen him my ownself you understand, but the local law claims a man answering his description has been hanging around the saloons." Gill sighed. "Well, Doc, now you know what you face. You've got a hill to climb and waiting won't make it smaller."

"Some advice, maybe?"

"I'm not about to face down Wolf Hartmann, so get on your horse and light a shuck out of Santa Fe. That's what I recommend."

"And go where?"

"Anywhere but here." Gill shook his head. "Hell, Doc, ain't you got friends, folks you've sopped gravy out of the same skillet with?"

Doc Holliday shook his head. "No. Nobody."

"Then you have two choices—fight or flee. Choose the first and I'll see you're buried decent. The second and, well, you have my best wishes."

A cockroach climbed up the wall near Doc's chair and for a while he watched it in silence. One of the old maids had dozed off and her knitting needles and pink yarn had slid from her lap onto the floor.

"There is someone who might give me refuge," Doc said. "His name is Jacob O'Brien and—"

"From down Glorieta Mesa way?" Gill looked surprised.

"I believe that's his location." Doc smiled.

"He's a gunfighter," Gill said. "In fact, the whole

O'Brien clan are gun hands, including their pa. But Jacob is the meanest of them."

"You know him?" Doc asked.

"I know of him. They say Jacob O'Brien has killed a dozen men and he always plays the piano before he guns a man."

"That's not quite true, Marshal. Jacob is good with a gun and he plays the piano, but never before he kills a man."

Gill said, "Well, I guess people say all kind of things."

"I'll be safe with the O'Briens, if I can make it that far."

"It's the only chance you got, Doc, so take it. Even James Stuart will think twice about stacking up against the O'Brien boys."

"Then I'll ride out at first light."

"Take my advice, Doc, ride out now. The place you're looking for is called Dromore. It's a big Southern mansion house in the middle of nowhere."

"But I'll be night riding and I don't know the country from here to the mesa."

"Dromore is less than a score of miles due south." Gill drained his glass of buttermilk. "You can't miss it."

Doc rose to his feet, frail and white as a china doll. "Thanks for the warning, Marshal. And the advice."

Gill stood and took Doc's skeletal white hand in his. "Good luck to you and ride careful."

By nature, Doc Holliday was a mischievous man and ill as he was he couldn't resist taking a poke at a lawman, never numbered among his favorite people.

"Gill, you should see a doctor about getting that growth at the end of your nose removed."

"What growth at the end of my nose?" the marshal asked.

Taken aback, Doc said, "Oh, sorry. I guess I was mistaken. The light in here is bad."

Grinning to himself, Gill rubbed the bristly hairs on his wart with his thumb as he watched Holliday step to the parlor door. "Doc," he called out, "now don't start a war down there at Dromore."

Doc stopped and looked back at the lawman. "Hell, that's the last thing I want to do."

*Yeah, but it will happen*, Gill thought. *As sure as eggs is eggs.*

If James Stuart and Shamus O'Brien butted heads, when it was all over only one of those proud old bulls would be left standing.

# Chapter Four

It had been in Colonel Shamus O'Brien's mind that Christmas at Dromore would be the best and most lavish ever, his family all together for the first time in years, even Jacob the Ishmael.

Doc Holliday threatened to be the specter at the feast.

"I couldn't turn him away, Colonel," Jacob said. "The man's dying on his feet and has nowhere else to turn."

Shamus lowered the heat under his simmering irritation. "No, of course you couldn't turn him away. To do that would be to defy the laws of hospitality and further empty the Irish vessel of its poetry."

"We could shoot him, I guess," Patrick said. "Put him out of his misery and ours." He smiled as he said it and Shamus let it go. Sometimes Patrick could be a scamp.

"I've heard of this James Stuart," Shamus said. "As a colonel of infantry he won the name the Lion of Lynchburg after he held a redoubt on Jubal Early's right flank for an entire day against repeated assaults by three Yankee brigades."

"He sounds like a man to be reckoned with, Pa," Samuel said.

"Colonel Stuart is a Scotsman, a fellow Celt, a hero of the Confederacy and a Southern gentleman. If he comes to Dromore I will receive him with great honor."

"Suppose he comes a-shooting, Colonel?" Jacob asked.

"Then I will do him the honor of returning his fire." Shamus waved a huge, work-hardened hand. "But I am sure it will not come to that."

"He wants to hang Doc for killing his son," Jacob said. "You know he's going to come looking for him."

Shamus didn't hesitate for even the space of a heartbeat. "While Doc Holliday is under the protection of my roof no harm will come to him."

"That lays it out clear enough for anybody to read," Samuel said.

"And what do my words spell out to you?" Shamus asked.

"That Doc Holliday could drag us into a war, Pa."

"Don't build the gate until you've built the corral, Samuel," Shamus said. "I'm sure Colonel Stuart is a reasonable man and we can talk over this situation like gentlemen."

That last dangled in the air and none of the O'Brien sons felt like taking hold of it, so Shamus stepped into the void. "Jacob, observe the laws of hospitality, but keep Doc Holliday away from little

Shamus. It's a harsh and cruel thing to say, but I don't want a consumptive anywhere near my grandson."

Jacob nodded. "I'll make sure your grandson and Doc don't breathe the same air, Pa."

"Jesus, Mary and Joseph, and all the saints in Heaven forgive me for crucifying a man on the cross of his terrible disease, but I want it done, Jacob."

Shamus waited until Jacob nodded, then said, "All right, we've discussed the matter, so now you can show the gentleman in."

"For God's sake, man, when did you last eat?" Shamus said, appalled. "You're skinny as a rail."

"I don't eat." Doc Holliday grinned, showing gray teeth in a pale mouth. "But I do drink."

"Well a glass of whiskey with you, then," Shamus said. "But we'll need to fatten you up. Patrick, will you do the honors for our guest?"

Shamus waited until Doc had a glass of Old Crow in hand, before he said, "My son Jacob says you're in a little trouble, sir."

"Jacob was always a master of understatement, Colonel. I expect a hanging posse to come knocking at your door any minute."

"Then state your intentions, sir. Come now, you're under my protection and you can speak freely."

Southern hospitality demanded politeness, but the sight of Doc repelled Shamus and made him want to turn away. The man was a walking corpse, white face, white hair, the light in his eyes burned out long before until only white ashes remained. He was young, but looked like a man who had survived eighty hard winters.

Shamus did not want Doc Holliday in his home. Not then. Not ever.

The man was talking again. "My intention, Colonel, is to head Colorado way to a place called Glenwood Springs where I'm told its healing waters will restore me to health. I do not believe this, but I must try."

"Then why did you come here?" Shamus already knew the answer to that question, but his dislike of this specter that had once been a man gave him a mean little pain in his belly and sharpened his words.

"I don't want to hang, Colonel," Doc said. "I think that sums it up. I've seen it done and hanging is a hell of a way to kill a man."

"You have a reputation as a gunfighter. You can defend yourself."

"I am a gambler who now and then used a gun. I am not a gunfighter, not like Jake, fast on the draw." Doc smiled. "Nor do I play the piano as well as Jake, but Schubert's waltzes bring me close to his standard, possibly because the composer was stark, raving mad when he wrote them."

"You must play for us sometime, Doc," Patrick said.

"Patrick, I don't think this is the time or place for piano playing," Shamus said. "We have other problems of the greatest moment that demand our attention."

Shamus and Jacob exchanged glances, something

Doc, a perceptive man, noticed. The O'Briens wanted to talk, but not with him in the room.

He rose to his feet and said, "With your permission, Colonel O'Brien, I'd like to retire to my room. These days I tire very easily."

"Of course." Shamus couldn't hide the relief on his face. "A nap will do you good." He managed a smile. "Then be off with you and we'll talk later."

After Doc left, Shamus said, "Samuel, Patrick, leave us. I wish to talk to Jacob alone. But ask Lorena if she'll care to join us. I value her common sense when it comes to family matters."

Patrick grinned. "You mean Sam and I don't have any common sense, Pa?"

Shamus's growing irritation over Doc made him boil over. "Patrick, do as I say and don't be so impertinent, young man."

Patrick looked at Jacob who said nothing. Instead, Patrick frowned and inclined his head in the direction of the door.

When they were alone, Jacob said to his father, "A bit hard on Pat, weren't you, Colonel?"

Shamus poured himself a whiskey then stepped to the window. Without turning he said, "Yes, I was hard on him, and I'm going to be hard on you and hard on myself."

For a few moments the colonel watched the wind-tossed snow and the mist of black cloud that shrouded the top of the mesa. "I want that man out of my house, Jacob. The stench of death hangs on him and he could bring ill fortune to me and mine."

"Colonel, Doc is all used up. Time had passed him by and he's a ghost of the West past. No one wants him. There's not a living soul who's glad when he arrives and sad when he leaves. What can you do with a man like that?"

"You mean we should invite him to stay and ruin the Christmas I plan and so look forward to? Is that your solution to the problem? Jacob, he's not kin. He's not anything. Like you say, he's just a lonely, unwanted and forlorn man, a coughing, diseased ghost who has outlived his time."

The door opened and Lorena stepped inside. She was a slender, pretty woman wearing a gray morning dress, its huge bustle following the dictates of the fashionable belles of Boston and New York.

Jacob rose to his feet. "Good morning, Lorena. You look beautiful this morning."

"Thank you, Jacob." Frowning, she said, "Your cat got into the butter again this morning."

"I'll talk to her," Jacob said.

"Yes, please do." The woman's frown deepened. "And she bit Lucy on the hand when she tried to lift her off the table."

"I'll talk to her about that as well. The cat, I mean."

Shamus harrumphed. "Lorena, we've more important matters to discuss than butter and a half wild calico cat."

"Of course," Lorena said. "But if the kitchen is to be run properly and without danger to the staff, it is a matter of the greatest importance that Jacob control his pet. The animal must be kept out of the kitchen."

"Yes, yes. I'm sure he will in the future." Shamus turned to his youngest son. "Jacob, see to your cat."

"Yes, Colonel. I'll surely do that."

"There, daughter-in-law, you have Jacob's assurance that he'll tame, or at least corral his cat."

Lorena nodded. "That is quite acceptable. Now, Colonel, what did you wish to talk to me about?"

"Doc Holliday."

"I suspected as much." Lorena sat in a chair by the fire and settled her hands on her lap. "He's a poor soul. As near as I can tell, Jacob is his only friend."

"I'm not Doc's friend, Lorena," Jacob said. "He almost got me hung twice, and he's mean enough to pitch his bathwater on a widder woman's kindling and laugh while he's doing it."

"No matter what he is, or was, you're all he's got now, Jacob," Lorena said. "There is no one else."

"Those are high sounding words, Lorena," Shamus said. "But what do you mean by them?"

"I don't know what I mean." Lorena shook her head and a strand of auburn hair fell over her forehead. "Maybe it's too late."

"It was too late for Doc the day he was born," Jacob said.

"It's too late for what?" Shamus grumbled. "Don't speak in riddles you two."

"Too late to save Doc Holliday." Lorena looked into Shamus's eyes. "He'll die soon."

"Before Christmas, I hope," Shamus said, aware and oddly ashamed at how heartless that sounded.

Lorena nodded, her gaze focused on a misty place the men couldn't see. "Yes, before Christmas. He will not live longer than that."

A silence grew in the room, broken only by the solemn tick of the grandfather clock against the wall and the crackling of the log fire.

Then a single gunshot shattered the quiet into a million cold pieces.

# Chapter Five

"What the hell was that?" Luther Ironside said, drawing rein on his horse.

"Sounds like a man in pain," Shawn O'Brien said. "Where?"

"I'd say directly ahead of us."

Both men, bundled into sheepskin coats, listened into the waning afternoon, a thin snow drifting around them.

Then came the sound again, a man's voice. "Oy, oy, oy . . ."

Ironside, always careful, slid the Winchester from the boot under his knee and yelled, "Who's there? Identify yourself and state your intentions. We're a dozen deputy marshals here, and we're well-armed and determined men."

The voice soared into a wail. "Oy, oy, oy."

Ironside and Shawn exchanged puzzled glances, and the older man kneed his mount forward. Shawn, holding his rifle in his gloved hands, followed.

A small, bearded man sat in a clearing in the timber, a shaggy black dog lying beside him, its head on his lap. The man glanced up when the riders entered the clearing, but his face registered no surprise, no fear, no expression at all, a man resigned to his fate.

"Oy, oy, oy," he said again, shaking his head.

Ironside looked around where the man sat. "Where's your gun? Speak up now. This rifle is primed and so is the man holding it."

The man made a W of his arms, his hands upturned. "Am I not a poor peddler who carries all he owns on his back? What do I know of a gun?"

"What brought you to this pass?" Ironside asked. "This is wild country, and dangerous."

"I was robbed," the man said. "Did the bandits not take my mule and my wagon and did they not shoot my dog?" He searched Ironside's eyes as though seeking the answer to a question he hadn't yet asked, then he asked it. "Why did they shoot my dog? What harm did he do?"

Shawn swung out of the saddle and kneeled by the man's side. "Are you hurt?"

The bearded man shook his head.

"Your dog is dead, mister," Shawn said.

"Oy, oy, oy, do I not I know he's dead? He was a good dog and sometimes he brought me a rabbit to eat. He was a dog so wise, I named him Solomon."

"My name is Luther Ironside and this here is Shawn O'Brien," Ironside said from the saddle. "How about you? Do you put your name out to folks?"

"Is not Abraham Grossman my name? Is it not a name for a peddler?"

"You're a Child of the Book, ain't you, Abe?" Ironside asked.

"Yes, I was a poor Jewish peddler and now I'm an even poorer Jewish peddler. And one of the robbers shot my dog." Grossman spat. "*A krenk zol im arayn in di yosles.*"

"What does that mean?"

"It is the language of my forefathers and it means may a disease enter his gums."

"Oh yeah, that will do fer him right quick," Ironside said, his raised eyebrows giving Shawn a *what-the-hell?* look.

"How many robbers were there?" Shawn asked.

"And answer in good ol' American," Ironside said.

"Three. There were three of them, all bandits."

"Describe them," Ironside said. "And be brief."

"Three big men, wearing sheepskin coats like yours, with revolvers strapped around their waists. They wore big hats like yours and one of the bandits"—Grossman traced a line down his left cheek—"had a scar right there."

"When did this happen?" Shawn asked.

"They took my grandfather's watch so I can't tell, but I think maybe an hour ago. Maybe more, maybe less, who can say?"

"What was in the wagon, Abe?" Ironside asked. "Anything valuable?"

"I am not, or was I not, a peddler? All my wares were valuable to the people who bought them. I had scissors, ribbons, needles, thread, pots, pans, medicine, candy sticks, children's shoes at cost, whiskey, coffee, sugar—"

"Yeah, I catch your drift," Ironside said.

"Ah, this one you see before you traveled all over, to farm wives, ranchers' daughters, miners, cowboys, soldiers, whoever would buy my goods. God have mercy on me, because of my wanderings I have properly observed the Sabbath fewer than ten times this past three years."

Grossman looked around him. "And now this. *Oy vey*, I must start all over again, just a poor peddler with boots on his feet, a pack on his back, and nothing but dust in his pockets."

"Here, let me take a look at that dog." Ironside stepped from the saddle and took a creaky knee beside the animal.

"Solomon was a good dog," Grossman said. "He walked into my camp one night and stayed. He didn't bother nobody but the rabbits."

Ironside took off his hat then put his face against the dog's muzzle. "He ain't dead yet. He's shot through and through, but he's still breathing."

"Can you save him, Luther?" Shawn looked down at the dog.

"I don't know, but I'm sure gonna try."

Ironside studied Grossman's face. Snow had collected on the man's eyebrows and beard and made him look like one of the Old Testament prophets who'd lived for a thousand years. "Abe, you and me got some gathering to do. I'll show you what we need."

Ironside rose and got a canteen from the saddle.

"We'll wash the wounds first. The bullet went into one shoulder and out the other."

Grossman gently laid his dog's head on the ground and then covered Solomon with his heavy wool coat.

"Hell man, you'll freeze," Ironside said.

The peddler shook his head. "It's for my dog. I won't feel the cold."

"Spoke like a good Protestant, Abe. You'll do." Ironside turned to Shawn. "I need to work on the dog. Go bring back the mule and the wagon. Oh, and the whiskey if there's any left."

Shawn nodded, mounted his horse, and rode out of the clearing, his eyes scanning the ground where wagon tracks scarred the mud.

It didn't enter Shawn's head to question Ironside's order, even though he faced odds of three to one. Luther expected him to handle it, and he would.

As for Ironside, he had taught the O'Brien brothers the ways of the Colt and he'd tutored them well. That Shawn was up against it never entered into his thinking.

The young O'Brien had sand and he was a Texas-trained gunfighter who would do what needed to be done, on the robbers' ground or any other.

But Abraham Grossman was not so sure. "Should he go alone?"

"Why not?" Ironside probed the trees and under-brush for the herbs and plants he needed.

"There are three robbers, all big men and well armed."

Ironside nodded. "I taught that boy. There ain't nothing he can't do. Well, he ain't much of a puncher, but I kinda overlook that part. Hey, look, Abe, there's willows over there on the bank of the creek. We need their bark."

But Grossman wouldn't let it go. "Are you his father?"

"Call me his second father. His real father was busy."

"Then aren't you worried? I mean he's like your own son."

"Nah, I'm not worried and Shawn isn't either."

Grossman shook his head. "Spoke like a good Protestant."

"Damn right," Ironside said.

He stepped toward the creek, then stopped and turned to the other man. "Hell, Abe, now you got me worried all of a sudden. Why do you go around putting thoughts like that into a man's head?"

# Chapter Six

Shawn O'Brien drew rein in a stand of aspen that clung to the crest of a shallow rock ridge overlooking a grass and brush meadow. Cottonwoods showed some distance off and from among them a thin column of smoke bent like a war bow to the prevailing east wind.

Three miles to the south soared the rugged peaks of the Sandia Mountains, their timbered towers and cliffs lost behind a veil of gray mist.

Shawn had no interest in the peaks, his attention fixed on the cottonwoods. Apart from the slow fall of the snow nothing moved down there and he heard no sound. But the wagon tracks led in that direction and he was sure that's where the robbers were camped. They hadn't gone far, one old man posing little threat.

The waning day had grown colder and Shawn's breath smoked in the chill air as he rode his long-legged blood bay along the aspen line then dropped down a rocky slope to the meadow.

He reined up the bay again and opened his sheepskin. The heavy coat was hip length and could impede a draw from the holster he wore high in the horseman style. He drew his short-barreled Colt, fed a round into the empty chamber under the hammer, and dropped the revolver into the right pocket of the sheepskin.

A draw from the leather was faster, but getting a Colt's front sight caught in a flapping coat was a mistake that could get a man killed.

He rode forward under a sky that looked as though it had been beaten out of a sheet of rusty iron. The wind had picked up a little and snow flurries swirled around him and tossed the bay's mane.

Pulling the glove off his gun hand, he lifted his head and smelled the air. Wood smoke, coffee, and frying bacon reached him, comforting as the odors of a friendly cookhouse. It was hard to believe he was fast closing in on armed outlaws, one of them vicious enough to shoot a dog for the sheer hell of it.

The three men had Shawn spotted when he was still a hundred yards away. They stood and watched him, long guns across their chests and let him come on.

When he rode close enough, Shawn saw a two-wheeled wagon and a grazing mule a short distance from the men and knew these were the men he'd been tracking. Still a dozen yards away, he drew rein and smiled. As politeness dictated, he called, "Hello, the camp."

So close, Shawn had run out of options. It was run or fight . . . and he wasn't about to run.

A tall man dressed in a sheepskin, a pearl gray

Stetson with a curled up brim tipped back on his head growled, "What the hell do you want?"

Shawn smiled again. His brother Jacob would've already gunned down all three robbers and be eating their bacon.

But Shawn was not Jacob.

"Been smelling your coffee for a spell," Shawn said, still smiling as though he was visiting kinfolk. "Wondered if you might have a cup to spare."

His eyes quickly scanned the camp. The man wearing the fancy hat was white, the two others with him were breeds, probably half-Mexican, half-Apache and all bad.

The tall man turned his head, revealing a vicious scar that gouged his right cheek. "Hey, Sanchez, how much you reckon the bay is worth?"

"If you was to buy it, Skate, unlikely as that is, you wouldn't see much change from a thousand dollar bill." Sanchez had the slanted, almond-shaped eyes of a snake and they didn't move from Shawn's face.

The man called Skate nodded. "Yup, that's what I reckoned." He grinned at Shawn. "So no coffee and no hard feelings, mister."

The rifle came down, leveling as Shawn drew from his pocket and fired.

The split second of surprise that made the difference in a gunfight was all Shawn's.

Skate died falling, a bullet between his eyes and a shocked expression on his face.

The breeds, caught flat-footed, came late to the ball.

A shotgun blasted, but the one-and-a-quarter-ounces of triple aught buck shredded the air where

Shawn no longer was. He'd dived off the bay, rolled to his left, and fired his Colt at the breed with the scattergun. The big .45 bullet smashed the man's face into a nightmare of blood and bone and, luckily for him, he was dead when he hit the ground.

The third man wanted no part of Shawn O'Brien or what he could bring to the fight. He tossed his rifle away and screamed, "Damn you, I'm out of it."

The one thing Shawn and his brother Jacob shared was Luther Ironside. Luther was not a merciful man in battle, and he'd taught the O'Brien brothers to be the same way. "Never trust a wolf until he's skun," he'd said. "And that means a lobo that's talkin' o' surrender."

Shawn slammed three shots into the breed and watched the man fall.

The breed had taken his chances and come up a loser. There was no right or wrong to the thing. It was the law of the gunfight and a harsh one at that.

By force of habit and the memory of cuffs on the head from Luther when he'd failed to do so, Shawn reloaded his Colt and shoved it into the leather.

He stepped to the fire, removed the frying bacon from the heat, and poured himself coffee. It was black and bitter, the way he liked it. When the bacon was cool enough to eat, he chewed up every strip and wondered why killing men gave him such an appetite.

After a killing, Jacob plunged into a black depression and sometimes for weeks on end, battled demons of his own making that tormented him night and day.

Shawn felt no such torment.

"When it's down to him or you, make damn sure it's you. And after the smoke clears be glad that it's his beard lying in the sawdust and not your'n," Luther once told him. "Killin' a man in a fair fight is like humpin' a saloon girl, Shawn. It's something you do and then forget. Don't let the ghost of any man come back and haunt you."

It was Ironside's code.

A glint of silver at the neck of the man called Skate caught Shawn's attention. He stepped to the outlaw's body, the bloody bullet hole between his wide open, sky-blue eyes a terrible thing to see.

A locket on a silver chain encircled Skate's neck. Shawn laid aside the tin coffee cup and his gloves and thumbed the locket open. Inside were portraits of an elderly couple, the man stern and bearded, the woman softer, smiling slightly.

"Your ma and pa back on the farm, huh?" Shawn said to the dead man. He closed the locket, settled it back on Skate's neck, and rose to his feet.

The awful finality of what he'd done nagged at him as he quickly put the mule into the traces and avoided looking at the dead breeds wearing shrouds of snow.

Shawn had made a bad mistake, something that, in all his tutoring, Luther Ironside had never prepared him for.

He'd opened the locket . . . and given death a human face.

# Chapter Seven

The racketing echoes of the gunshot outside Dromore had barely stilled when Shamus O'Brien stepped outside, his sons behind him, Patrick still fumbling with the buckle of his gunbelt.

A tall man sat a rangy buckskin, his Colt pointed at the sullen sky.

"That is no way to announce your presence when you visit a man's home," Shamus said, anger flaring on his cheekbones.

"It is my way, Shamus O'Brien." There was still yellow in the horseman's hair and beard and his chest and shoulders bulked large under a red plaid mackinaw. He holstered his gun. "The gunshot is to inform you that I come in peace or war, the choice is yours."

"You would be Colonel James Stuart who comes so bold and unfriendly to my front door," Shamus said.

"Aye, it is, and ye know why I'm here, Colonel O'Brien."

"I had thought to welcome you with honor," Shamus said.

"And so ye should, since I bear a king's name."

"And do I not bear a name as ancient and honorable as your own?"

"Aye, that ye do," Stuart said. "You'll get no argument from me on that score, Shamus O'Brien. But you harbor a murderer in your midst, and that I cannot and will not abide."

"You speak of Dr. Holliday, is that not so, James Stuart?"

Stuart's horse tossed its head and the bit rang like a silver bell. Falling snow drifted onto the man's shoulders and his breath smoked gray. "That is the criminal, as well ye know, Colonel."

"He is my guest and by the laws of hospitality he has my protection. Surely, being a fine gentleman yourself, you understand that?"

"I understand the laws of hospitality fine and that is why I came to your house alone and not with armed men behind me. Now, send him out," Stuart spat. "I will not say his name, and I will take him into my custody when he is no longer under your roof."

"And then what will you do?"

"I will hang him."

Shamus took a step toward Stuart and smiled. "Ah, man, come in and have a dram and meet my sons. We can parley and settle the dispute between us."

"I'm grieving for my own son, Shamus O'Brien, and I will not sit under the same roof as his murderer. I ask you again—will you send him out?"

Shamus shook his head, the pained expression in his eyes revealing a man torn apart. "That I will not do, James Stuart. My honor and the honor of my ancestors demands it."

"Then there is war between us, though it grieves me much to say it. We both wore the gray and there should be peace and goodwill between us as old comrades in arms."

"I say we send for a marshal, James Stuart, and let him decide this matter."

"No. The murderer you shelter harmed me and mine. I will avenge my son and not leave it to some nameless man with a star on his chest and no belly for a hanging."

"Then war it must be," Shamus said. "I will not dishonor the king's name I bear by bending the knee and begging for peace."

"The killings to come will be on your head, Shamus O'Brien. Before the winter snow melts from the top of yonder mesa, you will grieve for sons of your own."

"Then away with you, Colonel Stuart, and take up your sword if you must. You're a hard, unyielding man, so be damned to ye."

"From this day forth, Shamus O'Brien, we're all of us damned," James Stuart said.


"You could've stepped out and ended this thing," Jacob O'Brien said.

Doc Holliday sat on the edge of his bed, a scarlet-stained hand towel to his mouth. "Done the decent thing, you mean."

"That sums it up."

"I never do the decent thing, Jake. You know that as well as any man."

"Damn you, Doc, because of you a couple proud, stiff-necked old men have declared war and their young men will do the dying. I don't believe saving your hide is worth the life of a single vaquero."

"I won't put my head in the hangman's noose. Not for you, Jake. Not for anybody."

A rising wind sighed around the eaves of the house and made sport with the falling snow.

Jacob picked up the Colt from the table beside the bed. He spun the cylinder, checked the loads, then offered the revolver to Doc. "Take the Colt, Doc. Step outside and walk into the woods and blow your damned brains out. It's time the world was rid of your shadow."

Doc reached out and placed the muzzle of the revolver against his forehead. "You pull the trigger, Jake. Do it now for old times' sake and be a daisy."

"Damn you, Doc, if you don't have the decency to kill yourself, at least have the guts to leave this house," Jacob said, his anger rising.

"I won't kill myself, Jake. You're my friend and I want you to do it. Take the burden off me, you understand?" Doc bowed his head, inviting the bullet.

Jacob thumbed back the hammer of the Colt and shoved its muzzle into the parting of Doc Holliday's thin hair. "Damn you, Doc!" he yelled. "Damn you to the deepest pits of hell."

A woman shrieked.

Jacob turned. One of the Dromore chambermaids stood in the doorway, clean white sheets over her arm and a look of horror on her face. "Mr. O'Brien, what are you doing?" The maid was young and pretty and her blue eyes were open wide, the size of silver dollars.

Jacob lowered the Colt's hammer. "Nothing, Jane. Nothing at all." He tossed the revolver on the bed and stepped to the door.

"You failed me, Jake," Doc said after him, his face bleak. "You didn't have the guts to kill me, so you're no daisy."

"I told him to kill himself, but he wouldn't do it." Jacob and Shamus were alone in the parlor, the log in the grate reduced to a few feeble flames that guttered amid gray ashes. Only one lamp was lit and the room was filled with lilac shadow.

The colonel, wrapped in a red flannel robe, slippers on his feet, nodded but said nothing.

"He isn't worth a war, Pa."

"No, he isn't," Shamus said. "But the die has been cast."

"I tried to kill him myself," Jacob said.

"But you couldn't pull the trigger?"

"I don't know. A maid came in and stopped it."

"You wouldn't have killed him anyway, Jacob. My sons were not raised to commit murder."

"He's not worth a war," Jacob said again.

"Tell that to James Stuart. He's a hard, inflexible man. The black crow's curse on him."

"He grieves for his son. The man is not thinking straight."

"I invited him to parley and he refused. We could've worked something out, a compromise of sorts. There was no need for a declaration of war."

"I say tomorrow morning we throw Doc Holliday out of Dromore and end this trouble," Jacob said.

"Over my dead body," Shamus said, his thick white brows beetling over his eyes. "The day will never come that I'll kowtow to the likes of James Stuart, even though he was a hero of the South and bears a king's name."

"Colonel, we'll be asking men to fight and die to save Doc's worthless hide. Where's the sense in that?"

"Here's the sense, boy, and listen well. We'll be asking men to fight and die for the honor of Dromore. Damn it, Jacob, there are some things a man must be willing to give his life for. Or has all notion of honor fled my family and my nation in these modern times?"

"Our country, the flag, the future of our race, yes, these are things still worth dying for, Colonel. But the worthless life of Doc Holliday doesn't make that list."

"Perhaps it will all come to nothing in the end," Shamus said. "Holliday will leave one day and Stuart's *cassis belli* will no longer exist."

Jacob smiled. "Pa, you've been talking with Patrick again."

That tickled Shamus and he grinned like an imp.

"You're right. I would never have come up with cassis belli on my own. But it's true, with Holliday gone Stuart would lose his reason for war."

"Pat knows some strange things. One time Luther got my brother to teach him how to cuss in Chinese."

"And did he?"

"Damn right."

Shamus yawned. "Well, the hour grows late. It's me for my bed."

"Suppose he doesn't leave?"

"Tonight before I sleep, I'll say a rosary that he does."

"But Colonel—"

"No, Jacob. I will not discuss this matter further tonight. We'll look at it with fresh eyes in the morning."

After his father left, Jacob poured himself a drink and sat by the dying fire. He rolled and lit a cigarette and let the tobacco and brandy relax him.

As the grandfather clock struck midnight the house was quiet, but outside in the cold, bone-white night, coyotes wailed their hunger to the frosted land and hunting, silent owls glided through the pines like winged assassins.

Jacob heard a shriek, then silence . . . a small death somewhere out in the darkness. He laid his glass on the table and stared down at his big, muscular hands, work-hardened, strong, supple, and capable.

How easy it would be for him to use those hands

to kill Doc Holliday, snap his scrawny neck and end the nightmare that was about to befall Dromore.

Kill him in his sleep.

Jacob let his head fall back on the chair and closed his eyes. How easy it would be.

# Chapter Eight

Luther Ironside had a fire going and coffee simmered on the coals when Shawn drove the peddler wagon into camp.

Abraham Grossman stood in silence as Shawn came in, his eyes wide and his chin near to his top shirt button. When the peddler finally found his voice, he said, "You found it? And my mule."

Shawn nodded. "Looks like, and everything is there as far as I can tell. Hell, a wagon isn't much good without a mule."

Ironside was more aware than the peddler. "Did you have any trouble?"

"No trouble," Shawn answered.

"All three of them?"

"That's how it played out."

Ironside looked into Shawn's gray eyes and saw what he'd so often seen in Jacob's, a small wound that could sometimes fester. "You feelin' all right boy?"

"Just fine, Luther." Then, because he felt he owed

Ironside some kind of explanation, he added, "One of them wore a locket around his neck. It had his ma and pa's pictures inside. A fine old couple."

"Set by the fire and I'll get you some coffee," Ironside said.

"How's the dog?" Shawn asked.

"He's still alive and his eyes are open," Grossman said. "Come see."

Solomon lay by the fire. The peddler had torn strips from his shirt to bandage the dog's wounds. Shawn kneeled and took Solomon's head in his hands. The dog's eyes were bright and he made an effort to lick Shawn's face.

"He's much better, I think," Grossman said. "Mr. Ironside made a potion of herbs and other stuff—"

"A heap of willow bark," Ironside said.

"Yes," Grossman said, "willow bark for pain. He poured it onto Solomon's wounds—"

"And down his throat." Ironside handed a cup of coffee to Shawn. "I reckon he'll live. He's only a cur dog, but he's tough and he's got sand."

Ironside lit a cigar with a brand from the fire. "Abe, you know what you've got to do, right?"

"Yes. I stay here a few days until Solomon gets some strength back and then he travels in the wagon until he can walk."

"Good for you," Ironside said. "It seems like you remember stuff spoken by wise men like myself."

Grossman smiled. "I'm a Child of the Book, remember?"

"That you are, Abe," Ironside said, "and I don't

hold that against you none. You're true blue because you don't preach at folks and you do like I tell you."

"Be dark soon, Luther," Shawn said, stroking the dog's head. "I guess we'll camp here and push on at first light."

"That was my intention, Shawn. We still have ground to cover." Ironside looked at Grossman. "Hey, Abe, you got any candy sticks in that there wagon? I'm sure partial to them."

"Am I not a peddler? Of course I do." Grossman rose and stepped to the wagon. After a few moments of rummaging around, he called over to Ironside, "I have blueberry and peppermint."

"Peppermint is just fine."

The peddler returned to the fire and presented Ironside with a bright red and white candy twist, bowing ceremoniously as though he was bestowing a field marshal's baton. "That will be five cents, Mr. Ironside."

"Right nice feller, that peddler," Luther Ironside said. "Wasn't he a nice feller?"

Shawn O'Brien smiled. "Still sore about the five cents, huh?"

"Hell, he's a businessman. That's how I see it."

"And Abe's expensive candy cane gave you a toothache."

"Yeah it did. Punished me all night. Damn that peddler."

"When we get to Albuquerque you're seeing a dentist, Luther."

"The hell I will. I don't hold with dentists . . . nor doctors either."

"No arguments now, Luther. You need that aching tooth pulled."

Ironside turned in the saddle. "Shawn, you know how I am around dentists and their tools o' torture? How many have I plugged?"

"None, because in all the years I've known you, you've never gone to a dentist."

"Well, if I had gone to one I would've probably plugged him, so there. Damn it, Shawn, all your talk about dentists is making my tooth hurt again."

The Rio Grande was a couple miles ahead of the Dromore riders as they followed a well-marked trail that wound through the northern foothills of the Sandia Mountains. A high-country wind blew strong and cold, driving snow flurries ahead of it. Both men had turned up the collars of their sheepskins and Ironside rode with a woolen scarf wound around his neck and over his mouth. "It's the damned cold wind."

"It's the damned cold wind what?" Shawn asked.

"That's making my tooth hurt."

"It's got to come out."

"Hell, there ain't no dentists in Albuquerque," Ironside said. "Everybody knows that. All the damned dentists are back east."

"Albuquerque is full of dentists. We'll find you one you like."

"I don't like any of them."

"All right, we'll find one you don't like." Shawn pointed. "Hold up, Luther. Look down there."

Below them on the flat, a dozen mounted men rode through brush and nopal country. They seemed to be using the land for cover, coming together then spreading apart again, depending on the terrain.

"What do you make of them?" Shawn asked.

A far-seeing man, Ironside followed the riders with his eyes for a few moments. "I'm bettin' them boys are on the scout. Wouldn't surprise me none if we see a posse after them by and by."

But as the riders faded into snow and distance, there was no sign of a posse.

"Headed for Albuquerque, I reckon," Ironside said. "Good place for outlaws to drop out of sight."

"We'll keep some daylight between them and us, Luther," Shawn said. "We came to collect a bull, not tangle with outlaws and we've already done that once."

"Fine by me. We ride slow and easy until we get to town."

"Well-mounted men," Shawn said slowly. "I wonder who they are?"

"Let's hope we don't find out," Ironside said. "A man with a sore tooth ain't fit for a shooting scrape."

There were still two hours of daylight left when Ironside and Shawn rode into Albuquerque. The arrangement made by letter was that they'd meet Sir James Lovell at the Ambassador Hotel and then accompany him to wherever he'd penned up Bonnie Prince Charlie.

As they rode through crowded streets, past saloons brightly lit with electric lights that thrilled and fascinated Shawn, Ironside paid little heed to his surroundings. Wrapped in a cocoon of misery, he nursed his aching tooth and was in such bad humor he loudly cussed after Shawn lectured, "Hell, Luther, you should've brushed all your teeth, not just the ones you wanted to keep."

# Chapter Nine

"Well, it's pretty obvious we can't say howdy to Sir James with you in this state," Shawn said to Luther.

"Hell, all I need is whiskey. It will dull the pain. We'll find one o' them fancy saloons and down a few afore we meet the Englishman."

"Yeah, show up drunk to meet the representative of the most powerful woman in the world. Hell, Luther, old Vic could have your head chopped off."

"It would be an act of mercy," Ironside groaned.

A man wearing an expensive broadcloth suit stood smoking a cigar outside a saloon. "Is there a good dentist around here?" Shawn asked him.

"I don't know if he's good, bad, or indifferent, but there's a dentist office just down the street past the Masonic temple there. You can't miss it."

Shawn touched his hat. "Much obliged."

"Anytime," the man said. "It looks like your friend is hurting."

After allowing a freight wagon to pass, Shawn grabbed the reins of Ironside's horse and led the way to the dentist's surgery.

"Hell, Shawn, first we'd better go meet Sir Whatever-the-hell-is-his-name. When we get to back to Dromore I'll head up to Santa Fe an' get my tooth fixed, I promise."

Shawn ignored that and swung out of the saddle. He looped his horse to the hitching rail and said, "Get down, Luther."

"Shawn," Ironside wailed, "you're not going to do this to me. Are you?"

"I sure am. You can't meet Sir James Lovell with a toothache. I swear, you're such a baby."

Ironside dismounted. "Shawn, I'm never going to forget this. I'm gonna tell the colonel what you done and how you treated me so bad."

"Inside, Luther." Shawn gave him a slight shove. "And give me your gun."

"Hell, Shawn, suppose I want to plug this damned dentist?"

"That's why I want your gun."

Shawn shoved Ironside's Colt into his waistband and pushed him in the direction of the door. Under a stained-glass panel that depicted a buxom woman with white teeth grabbing a russet apple from a bowl was a polished brass sign.

## DR. WILLIAM C. CARSTAIRS
*Dental Surgeon*

Ironside studied the picture of the woman, then the sign. "I feel like a condemned man walking to the gallows."

"You won't feel a thing, Luther," Shawn said. "Dentistry is painless in this modern age."

"Then have him pull one o' your'n first, to show me how painless it is," Ironside whined.

"I don't have a bad tooth," Shawn said, opening the door and ushering the older man inside. "But you do."

"I always knew I never raised you right, boy. You got no respect for your elders and I blame myself for that." Ironside stopped and grabbed Shawn's arm. "Now prove to me that I'm wrong and get me the hell out of here."

"No, Luther, you're so right," Shawn said. "I love dragging old folks to the dentist. It's the way I was raised."

"Shawn, I swear—"

"And what seems to be our problem today?"

The nurse was young and pretty. She wore a gray dress, starched white apron, and hat. Shawn reckoned her smile was as bright as the electric lights in the saloons. Her teeth were perfect, white, and even.

"I'm the only one with a problem," Ironside growled. "I got a toothache."

"The doctor is busy with another patient, but he should be with you shortly. In the meantime, please make yourselves comfortable in the waiting room." The nurse showed Ironside and Shawn into a room furnished with an overstuffed horsehide sofa and a couple wooden chairs. A portrait of the gallant Custer, draped with black crepe, hung on one wall.

After glowering at the general, Ironside said, "The lady said get comfortable an' that's what I'm gonna do. Shawn, go fetch the bottle of whiskey from my saddlebags."

"Luther, are you sure?" Shawn asked. "The doc may give you ether and I don't think it's a good mix with alcohol."

"Shawn, damn it, I'm suffering here. Get the Old Crow like I told you."

"You'll regret it." Shawn shook his head. "I promise you, Luther, whiskey and ether isn't a good mix."

Ironside held his jaw and moaned. "The hell I'll regret it."

It amused Shawn that a tall, lean man who moved like a panther and was afraid of nothing or no one could be reduced to a babbling wreck by the thought of a dentist's chair.

When he returned with the whiskey, Ironside immediately popped the cork and drank greedily, his Adam's apple bobbing. After downing about four inches of Old Crow, he wiped his mouth and held up the bottle to the Custer portrait. "Here's to you, General. Wherever you are, in heaven or hell, I hope you remember that I almost rammed my saber through your brisket at Brandy Station."

Ironside turned his head and said to Shawn, "He was lucky that day. My damned horse stumbled."

Ironside drank deep again. "Right, Shawn, let's

go see Lord What's-his-name. My tooth is feeling a sight better."

"When the whiskey wears off, the pain will come back, Luther. You're getting that bad tooth pulled and there's an end to it."

"You're a traitor, Shawn O'Brien." Whiskey tears welled in Ironside's eyes. "I never took you fer a traitor . . . never . . . ever." He dashed a hand across his eyes. "Shawn, when the end comes, will you hold my hand?"

"Luther, you're only having a tooth pulled, not dying."

"It feels like I'm dying, boy."

"The doctor will see you now," the pretty nurse said, smiling her dazzling white smile.


Shawn stepped aside to let a big man pass him in the narrow hallway leading to the surgery. The man's mouth was padded with gauze, but it did nothing to soften the brutal thrust of his massive jaw or the hard gray eyes that raked across Shawn's face like claws.

It was a look of hatred—raw, inhuman, savage, and dangerous.

Shawn had never seen the big man before and knew the man's venom was not directed at him, but at all humanity—every man, woman, and child on earth.

That look, fleeting though it was, branded itself

into Shawn's consciousness and he felt as though he'd just been horsewhipped.

Whoever he was, the man was a hardcase to avoid.


Once in the dentist's chair Luther Ironside was a changed man, or so it seemed to Shawn.

"I can give you ether, Mr. Ironside," Dr. Carstairs said. "It will put you out and you won't feel a thing." He was a young man with sympathetic brown eyes and pleasant bedside manner. He'd been a dentist for just six months and was slowly building his practice.

"Hell, Doc, I don't need ether," Ironside said, puffing up a little as he sat back in the chair. "I was fighting Yankees at your age, an' I fit Apaches more'n wunst, so a little thing like a tooth pullin' don't scare me none." He held out the bottle of whiskey. "Here, afore you start have another drink."

"Well, I don't mind if I do," Carstairs said. "It's been a long day."

The young man chugged from the bottle as Ironside said, "Old Crow is good drinkin' whiskey, an' don't let anybody tell you different."

Shawn smiled and shook his head. Now that he was putting on a performance for a stranger, Luther was back to his old, boastful ways.

Ironside peered at the dentist, then blinked like an owl. "You see how a fighting man like me don't need no lousy ether, huh?"

Carstairs nodded. "Yes I do. You're a war hero, Mr. Ironside, that's what's exac . . . exec . . . exactly what you are. Let's drink to that."

"Sure, let's have another, Doc. You're damn right. A war hero who almost rammed a saber into the gallant Custer's brisket, don't need ether."

Carstairs hiccupped. "No, they surely don't." He shook his head. "None at all. All they need is guts."

"Damn right," Ironside said again. "And I got plenty of those."

The bottle passed back and forth until it was drained.

By that time, Carstairs was a little unsteady on his feet. "Right, Mr. Ironside, open wide and let's get started." He hiccupped, then picked up a pair of shiny steel pliers. "Now, let's find that itty-bitty, naughty tooth."

For a moment, Ironside seemed mesmerized by the dreadful sight of the gleaming steel pliers coming toward his open mouth. Then he shrieked, "Ether! For God's sake get the ether!"

"Of course it hurts," Shawn said as he and Ironside untied their horses. "You got the dentist so drunk he couldn't even see the tooth he was supposed to pull. Either that or he was seeing two or three of them."

Ironside stood in the street, and around a mouthful of gauze yelled at the glass door, "Carstairs, you're a damned butcher!"

He held out a hand to Shawn. "Gimme my gun an' I'll go plug the son of a gun."

Shawn shook his head. "No gun, Luther. That's

the ether talking. It's getting dark, we'd better go find Sir James."

"He's another Limey son of a gun."

"How can you say that when you've never met the man, Luther?"

"I just know." Ironside turned toward his horse. "God, I feel sick."

# Chapter Ten

"I'm sorry our ranch segundo couldn't be here, Sir James," Shawn O'Brien said. "He had dental work done earlier today and is indisposed."

"Oh the poor man," the Englishman said. "I trust he'll soon be well."

"I'm sure he will be once the effects of the ether wears off."

*And the whiskey,* Shawn thought.

Sir James reached into the inside pocket of his impeccable dark gray suit, tailored in the slim English fashion, and produced a long, cream-colored envelope. "I am instructed by Her Majesty that this be delivered into the hand of Colonel O'Brien. You will recognize the royal seal of course."

"Of course." Shawn figured that Sir James was talking about the circle of red wax that closed the envelope.

"It is Her Majesty's wish that I express her special thanks to the colonel for his past purchases of stud Hereford bulls from her private herds at Sandringham and Balmoral, and wishes this arrangement to continue in the future, to the betterment of both parties involved."

"I'll pass that message on to the colonel, Sir James. I'm sure he will deeply appreciate Her Majesty's kind words."

"And now I suppose you wish to meet Bonnie Prince Charlie?"

"If that's convenient.

"A black bull does not show to his best advantage at night," Sir James said. "But I'm sure we can borrow a lamp from somewhere."

The Lovell suite took up most of the hotel's top floor. One of the doors that led into the living room opened and a girl entered.

For Shawn O'Brien it was love at first sight.

"Ah, Judith. I'm so glad you decided to join us," Sir James said. "Mr. O'Brien may I introduce my daughter, Lady Judith Ashenhurst. Mr. O'Brien's father is the owner of Dromore and one of Her Majesty's favorite cattle ranchers."

The girl smiled and extended her hand. "I'm so glad to meet you, Mr. O'Brien."

"Likewise, I'm sure," Shawn said, taking Judith's tiny hand in his.

Suddenly, he felt big and awkward in his chaps, scuffed mud-spattered boots, and sheepskin, his battered hat clutched in his hands. He figured he smelled of horse dung and trail sweat, like a country rube fresh off the farm.

In fact, Shawn carried with him the odor of wood smoke, pines, and saddle leather, something Judith noticed, but he didn't even suspect.

Judith Lovell was a slender blonde with eyes the same jade as the sky when the sun sets. She wore a lacy white dress, her shapely shoulders bare, and a silver necklace that suspended a love knot brooch studded with diamonds graced her beautiful neck.

"You've come for Bonnie Prince Charlie, Mr. O'Brien. He's a wonderful bull, a pet really." Judith's voice was low and slightly husky, and Shawn was smitten.

"Sir James has offered to take me to see the bull. Will you join us . . . um . . ." Shawn stumbled a bit over his words.

"Judith is just fine, Mr. O'Brien."

"And please call me Shawn."

Judith smiled and nodded. "Then Shawn it is. I'd love to join you and say my farewells to the Prince. Let me just get my wrap."

After Judith disappeared into the bedroom, Shawn said, "You have a beautiful daughter, Sir James."

"Yes, she is indeed. I thought this trip to the American West would do her good. Her husband was killed by bandits in India two years ago and she's never quite gotten over it, poor thing."

"He was a soldier?" Shawn asked.

"Yes. Lord John Ashenhurst was the colonel of the Seventeenth Lancers stationed at Lucknow. He was considerably older than Judith, but everyone agreed, including myself I must add, that it was a love match. She was devastated when John died and, as I said, she's never quite recovered."

Sir James stepped to a decanter on the table. "I believe we have time for a sherry. When a woman says, 'let me get my wrap,' it means she'll be gone for quite some time."

Shawn accepted his drink. "Was Judith with her husband when he died?"

"No. She was visiting my wife and I in England. When she returned to India, John was already dead and buried."

"I'm sorry to hear that."

Sir James nodded. "A tragedy all round, I'm afraid. Judith was in such a state of shock she lost the child she was carrying and the doctors told her she can never have another."

That last came as a slap of cold reality to Shawn. He'd always imagined a future that included a wife and children. A childless marriage had never entered his thinking—until now.

"How is the sherry?" A perceptive man, used to the mood and manners of Victoria's court, Sir John detected a subtle change in Shawn's attitude, a certain stiffening of his handsome features that hadn't been there before.

"It's very good, Sir James," Shawn said, his words flat.

"Yes, I agree. The hotel manager recommended it and he certainly knows his wines." Sir James looked into Shawn's eyes. "Judith is just twenty-three years old, Mr. O'Brien and she's already had two tragedies in her life. I don't want her to experience a third."

"I can understand that."

Sir James Lovell nodded. "Yes, I'm sure you do."

\* \* \*

"He's a fine-looking animal, Sir James," Shawn said as he held the railroad lantern aloft. "He'll do much to improve the Dromore herds."

"The Aberdeen Black Angus is the finest beef breed in the world and they thrive in all kinds of weather," Sir James said. "The bulls pass on the hornless trait to their calves, so they're ideal for breeding with longhorns."

"We still have a small longhorn herd at Dromore."

"Then Bonnie Prince Charlie will do you proud." Judith scratched the bull between his ears. "Won't you, Prince?" She wore a hooded red cloak over her dress and Shawn thought she was the most beautiful woman on earth.

The Angus was penned up close to the railroad station and his glossy coat reflected the crimson light of the lamp. His massive, two-thousand pound weight was supported by short, sturdy legs and it looked to Shawn that if Bonnie Prince Charlie put his mind to it, nothing on earth could move him.

Judith shivered and pulled her cloak around her.

Sir James said, "Take leave of the Prince, Judith. We'd better get you back to the hotel."

The night was chill and snow tossed in the wind. Only the bright scarlet splash of Judith's cloak relived the gray and black gloom of the cattle pens. Over at the train station a single oil lamp swung from a platform roof and cast a dim cone of yellow light where the falling snow flakes fluttered like white moths.

"Father," Judith said quietly.

"I see them, dear," Sir James said.

Shawn, raised by Luther Ironside to have the alertness of a wolf, heard the changed tone of Judith's voice and followed Sir James's gaze to the muddy, open area beyond the cattle pens where two men stood in the dim light. They had their eyes fixed on Judith.

The men were big, made bigger by the fur coats and hats they wore, and one of them held a brass-studded club.

Alarm bells rang in Shawn's brain. He'd seen their kind before. Every settlement had men like these, bullies with no real depth or sand, men who preyed on the weak and the timid and laughed while they stomped faces to prove how tough they were. They were the scum of the earth and deep inside their worthless carcasses they knew it.

Shawn's gun was in his hotel room and why not? He was in a big city with a regular police force where no one walked around heeled. Besides, a man who's inspecting a prize bull with an English knight and his beautiful daughter hardly prepared himself for gunfight.

He'd made a mistake, and as the grinning toughs walked toward him and the others, Shawn knew he'd have to deal with the consequences.

"Perhaps we should walk away," Sir James said. "Those two look like ruffians and they're up to no good, I'll be bound."

"It's too late for that," Shawn said. Then to Judith, "Get behind us."

The woman did as she was told.

The two men walked closer, still grinning, human coyotes confident of an easy kill.

When they were a couple feet away the men stopped. To Shawn's dismay they were even bigger up close, blackjack and boot fighters who would know how to down a man.

"Come out from behind there, missy," said the one to Shawn's left, a man with a broken nose and tight, mean eyes. "You an' us are gonna have a little fun. Huh? What do you say?" He held out a bottle. "Here, have a drink, little lady.

"Be off with you," Sir James ordered. "My daughter is going home, where you should be."

"What the hell are you?" Mean Eyes said.

"My name is Sir James Lovell and I'll have the law on you if you don't leave this very instant."

The other man, just as mean as the first, looked at Shawn. "Hey, cowboy, are you this old goat's pretty boy? Well, you two don't need a woman and we do."

"Go fetch her, Jeb," the first man said.

The man called Jeb stepped forward, pushed Sir James roughly aside, and reached for Judith who screamed and shrank from the man's grasping hand.

Shawn thanked his lucky stars. Jeb's chin was outthrust and angled slightly upward. Perfect.

Shawn's hard-knuckled fist swung fast in a splendid uppercut that connected with the man's chin and snapped his head back so hard his fur hat flew off. Jeb dropped his club and staggered back, his eyes glazed. Shawn didn't give him time to recover. He hit him again, a straight right that landed a little too high and caught the man on his upper lip. Shawn felt Jeb's nose shatter under his fist and the man screamed and fell, blood splattering all over his face.

Shawn swung to face the other man. Too late.

The thug's fist came up fast . . . with a Colt self-cocker in it.

A gunshot racketed through the night, then another.

Shawn watched in stunned disbelief as the gunman took two bullets in the chest and staggered back a step, his face shocked.

"Ride this one into hell, you damn bully!"

Luther Ironside's voice. His gun fired again.

The thug dropped, stiff and dead as a wooden Indian.

The man called Jeb pushed himself to his feet, his face a scarlet mask of blood, bone, and horror. "Don't shoot me, mister!" he screamed, backing away, his hands up in front of him. "We were just having a little fun with missy was all."

Ironside was a harsh, pitiless fighting man who learned his trade in a hard school. "Boy, everybody lives, but not everybody deserves to."

He pumped two bullets into Jeb and coolly watched the man fall.

Then, totally unconcerned about Judith's screams and Sir James, who looked like he'd been kicked in the belly, Ironside rounded on Shawn. "Where the hell is your gun? Don't tell me, I know where it is. It's in your hotel room."

Suddenly, Shawn was ten years old again, trying to justify some boyhood transgression to his tall, grim teacher. "I didn't think I would need it, Luther."

"You did need it, and you needed it mighty

sudden. I thought I teached you better than that. Your brother Jacob wouldn't have gone prancing around in the dark in a strange city without a gun. Well, boy, speak up. Let me hear you whitewash it."

"I'm sorry, Luther."

"Sorry doesn't cut it, Shawn. Damn it boy, just be glad I was here to pull your balls out of the rat-trap." Ironside, suddenly aware of Judith, touched his hat. "Beggin' your pardon, ma'am, for my coarse, cowboy talk."

Judith threw herself into Sir James's arms and sobbed. "Take me home, Father, far from here. Home to England."

Sir James looked over the woman's head at Shawn. "I'll take Judith back to the hotel, and let the local constabulary know what happened." His eyes shifted to Ironside. "You did nothing wrong here tonight."

"I'm a rough and ready man," Ironside said. "My ways are not the ways of England."

"No," Sir James said. "Indeed they're not. But I understand your ways, Mr. Ironside. I served with the British army in the Sudan and I've taken part in my share of slaughter." He put his arm around Judith's waist. "Come, my dear, I'll take you back to the hotel."

As Judith left, Shawn tried to catch her eyes, but she kept her head bent and didn't look at him.

# Chapter Eleven

Doc Holliday stood at his bedroom window and looked out into darkness. Snow was falling lightly, just a few flakes drifting without sound past the glass panes.

Because of the terrible night sweats, one of the children of his disease, Doc had given up lying in bed and preferred to doze in a chair. He didn't dream much. He was sick in his dreams, just as he was while awake. Unable to sleep, he'd risen and wandered to the window.

He knew enough about medicine to be aware that people in the last stages of tuberculosis got a bluish tinge to their skin and turned almost transparent.

The mirror told Doc that he was slowly fading away, like an image on an old tintype, and soon there would be nothing left of him. Only his eyes would remain until finally they closed and all that once had been Doc Holliday would be gone. And forgotten.

That night, he was dying a little faster, a fact that greatly pleased him.

He pulled his shawl closer around him and shivered. The night was cold and getting colder. He poured himself bourbon, tossed another log on the fire, and sat by the crackling blaze.

Someone knocked on the door, and he said, "Come in, it's open."

Patrick O'Brien stepped inside, a book in his hand.

Doc saw an earnest young man whose round spectacles made him look like an intelligent owl. He was personable enough and Doc was in the mood for company.

Patrick extended the book to him. "I brought you Alexander Pope's translation of the *Iliad*. I thought you might like to read it."

"I read it many years ago," Doc said. "At the time, I decided it was pretty poetry, but not Homer." He smiled. "But I'll make an assay of it again. Perhaps now I'll have a better understanding of it."

He laid his white head on the back of his chair and said,

"The wrath of Peleus' Son, the direful Spring
    Of all the Grecian woes, O Goddess, sing!"

Patrick smiled. "The first lines of the *Iliad*. Very good."

"Well, Pope's version, anyway." Doc took the book and laid it on the table beside his chair. "Singularly cold tonight."

"This is high country," Patrick said. "We get snow and cold and the air gets thinner, like glass."

"Indeed. Why are you here? Most of the others in this household avoid me as though I was a pariah. Are you about to ask me to leave or demand that I shoot myself?"

"No. Doc, I wanted to ask you why you stay."

"I don't want to hang."

"I can't believe that's the only reason. There must be more."

"Then believe what you want."

"You're not the kind of man who fears death, Doc," Patrick said.

"I live with death, young man. And you're right. I don't fear it. Death is just stepping from a dark room into another that's full of light."

"I don't think you fear a noose, either."

"Then why do I stay here, in a place where I'm not wanted?"

"I don't know, Doc. But I'm working on it. That's why I wanted to talk with you."

"You fear a war between your father and the Scotsman . . . what's his name? I can't remember."

"James Stuart."

"Yes, of course. Well, do you fear this man?"

"I don't fear him, but I don't want to fight him either, especially over—"

"A dying reprobate like me?"

"That's the gist of it, Doc." Patrick pushed his glasses higher on his nose. "I'm sorry to lay it out so plain."

"Don't be sorry for telling the truth, Patrick. I

know what I am and I know what I'm worth—less then the dregs of the whiskey in my glass."

"I heard that you proved your worth in Tombstone in the Arizona Territory a few years back."

"Really? It was a street brawl in a dung heap, nothing more. Where was the glory in gunning down a bunch of scared, fumble-fingered cowboys? If the Tombstone fight was a measure of my worth, then I count for little." Doc was silent for a while, and then he said, "Patrick, I really don't want to hang. It's a dog's death."

"The colonel is thinking about getting a marshal down here to escort you to wherever you want to go. It's worth thinking about, Doc."

"I wouldn't get far. A marshal isn't going to give up his life to protect good ol' Doc Holliday. He'd probably be glad to hand me over to Stuart. Good riddance to bad rubbish and all that."

Doc's breath wheezed in his narrow chest and he put a handkerchief to his mouth as his cough rattled. When he removed it again the white cloth was stained with blotches of scarlet and there was blood on his lips.

He fumbled for the whiskey bottle and Patrick moved to help him.

"I can do it myself," Doc snapped. He poured himself whiskey, drank it down, and poured another. Breathing heavily, he said, "Don't help me. Don't try to help me ever again. Let me do my own damned dying."

"Sorry, Doc," Patrick said.

"Under the bed there's a carpetbag," Doc said,

gasping. "Bring me the Colt." He waved a thin, translucent hand. "It's . . . it's there . . . in the bag."

Patrick rose and took a blue Colt with a seven-and-a-half-inch barrel and a mahogany handle. There was nothing remarkable about the big revolver. Its like could be had for twelve dollars in any hardware store.

"Give it to me," Doc said, his breathing finally evening out.

Patrick smiled. "Is this thing loaded, Doc?"

"An unloaded gun is only a club. Give it here."

Doc took the Colt and raised it to eye level, his right arm straight. After a few moments, he lowered the revolver. "Put it back, Patrick."

Patrick put the gun back in the carpetbag. "For a minute there I thought you were about to do some target shooting, Doc."

"I wanted to see if I could still lift the thing. I can, but barely." Doc drank whiskey and refilled his glass. "You understand what it was all about, don't you?"

Patrick shook his head. "I don't know. A test of strength, maybe."

"Exactly that. There will come a day when I won't have the strength to raise my gun. You catch my drift?"

Patrick thought that through for a few moments. A log dropped in the fire and sent up a shower of sparks and snow floated thicker past the bedroom window. Doc lifted his gray shawl higher on his shoulders as though he felt a draft.

Finally Patrick said, "No, Doc, I don't catch your drift."

"I want to die before I can no longer lift a Colt. Is that difficult to understand?"

"No, I guess not."

Suddenly, the reason for everything Doc had said became clear. "You want to die with a gun in your hand. In one last gunfight."

"Yes, and in honorable battle, not in a scrape near a corral that killed three drovers and made my shoes smell of horse crap for a week."

"Fighting for Dromore fits the bill."

Doc smiled. "Exactly. I will help Dromore fight a battle for its very existence against James Stuart and I will die honorably, gun in hand. That's how history will remember me, Patrick, as the hero of the Dromore War and not for a squalid little street fracas in Tombstone."

Patrick was stunned. "Doc . . . that's . . . I mean, it's insane. You know how many men will die if it comes to a fight between the colonel and James Stuart?"

Doc held up a hand. "Please, Patrick, I can only handle one death at a time—my own."

Patrick rose from his chair and stepped toward the door. "Doc, it's not going to happen like that. You will have to leave."

"I don't plan to leave. I intend to stay right here until the shooting starts."

"You're a madman. Doc, you're plumb loco."

"Perhaps. But I'm not moving. Here I am and here I stay."

"When the colonel hears what you've planned, he'll force you to leave. He doesn't want you to fight on his side, or on anybody's side."

"Then I'll camp outside Colonel O'Brien's front door. Somehow I don't think he'll allow Stuart and his hemp posse to take me."

Patrick felt as though he was banging his head against a brick wall.

The Colt was in the carpetbag. All he had to do was pick it up and end the standoff once and for all.

But he knew he couldn't do it. He couldn't murder a man in cold blood, even vermin like Doc Holliday.

"You thought about going for my gun, didn't you, Patrick?"

"Yes, I thought about it."

"Murder is a hard thing. Killing a man is a hard thing."

"Doc . . . just leave here. Go to Glendale Springs and never come back."

"And die between white sheets with my boots off? I don't think so. What kind of end is that for a man?"

"Maybe the kind you deserve, Doc. You're no hero. You're just a narrow, selfish man who wants to write his own obituary, no matter the cost to others."

"It's all I've got left to me that's worth a damn," Doc said.

"Not at the expense of Dromore and my family. Go die somewhere else, Doc." Patrick opened the door and stepped out of the room.

Doc called after him, "Thank you for the *Iliad,* Patrick. It will keep me occupied for a while."

Patrick shut the door behind him. Standing alone in the hallway, he tried to rationalize his conflicted emotions. Then he summed it up in his mind. It was simple really . . . he pitied Doc Holliday . . . and hated his guts.

# Chapter Twelve

"How are you feeling this morning, Luther?" Shawn O'Brien took a bite of his pancakes and sausage.

"Like hell. I got a hole in my gum you could drive a Studebaker wagon through and my jaw feels like it's broke."

"I want to thank you again for last night. You snatched me out of the fire in the nick of time."

"We'll talk about that at another time, boy," Ironside said. "I may decide to take a switch to you. Hell, you're as bad as Patrick. Worse, maybe."

Shawn smiled. "I don't reckon so, Luther. Pat hunts butterflies without a gun, remember?"

"Yeah, and you hunt trouble without one." It took a while, but Ironside smiled. "Well, Shawn, at least now you know that you can depend on ol' Luther when heroin' is to be done."

He lifted his cup and drank coffee . . . then let out a loud howl that alarmed the dozen or so guests who were breakfasting in the hotel dining room.

"Damn. Hot, hot, hot. Hurt my tooth hole!" he yelled. "Hell, I should've plugged that dentist just on general principle."

Shawn ignored the horrified eyes cast in their direction and said, "Drink on the other side of your mouth, Luther, and finish your coffee. We have to meet Sir James at the stockyards early."

"Is his daughter comin'?"

"No, I don't think so."

"Good. She doesn't like me."

"Luther, last night she'd just seen you kill two men. She was scared."

"So, she likes me?"

"I don't know."

"I don't think she likes me." Ironside clattered his coffee cup onto his saucer. "Hell, I can't drink this swill. Let's get the Angus bull and head back to Dromore."

Shawn and Ironside had left their horses at a livery stable close to their hotel. They saddled up and headed directly for the station and Bonnie Prince Charlie.

When they got closer, they saw Sir James and a knot of men near the cattle pen arguing, if the Englishman's red face and a railroad man throwing his arms around was any indication.

Sir James spotted the two riders and stalked toward them, his features livid. "He's gone, stolen." Lovell waved a hand at two railroad agents and a couple belligerent men who looked like stockyard employees. "These damned fools say they didn't even know the Prince was missing until I told them."

A railroad man with silver buttons on his dark blue coat and a watch chain across his ample middle stepped toward Shawn and stood in front of his horse. "Two men were killed here last night and the law was here until late."

"We know that," Sir James said, his irritation showing. "I'm the one who informed the constabulary. They didn't seem too much concerned."

"I don't know about that, mister," the railroader said, "but they were here until about one o'clock this morning, tramping back and forth before the undertaker carried them dead boys away."

"So the bull was stolen between one this morning and the time Sir James got here," Shawn said. "When was that?"

"At seven o'clock," Sir James answered. "I wanted to make sure all was well with Bonnie Prince Charlie, and that's when I found his pen empty."

Shawn looked at Ironside, snow drifting between them. "Can we pick up tracks, Luther?"

"Maybe. He's a mighty big bull and he'll cut deep." Ironside kneed his horse forward. "I'll take a scout around."

After Ironside rode away, the railroad man, pompous as a small town politician, said, "I wish to make it known right here and now that the Atchison, Topeka, and Santa Fe Railroad is not responsible for the theft of the animal. Compensation of any kind is out of the question. My name is

Edward T. Goldwell, the representative of the ATSF in Albuquerque, and I am adamant on this."

Shawn grinned and leaned forward in the saddle. "Well, Eddie, you'd better take that up with the queen of England. She owns the bull."

The man was aghast. "He's Queen Victoria's bull?"

"He is. And he was stolen while he was in your care," Sir James said.

Goldwell retreated into bluster. "I will take this to a higher authority. I am not to blame for this . . . this . . . outrage."

"You'd better not be to blame, Eddie," Shawn said. "Old Queen Vic could view the theft of her prize bull as a reason for war."

Goldwell looked at Sir James. "Is this true?"

The Englishman nodded. "Her Majesty told me in confidence that every time she thinks about the loss of the American colonies her poor old heart breaks. I imagine she's looking for any excuse to send in an invasion force and set things to right."

"I would not," Shawn said seriously, "care to be the man responsible for plunging our United States into another conflict with the British Empire. Heads will roll and I reckon yours will be first."

Goldwell paled. "I will take this up with the ATSF. Given the circumstances, perhaps we can reach some kind of accommodation since the animal was stolen on railroad property. How much is the bull worth?"

"Officially, five thousand dollars American," Sir James said. "But I suspect he's worth a lot more than that."

"Five thou . . ." Goldwell gulped. "I'll contact my superiors at once. This is indeed a very serious matter."

"Damn right it is," Shawn said. "Hell, Eddie, you could be the Benedict Arnold of the Atchison, Topeka, and Santa Fe railroad."

Goldwell, a worried man, hurried away.

Ironside rode past the railroad man and up to Shawn. "Two men hazed the bull out of the pen, drove him to the back of the station. Near as I can tell there were maybe a dozen men waiting there. Hard to say since the ground is muddy and considerably cut up."

"Any idea where they're headed, Luther?" Shawn asked.

"North along the river. I didn't track them too far."

"Then we'd better get after them. Let's ride."

"Hold on, I'm coming with you." Sir James glanced at the sky where snow clouds looked like vast sheets of curling lead. An icy wind scudded from the north, frost on its breath. "The weather is closing in fast. I don't think the bandits will plan on riding far today."

"Hell, James, Sir, I mean—"

"Oh for heaven's sake, Luther, just call me James."

"All right, James. Can you ride a hoss?"

"Of course I can. I was a cavalryman in the army and at home I ride to hounds. Judith is also an expert horsewoman and she'll be coming with me, of course. I can't leave her alone in a strange city."

"She can't come on this trip," Ironside said,

"when there's shootin' and killin' to be done. Your daughter can't cry for her mama on the trail, because there ain't nobody gonna pay heed to her."

"Don't judge Judith by her reaction last night, Luther," Sir James said. "I think the shooting brought back memories of her husband's violent death."

"I'll tell you about that later, Luther," Shawn said. "You'd better rent horses, Sir James, and buy blankets for the trail. Luther, you find a grocery store and sack us up some grub. And make sure there's bedrolls for Sir James and Judith before you leave Albuquerque."

"And, Shawn, what are you gonna be doin' when I'm doing all this sackin' and makin' sure-in'?" Ironside asked.

"I'm going after Bonnie Prince Charlie before the snow covers the bandits' trail." Shawn looked at the sky. "Which might be real soon, I reckon."

"And how the hell do I foller your trail?" Ironside grumbled. "Didn't think of that, did you?"

"Luther, I've every confidence in you," Shawn said. "You're an Injun on the trail. You'll find me."

"Then let me go after the damned bandits," Ironside said.

"No. You're just like my brother Jake, you'd go off half-cocked and charge a dozen outlaws without giving it a thought. You pick up the supplies like I said and see that Sir James and Judith get good mounts."

"Damn it, Shawn, when you and me get back to Dromore you're in for some lessons on how to treat the hired help." Ironside's eyebrows lowered. "Did you remember to bring your gun or have you took a notion not to carry one anymore?"

Shawn smiled. "I've got my gun right on my hip, Luther. Sir James, I'll see you and Judith on the trail."

"Be careful, Shawn," Sir James said. "I think the recovery of the Prince may be fraught with the most singular peril to your person."

"Damn right," Ironside said, even though he had no idea what the hell the Englishman was talking about.

# Chapter Thirteen

Shawn O'Brien followed the tracks of the bandits north along the east bank of the Rio Grande, riding across flat sage country studded with prickly pear, cholla, and piñon.

The sky had not yet made good on its threat to dump more snow, but the wind was bitter and cut like a knife through every seam and tear in Shawn's sheepskin. Around him lay a lost and lonely land where a man could be killed and no one around to ask the why of it.

After an hour, the tracks swung to the east in the direction of the Sandia Mountains. A two-thousand-pound bull was not to be hurried and its tracks were relatively fresh, making deep impressions in sand and the occasional patches of grass.

Shawn reckoned the rustlers were no more than a couple hours ahead of him, slowed as they were by the terrain and Bonnie Prince Charlie's stately gait.

Ahead of Shawn rose a pinnacle of mountain rock, so high it lost itself against the black of the sky.

Two men at its base caught his attention, one of them bent over as he examined the front left foreleg of his horse.

The tracks of the bull and the rustlers led close to the bottom of the rock cliff and that troubled Shawn enough that he opened his coat to clear his gun. It could be that one of the rustlers' mounts had gone lame and another man had stayed behind should the horse be incapable of going farther.

As he rode closer, the man who'd been looking at his mount's leg straightened and stared in Shawn's direction. Hurried words were exchanged between the two. They stood side by side and watched him.

Wary, Shawn slowed his horse and came on at a slow walk.

The man to his right shoved aside his blue plaid mackinaw and showed his holstered Colt. The other man's gun was already cleared.

Shawn figured that he was riding into big trouble and there was no backing away from it.

"Howdy," the man in the plaid mackinaw greeted, smiling.

Shawn nodded. "Howdy your ownself."

"My hoss pulled up lame and I been pushing him for an hour, but he can't take another step."

"Sorry to hear that," Shawn said. "I guess you boys will need to ride two up until you can swap for a sound mount. There are ranches ahead in the Cedar Mountain country."

"That was our intention." The other man was small and slender and looked as though he'd be quick. Gun-confidence had given him an arrogant tilt to the head that spoke of nothing but trouble. "But now we've changed our mind. I mean, you showing up on a good horse an' all."

"He isn't for sale," Shawn said tightly.

The man in the blue mackinaw spoke again. "Cowboy, we ain't in the market to buy. We're taking."

"You're pushing it, mister. Don't push any harder."

The small man looked at his companion. "Hell, he's scaring me, Bill. Is he scaring you?"

"Ooh, yeah. Right out of my wits." Bill's face hardened. "Git off that damned hoss before I blow you off it."

"You boys stole my black bull, huh?" Shawn said conversationally.

"And you came after it, all by yourself like a good little soldier," Bill said. "That was a big mistake and you're the one that made it."

Shawn shook his head, pulled off his gloves, and shoved them in a pocket. "No, you made the mistake. Instead of getting your rifles and bushwhacking me at a distance like your kind of trash do, you gave me an even break."

"Hear that, Luke?" Bill said. "What we got here is a big, bad, Texas draw fighter. Why don't you show this boy what a fast draw really is?"

"Sure will," Luke said, grinning. "Catch this'n, cowboy." He drew.

Shawn, a split second slower because of sitting his saddle, took a bullet in his left shoulder before his own shot smashed home. Hit hard in the center of his chest, Luke cried out in surprise and anger.

Shawn ignored him.

He turned on the man called Bill who had cleared leather, but shot way too fast. A startled exclamation point of mud and snow kicked up between the front hooves of Shawn's horse and Bill screamed in horror, knowing he was dead.

He was right.

Shawn gunned the man until he fell, three shots—two in the chest, the third tearing off Bill's lower jaw, leaving his face a mangled mask of meat, blood, and bone.

A bullet split the air next to Shawn's head.

The small man Luke lay on his back, his smoking Colt leveled. He desperately tried to thumb back the hammer with a slippery, scarlet hand.

The last round in Shawn's revolver ripped into the gunman's throat and all the life that was in Luke, named for the gentlest evangelist, left him.

Shawn slumped in the saddle as the snow came down and tumbled around him. He was hit hard, and already pain pounded at his shoulder. He lifted his coat and saw that his shirt was glistening red from his shoulder down to his gunbelt. He was in a sorry fix and he knew it.

Shivering in the cold wind, his body shaken with pain and shock, Shawn sat his saddle for a while and gathered his strength. Then he kneed his horse forward close to the base of the cliff and climbed wearily out of the saddle. There, the wind was less, but the eager snow found him. The air was laced with ice crystals and hard to breathe.

The lame horse, a stocky paint mare, hobbled to the meager shelter of the rock face and stood close to Shawn. Her head hung and the gusting wind whipped her black tail across her flank.

Shawn's back slid down the rock until he was in a squatting position. To his relief, his cigar case was undamaged. After three attempts and three matches, he managed to get a cigar lit, its glowing tip and smoke giving him the illusion of warmth.

Around him, land and sky merged into a single, gloomy wall of gray, the only sound the rush of the wind, the only movement the fluttering fall of the snow. The two dead men were very still.

Shawn felt weak and his head spun. A man much addicted to tobacco, the cigar helped keep his spirits up, as did the thought that Luther and the others would arrive soon . . . unless the worsening weather had them pinned down somewhere.

It was a sobering possibility and one that was growing more likely with every passing minute. The day was much colder and the wind stronger, the ominous signs of an aborning blizzard.

A wounded man could die real quickly when night fell and the temperature plunged.

Weak as he was, Shawn knew he had to find shelter before he could no longer sit the saddle or his horse foundered.

Heading south to meet up with Luther was out of the question. He'd ride into open brush country and in a blizzard that wiped out the delineation between earth and sky, enter a death trap.

Shawn struggled to his feet and stood for a few moments until his dizziness settled. The pain in his shoulder had grown less, but whether that was a good or a bad sign, he didn't know.

Using up the last of his strength he climbed into the saddle. His cigar had burned out and he tossed it away, then pushed his reluctant horse back into the full force of the wind and driving snow.

All the Dromore range was farther east, and Shawn had no real knowledge of the terrain around the Sandia Mountains, a fact that could kill him.

He rode north, keeping close to the timbered foothills, and after a mile or so he realized how foolhardy he'd been. His horse was slowing, the wind and cold wearing on him, and he was so weak he could barely stay in the saddle.

The icy cold had stopped the worst of his bleeding, but that did nothing to bolster his confidence. If he didn't find shelter soon, he was a dead man.

Riding head down against the north wind, Shawn and his mount were covered in snow as though they'd been sculpted from a block of alabaster. He wore leather gloves but his fingers were stiff from the cold and his breath had frozen on his mustache. The wind shrieked, cursing his persistence, and above him all the black sky offered was a dark shroud to cover him when he finally had the good sense to give up and die.

He crossed an ice-rimmed creek, the white corpses of dead willows on both banks, and rode onto a flat, dead wasteland of brush, piñon, and thickets of mesquite.

There was no shelter and no hope of any for miles. The only option he had was to choose his place to die.

From somewhere close, a dog barked.

# Chapter Fourteen

Shawn O'Brien peered, blinking, through the torn white fabric of the snow, but saw nothing.

The dog barked incessantly, its sensitive nose reading the wind.

Shawn drew rein and called out, "Who is there?"

It was a useless effort. The words were torn out of his mouth by the tempest and hurled away, unheard.

To his surprise, it seemed that the white world around him suddenly stood on end, and a moment later, his body hit something hard that jolted pain into his wound and left him breathless from shock. It took him a while to realize he was lying on the ground. His horse stood close by, head hanging, its tail turned to the wind.

The dog no longer barked and the only sound was the thud of Shawn's heart in his ears.

He tried to struggle to his feet, but fell back, spent. Snow cartwheeled around him and he knew it was the end. The storm had completely blanketed the trail and not even Luther could find tracks where there were none.

Shawn rolled onto his back and let the snow settle on him like a blessing. For the first time in hours he felt warm . . . and drowsy . . . ready for sleep . . . .

"Up! Get up!"

Hands tugged at Shawn's coat, but he lacked the will to even open his eyes.

"If you stay here will you not die?"

A man's voice, oddly familiar.

"Get away from me," Shawn whispered.

"And let you die? That I will not do."

Shawn opened his eyes. A concerned, bearded face, wrapped in a blanket, leaned over him.

"I know you," Shawn said. "I'm sure I've seen you before."

"And why shouldn't you? Am I not Abraham Grossman, the peddler?"

"But how . . ."

"Get up, Mr. O'Brien. If you lie here much longer, you will freeze to death."

"I'm shot through and through. Just leave me the hell alone. And bring Lorena here. She knows about gunshot wounds."

"There's no one by that name here. Only me," Grossman said. "Now, I'll help you to your feet."

"I'm in trouble, Abe, ain't I?" Shawn's face was a white mask of frozen snow.

"Oy vey, the troubles I have should fall on your head." Grossman sighed. "Two times I am robbed of my wagon and mule. Here, up now. There's no time to waste."

Revealing surprising strength, the peddler tugged Shawn to his feet. Grossman had lugged a heavy pack on his back for years and it was not a task for weaklings.

Shawn swayed on his feet and Grossman caught him just in time before his knees buckled.

After he looked around him, Shawn said, "Where's the colonel and Jake and them?"

Grossman ignored that. "I'll lead your horse, Mr. O'Brien. And you will hold onto me."

"Call me Shawn."

"Yes, I'll call you Shawn. Now, we must move or we'll both freeze to death."

Wind-driven snow wheeled around the two men and the icy cold bladed into them. His lungs on fire, his breath smoking, Shawn managed, "I'm crazy, aren't I?"

Grossman nodded. "*Bist meshugeh.*"

"What does that mean?"

"You're crazy."

Stumbling through savage wind and snow, Grossman led the way to a burned-out rock cabin situated near a shallow dry wash. Only the north wall of the cabin still stood, its top partially broken down by the spreading branch of a vagrant cottonwood.

The roof's heavy, charred beams had fallen in, but several angled from the wall and formed a lean-to of sorts. Across these Grossman had secured a canvas tarp. A small, unenthusiastic fire flaunted its feeble flames at the base of the wall.

Solomon, still heavily bandaged, lay close to the thin heat, his intelligent brown eyes watching as the peddler helped Shawn into his meager shelter and sat him near the fire with his back against the wall.

After adding a few almost dry sticks to the fire and settling the coffeepot onto the coals, Grossman shouted against the howl of the rising storm, "I'll unsaddle your horse and shelter him in the piñon on the rise on the other side of the dry wash. There's some graze on the slope and the trees cut the worst of the wind."

Shawn was beyond caring. His chin dropped to his chest and he slept.

When Grossman returned, wrapped like a cocoon in his blanket, he poured coffee and shook Shawn awake. "Drink this."

Shawn took the tin cup in his hand, shivering.

The peddler took it as a good sign. "Drink. It'll help you get warm."

After trying a taste, Shawn said, "Worse damned coffee I ever drank."

"So, you should try making coffee in a blizzard." Grossman rooted around in a sack and produced a pint of whiskey. "Here, try some of this." He poured a generous shot into Shawn's cup and waited.

After a sip Shawn said, "It's better, if I can call bad coffee and cheap whiskey *better*."

"Kiss my ass," Grossman said. "Now, let me take a look at your wound."

Because of the cold, the peddler didn't remove Shawn's coat, but pushed it off his shoulder. After examining him front and back, he said, "It's stopped bleeding, but the bullet is still in there. It has to come out."

"Abe, I'm not crazy anymore, so I know this will hurt like hell."

"Yes, that it will." Grossman shook his head. "That it will."

"Have you ever taken a bullet out before?"

"Only once, after a settler up Kansas way accidentally shot himself in the thigh with a hunting rifle. His wife was a Piute woman and she showed me how."

"Did the sodbuster live?"

"Oh yes. Wasn't he right as rain within a month?" Grossman poured more bourbon into Shawn's cup. "Drink."

He watched Shawn sip the raw whiskey for a while then said, "The settler's name was Lafe Grimes and he called his wife Three Horses. You know why he named her that?"

"Because that's what he paid for her?"

"No, it's because all she ever did was nag, nag, nag." Grossman smiled as he poured more whiskey. "Drink."

"Are you trying to get me drunk?" Shawn asked.

"Numb at least. I need to cut out the bullet."

"Abe, I'm not real brave when it comes to cutting."

"And who is? Any man who tells you he's brave enough to face the knife has his suspicions."

The wind flapped the canvas tarp like a wet flag and the snow fell in fat flakes. Off in the distance among the Sandia peaks a wolf pack, driven by hunger, hunted the high timber country and their howls pierced the relentless roar of the day. Solomon growled and bared his teeth, but it was more for show than any burning desire to tackle a wolf pack.

Shawn drank the whiskey bottle dry and Grossman judged that he was feeling no pain. "Are you ready?"

"I was tracking a black bull that was stolen," Shawn said. "He was a gift to my father from old Queen Vic."

"She's a generous lady, I'm sure."

"Raised it herself with her own two hands."

"Who?"

"Old Queen Vic, damn it."

"Ah, a very industrious lady. Now, are you ready?"

"Cut away, doc," Shawn grinned. "Your dog is real interested in all this."

"Yes, he likes to watch surgery. You'll need to strip to the waist," Grossman said. "I'll help you."

"It's damned cold." Shawn slurred his words. "The wind doesn't stop, or the snow. Nothing stops."

"I know."

The peddler took a Barlow knife from his pocket, opened it up, and plunged the blade into the fire. He manhandled Shawn to a sitting position then helped him strip off his coat, shirt, and underwear. Melted snow ticked from the tarp and hissed into the fire.

"Lie on your coat, Shawn," Grossman said. "I'll try to keep blood off it."

"That is very re . . . re . . . a . . ."

"Reassuring. Yes, I know," Grossman said. "Now lie back."

The bullet wound was ugly and raw and the peddler took a deep breath, steeling himself for what he had to do. He withdrew the knife, the blade black from carbon, but free of the germs that could cause an infection.

Shawn giggled. "Nag, nag, nag. That was a funny joke he played on his wife."

Then he gasped in agony as the blade of the Barlow dug deep.


Luther Ironside was thirty miles away to the southwest, stuck in Albuquerque by the blizzard, and he was a worried man.

"Shawn isn't the O'Brien brother to hole up somewhere and wait out the storm," he said to Sir James Lovell. "Jake could, and so could Sam, and even Patrick, but Shawn loves his comfort and he never took to roughing it like the others did."

"When will it blow over, Luther?" Judith glanced out the window at the steely day. "It looks as though it will go on forever."

"I reckon we'll be able to leave at first light," Ironside said.

"Is that wishful thinking, Luther?" Sir James asked. "Or do you really think that?"

"A little of both." Ironside stared moodily out the

hotel window. The blizzard had cleared the streets of people, but a dray drawn by mules trundled past, the drunken skinner at the ribbons singing "The Star of the County Down" at the top of his lungs.

"One thing I do know, James, is that blizzard or no, I'll take to the trail in the morning."

"Then let us pray that the weather settles by then," the Englishman said.

"If you're a praying man, then say a few for Shawn," Ironside said. "He's the one who needs them."

# Chapter Fifteen

"Sign it, pops, or I'll shoot the girl. Continue to refuse and I'll kill the boy. Ah, me, life's just full of choices, ain't it?"

The porcelain clock on the ranch house mantel struck midnight.

The big man with cruel eyes and a massive boulder of a chin grabbed the rancher by the back of his neck. "Once upon a midnight dreary, while I pondered weak and weary . . ." He grinned. "Don't ponder, pops, just sign the damned thing."

The rancher's name was Tom Johnson. His hair was gray, his manner mild, but he'd fought Apaches and he had sand. "Two thousand acres of grass, three hundred head of prime cattle, and my house for a dollar? You go to hell, mister."

"You got one last chance to sign the bill of sale, pops, and then I introduce your spawn to my good friend Johnny Sligo." The big man looked over at a rodent-faced man wearing crossed gunbelts and a sneer on his small mouth. "Ain't that right, Johnny?"

"Anything you say, Morg. Anything you say."

The big man called Morg grabbed Johnson by the hair and slammed his head again and again into the hard pine table. "Sign it . . . sign it . . . sign it . . ." he yelled.

Finally, Morg jerked back the rancher's bloody head and looked down at him. "Damn you, will you sign it? I had a tooth pulled recent, and I'm in a real bad mood, understand?"

"You go to hell," Johnson said again. His nose was broken and a scarlet torrent of blood ran over his mustache and chin.

"Johnny," Morgan said.

Sligo stepped away from the other gunmen with whom he'd been sharing a jug. "Which one first, Morg?"

"The girl."

Hannah Johnson was thirteen that winter. Blond and pretty, she still slept with the ragdoll her mother had made her for her second birthday.

Sligo drew his gun and smiled at the girl as he thumbed back the hammer. "Say good night, sweetie."

"No!" Johnson yelled.

Too late.

Sligo's bullet crashed into Hannah's forehead and the girl dropped like a puppet that just had its strings cut.

"Now sign!" Morg roared. "Damn you sign or I kill the boy."

"Spare my son," Johnson said, tears in his eyes. "Spare my boy. Let him go."

"Then sign, damn you. The blood of your daughter is already on your hands. Sign!"

Johnson scratched the pen across the bill of sale, unaware that he was signing his own death warrant.

Johnny Sligo, a man who enjoyed killing, a cold-eyed predator without conscience, shot the rancher and the fifteen-year-old son as casually as he'd pot jackrabbits.

"Damn it, we dragged Grossman's wagon all the way here for nothing," Morg said.

"You couldn't have let them live anyway, Mr. Rowlett," a tall gunman with the face of a whipped bloodhound said. "They'd have brung down the law on us."

"No, he could've put his kids in the wagon and drove away, but he chose to be obstinate." Morg Rowlett waved a hand at the three corpses on the wood floor. "As God is my witness, this was none of my doing."

"Hell, it was mine," Johnny Sligo said, grinning. "If you come right down to it."

"Not yours either, Johnny," Rowlett said. "Johnson's obstinacy brought it on himself. He made the wrong choices was all."

The smell of gun smoke was acrid in the small room.

The big man reached into the pocket of his coat and produced a tattered black Bible that he raised heavenward in both hands. He tilted back his head and roared, "Hear thy servant, Lord, and do not blame him for the transgressions committed here tonight. It was none of poor Morg's doing, but the deadly sin of pride in Tom Johnson that brought these terrible things to pass." He bowed his head. "Amen."

Furious at the silence that followed, Rowlett yelled, "Amen!"

The eight gunmen in the room, except Johnny Sligo, the only one of them who didn't fear Rowlett's draw, said "Amen" in unison.

"Good. Now we will give the deceased a decent burial," Rowlett said.

"Hell, boss. It's freezing out there."

"And snowing," another said.

"We'll bury them shallow," Rowlett said. "The snow will cover them pretty damned quick."

"I don't use a shovel, Morg." Sligo's green eyes were narrowed. "I signed on as a gun, not as a damned gravedigger."

A murmur of approval from the rest of the men followed and a couple of them folded their arms in a gesture of defiance. Gunfighters depended on their supple hands and undertaking manual labor never entered into their thinking.

Rowlett said, "Then we'll load them on the wagon and dump them somewhere. Hell, boys, we can't leave them lying underfoot until spring. The Rafter-J is our new home."

"Yeah, but only until you pay us off, Morg," Sligo said. "I don't use a shovel and I don't do cowboying, either."

"Johnny, I plan to build an empire here," Rowlett said. "It takes time and I want all of you to stick. When it comes to paying out, I guarantee every man jack of you will have enough gold in your poke to keep you in whores and whiskey for the rest of your lives."

A few men cheered and Sligo said, "The boss is right about one thing. At first light, we'll need to dump the bodies somewhere or they'll start to stink."

"No," Rowlett said. "We do it now. Look, they're bleeding all over my clean floor. There are arroyos all over this part of the country and we'll find one close and send the sinners to their last resting place."

"Bring lanterns, boys," Sligo said, a sigh in his voice. "We best get it done."

Morg Rowlett led the procession, a lantern raised in his right hand, a bobbing scarlet light. His left clutched the Bible to his chest. Behind him rolled a two-wheeled wagon, a gunman leading the mule in the traces, and then the rest of Rowlett's gunmen, walking two-by-two, a couple of them also holding lanterns.

Pummeled by wind, they trudged head down through the opalescent night, the only sounds the *crump, crump* of their feet in the snow and the creak of the wagon wheels.

Cedar Mountain, its dark bulk lost behind a curtain of falling snow, marked the western limit of the Rafter-J range, but the silent, solemn procession trudged on, men and wagon silhouetted against the white land.

The gunmen's muttered complaints reached Rowlett's ears. Their high-heeled boots, hand-sewn with thin awls on narrow, Texas lasts, were not made for walking in snow across rough country. In fact, they were not made for walking at all. Aching feet, like an empty belly or tobacco hunger, angers a man fast.

A yell from one of his gunmen made Rowlett lower his lantern and halt the march.

"Look, over there!" The man pointed north to a high wall of rock. "Ain't that a slot canyon?"

Others peered through the snow-flecked gloom and another man said, "Yeah, it is, by God."

Rowlett raised both lantern and Bible. "Hallelujah, the Lord has shown us the way! Yea, though we wandered in the wilderness, He led us unto this place."

"All right. Let's get over there and dump 'em," Johnny Sligo said.


The canyon was wide enough to allow the passage of the wagon and the reluctant mule was led deeper until the way was blocked by a rock fall and thick brush. Orange light from the lamps splashed on the canyon walls as the bodies of Johnson and his children were dragged off the wagon and thrown on the wet ground.

"Back the mule up, boys," Rowlett said. "The wagon will come in handy for bringing in wood an' sich."

The gunmen gathered at the mouth of the canyon and a few started to head back for the ranch house.

Rowlett stopped them. "Tarry a few moments longer. And stand close to me."

Once the gunmen, shuffling their feet and blowing on their hands, surrounded Rowlett, he opened his mouth and in a loud baritone sang

*Shall we gather at the river,*
*Where bright angel feet have trod,*
*With its crystal tide forever,*
*Flowing by the throne of God?*

Rowlett looked around him and yelled, "Now, boys, join in the refrain. Sing aloud your praise to the Lord."

He led the way and one by one the gunmen reluctantly joined in.

*Yes, we'll gather at the river,*
*The beautiful, the beautiful river.*
*Gather with the saints at the river*
*That flows by the throne of God.*

The hymn petered out and since there seemed to be no more forthcoming from the grim-faced gunmen, Rowlett said, "Then let us return to the ranch and warmth. And just remember, this day the Lord has seen fit to bestow on us a fine ranch and a prize black bull. Praise His name. Amen."

There were no "Amens" from the gunmen and Rowlett, sensing their angry mood, didn't push it.

# Chapter Sixteen

Shawn O'Brien woke to find Abraham Grossman's sensitive, Semitic face so close to his he could smell coffee on the man's breath. "Are you Saint Peter?" he whispered.

"No, I'm plain old Abe Grossman the peddler. How do you feel?"

"I don't know yet."

"It's morning. "The sun is shining and the birds are singing."

"Is that a fact?"

"No, it's a lie. The wind is howling, the snow is falling, and overnight the temperature dropped. It must be close to freezing."

"That's a hell of a thing to tell a sick man."

"It's a hell of a thing to tell a well man. Can you sit up and drink coffee?"

"From the same pot as you had last night?"

"The same, only worse."

"Well, it's better than nothing."

"Ass kisser." Grossman helped Shawn to a sitting position, his back against the rock wall.

It was then he saw that he was covered in a blanket and that the peddler had on only his old black coat, the collar pulled up around his ears.

"Where's your blanket?" Shawn asked.

"Are you not covered with it?" Grossman said. "The storm covered me. You needed the blanket more than I did. Besides, I had the fire."

"Not much of a fire to keep a man warm, Abe." Shawn pulled off the blanket and handed it to Grossman. "I can get back into my coat."

It was only when the peddler helped him into the sheepskin that the pain hit like a knife blade driven by a sledgehammer. Like nothing Shawn had ever felt before. He gasped, fought to keep back the cry that tried to escape his lips.

Grossman waited.

Defeated, the sheepskin coat hanging loose from his shoulder, Shawn let his head rest against the cold rock, willing the pain to pass.

"I had to cut deep. "You'll need a doctor soon." Grossman poured coffee from the pot he took from the small fire. "This will warm you."

"Give me a minute," Shawn said, his breath heaving fast. "All right, I'll try it." He took the steaming cup in both hands and sipped. "You're right, Abe. It's even worse than last night."

"It's been biling for hours, a black soul in a pot, tormented by hell fire."

"Tastes like it. I have cigars in my coat pocket. Can you get them without moving me too much?"

It took awhile, but Grossman finally extracted Shawn's cigar case from the inside pocket of the sheepskin.

Shawn took a cigar and passed the case to the peddler. "Help yourself."

"I don't mind if I do," Grossman said. "The men who stole your bull also stole my wagon and mule. They took my cigars and threw everything else in the snow. Look around you, this is all I own, a dog and a canvas tarp."

Suddenly, Shawn was alert. "They had an Aberdeen Angus bull with them?"

"What do I know from a bull? It was black."

"The men with him, what did they look like and where were they headed?"

Grossman shrugged. "Big, rough men riding horses with rifles attached to them. They didn't like me."

"Why?"

"Because I'm a Jew."

"How did they know?"

"Who but a Jew is crazy enough to become a peddler?"

"You were lucky they didn't kill you, Abe."

"They felt pity for the dog. They spared me so I could care for him. To some people a dog is more worthy of life than a Jew."

"I reckon you exaggerate," Shawn said. "Most people don't think like that, even Luther Ironside who hates everybody." Despite the cold, sweat beaded on his forehead.

Grossman, seeing it, worried about fever. "We are

a persecuted people," the peddler said after a while. "From long times past."

"That's all ended. The Children of the Book will never be persecuted again, not in this country or in any other. These are modern times, Abe, not the Dark Ages."

"Then I will pray that this is the case," Grossman said.

Shawn smiled. "Depend on it." Pain slammed at him again.

When Luther Ironside found him, Shawn O'Brien was in the grip of a raging fever.

"We heard the dog bark and that's how we found you," Ironside said.

"I told him to keep watch," Grossman said, "and he did. He's a very wise dog."

"I don't know how he saw us. We were a ways off Shawn's trail."

"A dog sees pictures in the wind, that's why Solomon was able to summon you."

Ironside patted the dog's head. "A steak for you, boy, first chance I get."

Judith Lovell kneeled beside Shawn, her hand on his forehead. "He's burning up, Luther. He's got a really high fever."

"Let me, Judith." Sir James took his daughter's place and placed his hand on Shawn's neck and chest. "This is bad. His fever is dangerously high."

Ironside kneeled beside the Englishman. He removed the pad of cloth from Shawn's shoulder.

"I tore it from his shirt," Grossman said. "It was cleaner than mine."

The wound was red and raw, like an opening scarlet rose, but Ironside didn't detect the rotten meat smell of gangrene. "You did a good job, Abe. Cut him up just fine."

"A Piute woman taught me. "Her name was Three Horses."

"It's not the wound that will kill him, it's the fever it brings," Sir James said.

Shawn shivered, muttering as his mind wandered. Judith took off her heavy woolen cloak and placed it over him. She looked up at her father. "What do we do? We must do something."

"Stay with him, my dear. Be here when he dies. That's all we can do."

"The hell with that," Ironside said. "I'm not going to let one of my boys die like this."

He thought for a while, then said, "Listen to this. One time after the Battle of Bean's Station in the winter of sixty-three, I seen General Longstreet's personal doc break a young lieutenant's fever. Saved the boy's life and with him near dead afore."

"How, Luther?" Judith said, interpreting Ironside's mangled syntax. The wind tangled snow in her hair, the tarp too small to shelter five people.

"Well the doc lowered the lieutenant into a stream that had ice along its banks and the cold water broke his fever pretty quick. Me, I watched it happen with my own eyes. I know we don't have a stream, but we got deep snow drifts."

"Luther, it could kill him," Sir James said. "Shawn could freeze to death."

"Is it not worth the risk?" Grossman asked. "Without the snow, he'll die anyway."

"This ain't a matter for cussin' and discussin'," Ironside said. "Miss Judith, you might want to step away. I'm gonna strip Shawn naked as the day he was born."

"I've seen a naked man before, Luther," Judith said. "But I'll close my eyes if you wish."

"Yeah, do that. A buck naked man ain't no Christian sight for a well-bred lady."

Judith smiled and stepped from under the tarp. Around her the snow and wind danced their frenetic quadrille and without her cloak she shivered, her green velvet riding costume doing little to keep the cold at bay.

A few minutes later, Ironside stooped under the tarp, Shawn naked in his arms. He put his unshaven cheek against Shawn's forehead and said, "Hell, this boy is on fire. Abe, dig me a hole in the snow somewhere close. Hurry!"

A deep, wedge-shaped drift had piled up on the south bank of the dry wash and Grossman ran to it. He fell on his hands and knees and began to dig like a dog at a rabbit hole.

Sir James joined him and between them they excavated a cavity in the snow about three feet deep and twice that long.

Ironside carried Shawn to the drift. "Stand aside, boys. I'll lower him. And let's hope this works."

Under his mustache, Shawn's lips were pale and

his breathing shallow, barely raising his chest. The wind tugged at his hair and snow fell on his face, then melted at the touch of his burning skin.

Ironside gently lowered Shawn into the snow. "Quick, cover him up."

Pushing snow on top of Shawn with his bare hands, Sir James said, "Luther, I hope you know what you're doing."

"So do I." Ironside's grim face was set as fear and doubt thrashed at him. "So do I."


Later, when Luther Ironside talked about it, he said that after Shawn had lain in the snow for fifteen minutes, closer to death than life, God performed one of his small miracles.

For a fleeting moment the black clouds parted and a beam of sunlight fell on the anvil-hard land. Borne upward by the wind, snowflakes fluttered in the golden column like the rising of souls . . . and then the clouds slammed shut again and the earth returned to darkness.

Ironside, as superstitious as any vaquero at Dromore, took the sunbeam as a sign. "The fever's broke. Get me a blanket."

Judith, who'd been standing close to her father, ran back to the ruined rock house and returned with the blanket.

Ironside lifted Shawn from the snow and wrapped him in the blanket like a cocoon. He again shoved his unshaven chin against Shawn's cheek. "He feels cooler."

"He's been buried in snow, Luther," Grossman said.

"I know, Abe, but I'm clutching at straws here."

"My God, Luther, is he breathing?" Sir James impatiently. "He's cold as ice."

"I reckon so," Ironside said, but there was doubt in his face.

Judith leaned over and put her mouth on Shawn's, her lips parted. After a few moments, she straightened. "He's breathing."

"That's one way to find out." Ironside said.

# Chapter Seventeen

Shamus O'Brien stood at his study window and stared moodily out at the snow, wind, and failing day. "I hope Luther and Shawn had the good sense to find shelter until this storm passes."

Samuel smiled. "Luther has. I'm not too sure about my brother."

Shamus was silent for a while, then said, "Why hasn't James Stuart made a move against us? Our unwelcome guest is holed up in the attic, yet Colonel Stuart does nothing. Why?"

"Weather maybe, Pa," Samuel said. "Even angry men don't ride out in a blizzard."

Shamus turned to his youngest. "Jacob, you know about these things. Do you think Samuel is right?"

The lamps were not yet lit and the log fire cast a shimmering scarlet glow, its flames reflecting in the cut crystal decanters lined up on the colonel's old campaign table. Jacob had just lately returned from the range and he poured himself a whiskey to keep out the chill. "Colonel Stuart is essentially an honorable man, Colonel. He won't stand off and bushwhack a man or set his hayricks on fire . . . or rustle his cattle, either."

"What are you telling me, Jacob?"

"That if Stuart decides to move against Dromore, he'll ride up to our front door with his gun drawn."

Shawn nodded. "He's a gallant Southern gentleman. You will get no argument from me on that score." He tapped his whiskey glass against a window pane blinded by frost. "Damn that hollowed-out excuse for a man."

"You mean Doc, of course." Samuel said.

Irritably, Shamus answered, "Of course I mean Holliday. I would not speak of Colonel James Stuart in those terms."

"You heard what Pat said, Pa," Samuel said. "He means to die a hero's death. It's how he wants posterity to remember him."

Jacob said, "I guess he thinks dying for Dromore a nobler legacy than his dusty little street fight in Tombstone. It seems that in Doc's mind there's no honor in gunning drovers."

"Then I won't let him die the death he seeks," Shamus said. "If James Stuart forces me into a fight, by God, Doc Holliday will have no part of it."

"Another drink, Pa?" Samuel asked.

Shamus declined. "I must retire to my room and say a rosary to the holy saint Child of Atocha that the clouds part and Shawn and Luther survive the storm."

Jacob managed to keep his grin in check. "He's a new one on me, Colonel."

"Your knowledge of the holy saints is sadly lacking,

Jacob, and Luther, benighted heathen that he is, must take the blame." Shamus laid his empty glass on the campaign table.

"The Child of Atocha is the patron saint of travelers and those in peril. When the Moors captured the Spanish city of Atocha, they allowed only children to care for their Christian prisoners. Then a boy child appeared among them wearing the garb of a holy pilgrim. He carried a basket of food and a gourd of water and gave these to the suffering prisoners. Miraculously, no matter how much water he poured or food he distributed, his basket and gourd always remained full."

Shamus took a coral rosary from his pocket. "The Child of Atocha is a very devout and powerful saint and I'm sure he sits at the right hand of God."

"Well, now I know," Jacob said.

"Yes, now you know, but you should've known years ago." Shamus nodded good night and left the study.

After the colonel left, Jacob turned to his older brother. "Sam, had you ever heard of the—"

"Child of Atocha?"

"Yeah."

"Hell, no. Luther was never real big on the saints of Holy Mother Church." He smiled. "But when I'm around Pa, unlike you, I know when to keep my mouth shut."


When Luther Ironside halted his party a mile south of Lone Mountain, the gray day was shading into night and a cold north wind cut to the bone. "We'll camp in the arroyo and head for Dromore at first light."

He looked around at his snow-covered companions, all of them showing the effect of the afternoon's ride through rough, sullen country.

Snow and wind had bullied Judith into a stiff, frozen silence and Sir James was in no better shape. Abe Grossman rode double with Shawn, holding him erect in the saddle. The little peddler, well used to roughing it, was enduring and looked to be in better shape than any of the others.

"As soon as we get a fire lit, I'll rustle up some grub," Ironside said. "It will be simple cowboy fare, Miss Judith, hardly fitting for a fine lady like yourself."

The girl managed a small smile. Her voice weak she said, "I'm sure it will be just fine."

Ironside nodded. "As fine as I can make it, ma'am." He looked at Grossman. "Can you eat salt pork, Abe? Ain't that against your religion?"

"It's not salt pork, Luther. It's fish," Grossman said.

Ironside grinned. "Why so it is. Fresh caught months ago."

The arroyo was more like a great cleft in a rugged rock plateau, created after some mighty earthquakes in ages past. A few stunted juniper and piñon struggled for a living on the plateau itself, and here and there sage and clumps of bunch grass had taken root.

High walls cut the wind when Ironside led the way inside and the trees filtered some of the falling snow.

"It's widening out," he called out over his shoulder. "I see some sort of open area ahead."

Abe Grossman struggled to keep Shawn in the saddle. The young man was unconscious, mumbling in shadowed dreams, and only the peddler's strong arms kept him from falling.

To Ironside's joy the arroyo opened up into what was almost a small pasture about an acre in extent. A rock overhang promised shelter of a sort and as he rode closer he saw a few black fire rings indicating the place had been used before as a campsite, probably by Apache hunting parties.

After Shawn was carried under the overhang and laid on a bed of sand, Ironside found enough wood and kindling scattered around by past campers to start a fire.

Solomon, who'd been riding with Ironside, remained by his side. The dog staggered a little, but he'd figured out that the tall, lean man gathering wood would be the source of grub on this trip and he kept a wary eye on his meal ticket.

The horses discovered grass under an inch of snow, aided by Grossman who cleared a large area with his booted feet. He seemed tireless.

"Shawn's fever is completely gone, Luther," Judith told Ironside. "You saved his life and now all he has to do is recover."

"We saved his life, all of us and that includes the dog," Ironside said. "When he wakes and sees a pretty woman sitting beside him, he'll get better right quick."

But by morning, Shawn O'Brien's breathing was labored and he had not regained consciousness.

# Chapter Eighteen

To say that Morgan Rowlett was concerned about his two missing men would be an exaggeration. At best, he was mildly interested. "What do you figure happened to them, Johnny?"

Johnny Sligo sprawled in a chair by the fire. "Hell if I know."

"They got lost in the blizzard, maybe," Rowlett said. "Easy to do around here."

"Maybe."

"Or they just gave up on me and rode off somewhere."

"Hell, Morg, why talk so much about a pair of nobodies. Do you give a damn?"

"No. I was just saying."

"They weren't worth much," Sligo said. "I didn't like Luke Wilson's face. It was in the back of my mind to gun him one day."

The ranch house that had always been clean, swept, and polished already looked like a garbage dump. Empty bottles and cigarette butts littered the wood floor. Dirty dishes were piled high in the kitchen sink and the place smelled of urine and man sweat.

Rowlett had no idea of his range conditions or how the cattle fared, nor had he any real interest. He was an outlaw, as shiftless and lazy as the worst of the breed. But he had a plan for the Rafter-J that he outlined to Johnny Sligo. "We add to our cattle head count, just lifting a few at a time from the surrounding ranches, and when I reckon we're big enough, we sell the place."

"How long will that take?" Sligo asked.

"Not long. I want to sell an empire, Johnny, not a one-loop ranch."

"Who the hell's gonna to buy the place, Morg?"

"I already have a buyer. Black Tom Church."

Sligo wanted to say, "You're a damned liar," but bit his tongue. Rowlett wasn't a fast gun, but he was mean and big enough to take his hits and keep coming. Sligo settled for, "Black Tom never struck me as the rancher type."

"Me neither, but he told me if I find him a suitable place, he'll pay top dollar."

"But he's in the bank-robbing business. I mean, that's how he made his name. He ain't cut out to be a rancher."

"He thinks he is now, Johnny. Times are changing in the West and Black Tom figures it's high time he quit riding them night trails and becomes legit. And who's more respectable than a prosperous rancher?"

Sligo shook his head. "Black Tom Church a cow rassler. That's hard to believe."

"I know, but it's the truth, right down the middle."

"How much?" Sligo asked.

"With enough cattle on the range, I'd say the sky's the limit."

"How much?" Sligo asked again.

"Fifty thousand, maybe more now we have the Angus bull."

"Black Tom has that much money?"

"No, but he has partners."

"Who?"

"I don't know," Rowlett said. "Does it matter?"

"Including you, there's nine of us. Fifty thousand don't go far in that kind of split."

"Who says we need to split the money nine ways? I was thinking fifty-fifty, me and you."

"What about the others?"

"We pay them a few dollars for their trouble."

"The boys will expect gun wages and those come high," Sligo said.

"Johnny, you'll take care of it. You got the credentials and that's why I hired you."

Sligo smiled. "Not if they come at me all at once."

"Well, I leave it to you to work it out. But only after we stock the range."

"I can whittle them down, I guess."

"You may have help, if Black Tom comes here. When it comes payoff time, he's mighty tightfisted, but he's slick with a gun."

Reading the question on Sligo's face, Rowlett said, "I sent a rider to Albuquerque to tell Tom where we're at. I reckon he'll show to protect his investment, you might say."

"Hell, Morg, you know how Black Tom is around

women," Sligo said. "He could bring the law down on us."

Rowlett smiled. "Johnny, Johnny, can't you tell that I'm funnin' you?"

Sligo's voice iced. "Don't make fun of me, Morg. Not ever again. Was that all a lie about Black Tom Church?" He stood, clearing his guns. "Think real careful before you answer that."

Rowlett, a massive man, sat at ease in his chair. "I didn't tell you no lies, Johnny. But, see, my constant prayer has made me smart, way smarter than you. Call it a blessing."

"Talk," Sligo said. "And speak clear."

"All right. We sell this place to Black Tom, only we don't really sell it. You catching my drift, Johnny?"

"Maybe. Talk."

"We get the fifty thousand from Tom and his partners, give them a bill of sale"—he made a gun of his forefinger and thumb—"then pop! pop! pop! Goodbye Tom. Good-bye partners."

"And we can sell the ranch again?" Sligo asked.

"You catch on quick, Johnny." Rowlett smiled. "That is, if you think you can shade Black Tom."

"There ain't nobody I can't shade"

"I agree with you there, Johnny. I've never seen anybody faster."

"And you never will." Sligo sat again and thought for a few moments. "All right, Morg, I'll go along with you on a fifty-fifty basis and I'll do any killing that's needed. But I say we set tight and don't lift any cattle. That way we won't attract unwelcome attention."

"How many cows do we really have, Johnny?" Rowlett asked.

"Hell, I don't know. How do you count heads in the middle of winter?"

"I don't know either, but we'll lift a few, just to keep the boys busy. The ranchers around here will never miss them, figure they died or something."

"A few then, Morg. A big-time rustling operation could land us in deep trouble, and I mean shooting trouble. The ranchers around here don't sit on their gun hands."

"I accept your advice, Johnny." Rowlett stood and picked up his Bible. "Now, would you like to pray with me for the success of our venture?"

Johnny Sligo frowned. "Go to hell."

# Chapter Nineteen

Jacob O'Brien was in the blacksmith's shop shoeing a draft Percheron when Luther Ironside led his small band to the front door of Dromore.

When Jacob saw Shawn supported on his horse by a small, bearded man, he threw down his hammer and left the shop at a run.

"Shawn is sick, Jake," Ironside yelled when Jacob was still at a distance. "He's real sick and we got to get him inside."

Jacob reached up and Abe Grossman helped Shawn into his arms.

"Luther, he's been shot," Jacob said.

"I know that, Jake. Now take your brother in the house."

The commotion brought out Shamus and Lorena and some of the servants.

"Jacob, what has happened to my son?" Shamus asked.

"He's been shot, Pa."

"Get Shawn inside," Lorena said. "Put him on the couch in the parlor where it's warm."

Jacob, followed by Lorena, rushed inside with Shawn in his arms.

Shamus rounded on Ironside. "Luther, what happened?"

"It's going to take some tellin', Colonel," Ironside said.

"You better come inside and tell it then," Shamus said, his face like stone. "And I'll be listening closely, Luther." As though he'd only just noticed them, he said, "Who are these people?"

Ironside made the introductions. "Abe is a peddler and a Child of the Book. The dog is his."

"You are all welcome to my home, including the dog." Shamus turned to a housemaid who was standing close by. "Milly, please assist Miss Lovell inside."

Ironside said, "Colonel, the black bull—"

"Tell me in the house, Luther," Shamus said. "Please, Sir James and you too Mr. Grossman, come inside. My men will see to the horses."

On the way to the door Shamus glared at Ironside. "Jesus, Mary, and Joseph, but this is a dark day at Dromore, Luther."

Before Ironside could respond, Shamus hurried inside. All his segundo could do was follow and close the door after him.

"Luther did what he thought was best, Colonel O'Brien," Sir James Lovell said. "If there is blame, then we must all share it. The snow was the only way to bring down your son's fever and save his life."

"Pneumonia, Lorena says. Shawn needs rest and good, healthy food," Shamus said. "There is no blame, Sir James. You all performed very well under trying circumstances."

"I commend Mr. Grossman to you, Colonel," Sir James said. "He was a pillar of strength on the trip to your home."

"You're a Child of the Book, Mr. Grossman," Shamus said.

"Indeed I am, sir, and a poor peddler with nothing left to peddle."

"Then will you bide awhile and celebrate Christmas with us? If there's anything I can do to accommodate your own beliefs, please let me know.

"And my dog? His name is Solomon and he's wise."

"Of course. I said before, Solomon is most welcome, too."

"Then I accept your kind offer."

Shamus cast a critical eye over Grossman. The little man had swapped his wet, muddy clothes for duds provided by Patrick and they were much too large for him.

"We must find you some clothes that fit. May I call you Abe?"

"Please do. But are these clothes not finer than any I have ever worn?"

"Then we'll get them altered. One of my household staff is a seamstress and she'll fit some clothing to you."

"Please, I don't wish to trouble you, Colonel," Grossman said.

"Nothing is too much trouble for the man who helped save my son's life."

Sir James also wore borrowed clothes and Judith looked beautiful in one of Lorena's dresses. The only O'Brien who didn't donate was Jacob, whose wardrobe was deemed by Shamus too worn and ragged for decent folks.

The parlor door opened and Lorena and Judith stepped inside.

"Shawn is resting comfortably," Lorena said. "He opened his eyes and saw Judith and smiled, so I'd say he's feeling much better."

"Thanks be to Jesus and his blessed mother," Shamus said.

The door opened again and a parlor maid ghosted through it. "Colonel, begging your pardon, but how many for dinner this evening?"

"The same as for lunch," Shamus said. "My sons will be out on the range until tomorrow."

The maid said, "Thank you," and left.

And the door opened a third time.

Doc Holliday, a spectral figure in a long white nightshirt, carpet slippers, a blanket wrapped around his shoulders stepped inside. He seemed surprised that there were other people present, and his bleached eyes lingered for a moment on Judith. "Pardon my intrusion, Colonel, I was not aware that you have guests."

Shamus made the introductions, then Sir James said to Doc, "Are you a doctor of medicine, sir?"

"No. I'm a dentist, or was."

"An honorable profession," Sir James said with all the courtliness of the English gentry.

"Maybe so. But for many years now I've pursued a profession less honorable, that of saloon gambler."

"Ah." It was a one syllable sound that implied dismissal, disdain, and contempt for a breed Sir James despised.

It was not lost on Doc. "You have no liking for gamblers, sir?"

"I've seen too many men ruined by them," Sir James said, "including my own father. After he gambled away everything he owned, he took his own life."

Shamus didn't care for the direction the conversation was taking and he stepped in quickly. "What can I do for you, Dr. Holliday?" His distaste for the man was obvious.

"I'm out of whiskey and almost out of laudanum, Colonel," Doc said. "I wonder if I could impose on you for a bottle of each."

Out of the corner of his eye, Shamus caught a glimpse of Ironside. Luther stood poised, stiff, a man of quick, lasting affections and terrible hatreds. He was a hard man, bred of a hard and lonely land and he'd been tempered by a savage war. His judgments of other men were quick, instinctive, and unerring. Shamus knew that Luther had judged Doc Holliday and found him wanting.

"Luther," Shamus said, "would you ask one of the maids to get a bottle from the cellar and take it to Dr. Holliday's room. And see if we have any laudanum."

Shamus saw it then, the slow turn of Ironside's head in his direction, the hammered steel in his eyes, the grim set of his mouth under the great, sweeping dragoon mustache.

"Please, Luther," he said, almost pleading. "If you would be so kind."

Doc had met men like Luther Ironside before, tall, rangy men who took a deal of killing. The big man's dislike of him was a palpable thing, and he felt as though he stood in an icy draft.

Without a word Ironside strode to the door and left the room.

His going left a vacuum that no one, not even the normally talkative Abe Grossman, felt inclined to fill.

Finally Doc said, "Once again, I apologize for the intrusion and my night attire." He gave a little bow. "Sir James, Miss Judith." Grossman he omitted, as though a peddler was of little importance.

After Doc left, Sir James said, "Colonel O'Brien, I apologize if I spoke out of turn."

"Many good men have been ruined by gambling, Sir James," Shamus said. "Your words were well chosen."

"What, pray, is wrong with that man?" Judith asked. "He looks awful."

"He's dying of consumption and whiskey is the only thing left to him," Shamus said. "Poor, lost creature, the crows' curse is on him to be sure."

# Chapter Twenty

Black Tom Church was taking his ease.

The shabby red velvet and brass confines of room seven in Madame Marie DuPont's cathouse smelled of cheap perfume, whiskey, cigar smoke, and ancient sweat. The cast iron clock on the mantel was there to remind gentlemen that time was fleeting and that sporting gals needed a high turnover of horny males to make ends meet.

But Black Tom ignored the clock. He had no intention of paying, anyway.

A man who'd been named for his shaggy mane of black hair and dark skin, the heritage of his Cheyenne mother, he sprawled in an easy chair, his appearance a stark contrast to the naked blonde who sat on his huge knees and fed him whiskey from a brown bottle that bore a label containing only the handwritten word—*RYE*.

Close to him on a table was his gunbelt and holstered Colt. There were those who said Black Tom Church had killed eighteen white men, but the number was closer to thirteen. He could never be sure.

His two business partners were in adjoining rooms separated from his by thin, plasterboard partitions.

Zeke Lawson had embezzled a small fortune from the Austin bank where he'd worked as a clerk. Black Tom had promised him a safe escort out of Texas and a partnership in a ranching venture in the New Mexico Territory. Small, mousy, and terrified of winding up in federal prison, Lawson had jumped at the chance.

Nate Sullivan was a successful bank and train robber, but like Black Tom he'd a vision of leaving the profession and going straight. He had twenty thousand dollars in his carpetbag and an engraved Colt that he handled well.

It was in Black Tom's mind that he would hurt the yellow-haired whore before he left the joint. But that would not be for a while yet. At the moment, he was enjoying her too much.

Marie DuPont's brothel didn't do a roaring trade in winter. Situated just across the New Mexico border from El Paso in a dung heap of a settlement named Springburn, Marie's girls were not the prettiest or the cleanest and working the line in cow towns had worn them out long before. The brothel was the last stop before a hog ranch, and the weary girls knew it.

If Black Tom was aware of this, he didn't given a damn. To him, a woman was a cheap mare to be ridden hard then tossed away.

It was probably better for his peace of mind that he didn't know of the man who stood in the foyer downstairs, in his pocket a yellowed newspaper clipping with a cascade of headlines.

### *MARSHAL JOSEPH LANE MURDERED!*

---

### *Tom Church's Deadly Revolver Does Its Work*

---

#### JOE LANE HURLED INTO ETERNITY IN A MOMENT

---

*Wife and Three Children Weep for Him*

##### BLACK TOM AND HIS COHORTS FLEE ABILENE—
##### BANK ROBBER'S WHEREABOUTS UNKNOWN

The man in the foyer was Joe Lane's brother. Tall and bearded, a pharmacist by profession, he pulled a Smith & Wesson American .44 from the pocket of his brown overcoat and said to the bouncer, "Rooms?"

"Mister, are you sure you want to do this?" The bouncer was a muscular Irishman with his thin hair parted in the middle. In a fist the size of a ham, he held the double eagle the stranger had given him. "Them boyos are hard men and dangerous."

"Rooms," the bearded man said again. He had mild blue eyes, spider webbed with red veins.

"Your funeral," the Irishman said. "Rooms four, six, and seven."

"Which one is Black Tom's?"

"I don't know. I saw the three gentlemen go upstairs with three girls. Madame DuPont told me the room numbers and said for me to make sure the gentlemen paid before they left."

"Are the rooms locked?"

"Sometimes the girls lock them from the inside, but more often they don't. Gentlemen who've been drinking can get violent and the girls don't like locked doors."

The bearded man nodded and made his way to the stairs.

"Mister," the bouncer said, "may God have mercy on you because Black Tom won't." He watched the man mount the steps, taking care to make no sound, a respectable looking gent wearing a bowler hat and good tweed clothes.

The Irishman shook his head and then looked at the gold coin in his hand. Ah well, what happened next was no concern of his.


The bearded man stood outside room four and listened. Inside a brass bed creaked in frantic rhythm and a practiced soiled dove made little *Ooh* and *Ah* sounds.

He tried the door and it opened.

There was a blur of movement inside. First, a man's naked butt pumping, then a scream from the girl. The man turned on his back and yellow lamplight stained his white body. He made a dive for the gun at the bedside, snarling.

The bearded man fired twice. At a range of ten feet he didn't miss. The naked man took two bullets to the chest and the bearded man left to the woman's screams.

In room six the man was already on his feet, his genitals dangling, and the woman in the bed had pulled the sheet over her breasts. He and the bearded man fired at the same time, and both scored a hit. But the naked man's Colt was fired in shocked haste and he hit the bearded man high in the right shoulder. His enemy's bullet was better aimed and took the naked man in the throat, smashing his Adam's apple back into his spine.

The bearded man didn't stay to watch him fall. He stepped into the hallway again where Black Tom Church pumped three bullets into him.

The bearded man's name was Ezra Lane and as he fell to the carpeted floor of the hallway he knew he'd failed. He tried to raise his revolver, but it seemed too heavy for him. With the last of his strength, he yelled, "This was for Joe, you horse's ass!"

Black Tom, unimpressed, shot the bearded man between the eyes.

The Irish bouncer ran up the stairs and went from room to room, seeing only terrified women and dead men.

When he stopped in the hallway, Black Tom said, "Who the hell was he?"

"Hell if I know," the bouncer said. "He just walked into the place and asked after you."

"He said, 'This was for Joe.' Who the hell is Joe? I don't know any damned Joe."

"Beats me, Mr. Church," the Irishman said. "He must have mistook you for somebody else."

Black Tom motioned down the hallway with his blue chin. "Did he do for Zeke and Nate? They're my partners in a business venture, like."

"They're both dead," the bouncer said. "They ain't anybody's partners now."

"Hell. Far as I recollect, they didn't know anybody called Joe either."

The Irishman shook his head. "It's a strange world, Mr. Church. People do crazy things."

The big man didn't respond, his brow wrinkled in thought. "Wait, I shot a marshal in Abilene a while back. Was his name Joe, do you figure?"

The Irishman shrugged. "I wouldn't know anything about that."

"Ah well, it doesn't matter a damn," Black Tom said.

The woman stood at the door, wrapped in a sheet. He grabbed her arm and pulled her into the hallway. "I ain't in the mood no more. Beat it."

"What about my money?" the woman said.

"Hell, you got slack tits and wrinkles around your mouth. I ain't paying you good money for that. Now, git the hell out of here."

"The girl should be paid," the Irishman said. "It's only fair."

"Then you pay her." Black Tom pushed the big, strong bouncer aside as easily as he would a twelve-year-old boy.

It only took a couple minutes for Black Tom to empty the wallets and carpetbags of the two dead men and strip them of their watches and rings. The man he knew as Nate had owned a nicely engraved Colt and this he stuck in his waistband.

Black Tom stuffed the money and jewelry into one of the bags and reckoned his haul would top out at around fifty thousand dollars. Not a bad night's work.

When he stepped back into the hallway, the enraged woman attacked him. Completely naked, she jumped on his back and pummeled his ears with her fists. "You swamp rat!" she yelled. "Give me my money."

Black Tom turned, slammed the woman's back against the wall again and again and when she finally fell he pulled the engraved Colt and shot her between her slack breasts. "I told you to beat it and shut the hell up," he said to the dying woman. "You didn't take my advice."

Madame DuPont, plump, blowsy and breathless, clumped up the stairs and gasped to the Irishman, "Timothy, the law is outside."

"How many?" Black Tom asked.

"The sheriff and two deputies."

"We got four dead up here, ma'am," stated the man called Timothy. "The man on the floor at your feet accounted for two of them and this man here"—he nodded in Black Tom's direction—"took care of the rest."

Madame DuPont's eyes had grown accustomed to the lamp-lit gloom of the hallway and she saw the woman's body. "Who . . . who killed Lottie?"

"Hell, I did," Black Tom said. "She wasn't worth a plug nickel let alone twenty dollars."

Her eyes round as dollar coins, Madame DuPont screamed. She turned, hiked up her skirts, and her fat legs pounded on the stairs. "Murder!" she yelled as she sped for the door. "Bloody murder!"

Unhurried, Black Tom went back to room seven, put on his hat and mackinaw, and tied a yellow woolen scarf around his neck. Then he took time to reload both revolvers.

A hick sheriff wasn't about to come barging through the cathouse door, not if he'd any sense he wasn't.

A few other women, in varying stages of undress, crowded around Lottie's body and one of them spat in Black Tom's direction. He grinned, then said to the Irishman, "You planning on being a hero?"

"Not me, mister," the man said. "They don't pay me enough. I'm out of it."

"Then ditch the shillelagh, Mick, and do it now."

The bouncer pulled a blackjack from his pants pocket and let it drop to the floor.

"Now walk downstairs," Black Tom said, a Colt in one hand, the carpetbag in the other. When they reached the door, he said, "Now open it."

"Mister, this isn't exactly healthy," the bouncer said. "Them boys outside are nervous and they'll be quick on the trigger."

"Things are tough all over. Now open it and step outside."

A moment later the Irishman made the last, and worst, mistake of his life.

He lunged for the door, threw it open wide, and ran onto the boardwalk. "Don't shoot!" he yelled. "It's only me!"

The inexperienced sheriff and two nervous young deputies could not be counted on to hold their fire.

The bouncer was cut down by a hail of lead, dead when he thudded like a sack of grain onto the boards.

And hell came right behind him.

Black Tom Church, a seasoned gunfighter against overgrown farm boys, stepped onto the boardwalk, his Colt blazing.

The sheriff went down, hit an inch to the right of the star on his vest, and then one of the deputies fell, gutshot and screaming.

Terrified, the third lawman, an eighteen-year-old towhead, dropped his gun and ran. Black Tom could've let him go, but he didn't. Hit twice in the back, the deputy did an odd little sprawling dance, then hit the snow-streaked mud of the street.

Black Tom holstered his gun, drew the fancy Colt from his waistband and walked into the middle of the street, the dead sheriff lying at his feet.

Springburn's only street consisted of a row of cabins, a couple stores, a blacksmith's shop and a saloon with a false front and canvas roof. The street was deserted, but oil lamps guttered in the saloon and its open door cast a rectangle of dim orange light onto the mud.

"All right, you damn chickens. Who wants to arrest ol' Tom Church?" he roared, his eyes burning with black fire.

A head popped out of the saloon door and Black Tom took a pot at it. Wood splintered off the door frame and the head ducked back inside.

"Is there anybody?" he yelled. "Come out you lowlifes and face me."

Black Tom got no takers that night.

But Madame Marie DuPont proved that she had more sand than the menfolk and staged a grand-stand play. The woman stomped out of the hotel on her stubby legs and without a word, cut loose at Black Tom with a Greener scattergun.

Unfortunately for Marie, her aim did not match her courage.

The buckshot ripped through the air a foot from Black Tom's head. He turned like a dancer, his gun coming up fast, and slammed two shots into the woman, a large, wide target.

Marie cried out, staggered, then fell backward in a flurry of white petticoats.

Echoes of Black Tom's shots racketed around the town as he shoved his gun back into his waistband and walked to the livery to claim his horse.

He rode out of town and grinned, exalting in the man-strength that surged through his powerful body. It had been his last, wild fling before he settled down to a respectable new life as a cattleman . . . and by God it had been crackerjack!

# Chapter Twenty-one

Four days after Luther Ironside returned to Dromore, a vaquero was murdered and a number of Herefords stolen west of Hurrado Mesa.

"How did it happen, Manuel?" Ironside asked, his grim face made grimmer by the news.

The vaquero turned his hat in his hand. "Quique was tending the fire as I went into the trees to find more dry wood. Because of the snows such wood was hard to find and I wandered far in my search." He glanced at Shamus O'Brien as though he feared the patron's wrath for leaving Quique alone.

But Shamus said gently, "Go on, Manuel. Just tell us what happened."

Patrick handed the vaquero a glass of brandy that he accepted eagerly and immediately downed in one gulp.

The brandy seemed to bolster the man's confidence. "I heard shots and made my way back to the camp. It took me some time because the underbrush was thick." He took a deep breath. "Quique lay on his face by the fire and I counted three bullets in his back. Then I saw that the cattle were gone."

"How many head, Manuel?" Ironside asked gruffly.

"There were five Hereford cows grazing near the mouth of Hurrado Canyon. They were all gone."

"Tracks?"

"It was snowing, senor, but I would say they were headed west."

"Did you see anybody, Manuel?" Shamus asked.

The vaquero shook his head. "No one, patron. There was a heavy snow and the day was coming on dark."

Shamus looked at Samuel. "What do you think? Rustlers or James Stuart?"

"I don't know, Pa. It depends how far Stuart is willing to go."

"By God, if it was him, then he's in for a war." Shamus smacked the table with his fist. "And if he was responsible for Quique Ortega's death, I'll hang him."

"Colonel, could this in any way be connected to the theft of the Aberdeen Angus bull?" Sir James Lovell wondered.

Shamus had persuaded the Englishman and his daughter to stay on at Dromore for Christmas and their trunks were being sent by rail and wagon from their hotel.

"This could very well have been Stuart's doing," Shamus said. "The curse of the seven snotty orphans on him."

Shawn, still pale and weak, sat by the parlor fire. "I believe the two men I killed over in the Sandia Mountains country may have been part of the gang that rustled the bull. I'd never seen them before, but they were not James Stuart's men. I'll lay to that."

He turned to Jacob. "What do you think, Jake?"

"Doesn't seem like Stuart's style. And I don't believe he'd sanction the killing of a Dromore vaquero. Not like that, not shot in the back."

"If he did take the bull, he may plan to keep it hostage in return for Doc," Patrick said. "I'd say that's a possibility."

"What about the vaquero?" Jacob asked.

"I agree with you, Jake. Stuart is not a murderer." Patrick thought for a moment. "Unless the death of his son tipped him over the edge."

Shamus rose from his chair and as was his habit he stood at the window and stared into the dying day.

Speaking to his back, Ironside said, "The way I see it, Colonel, we got two choices—plug Holliday or plug Stuart. Either way, it's done."

Shamus was silent for a long time. When he spoke, his voice was flat and strangely toneless. "Luther, go to the closet in the hallway where we keep the honored battle flag of the Confederacy. Beside it, you will find a stout blackthorn stick that I brought from Ireland as a boy. Leave it beside the front door because I'll have use for it tomorrow morning when I confront James Stuart."

Ironside grinned. "Now you're talkin', Colonel."

The O'Brien brothers exchanged horrified glances, then Samuel said, "Pa, what do you plan to do?"

"You will see tomorrow, Samuel. Until then, this matter is closed for discussion."

"God help us," Samuel whispered. "This doesn't bode well."

Sir James Lovell looked at Shamus with horrified eyes as though he'd just been struck.


Colonel James Stuart's ranch lay to the east of the San Pedro Mountains, a series of high country meadows watered by runoff from the nearby peaks. Like Shamus O'Brien, Stuart had few longhorns, his stock mostly made up of Herefords.

Though not as grand as Dromore, the ranch house was a sprawling, well-built timber structure with a fine shingle roof. Rooms had been added to keep pace with their growing family. Stuart's wife, a former schoolteacher, had produced two sons and five daughters.

A riding accident three years before had confined Alice Stuart to a wheelchair, but she'd then turned her energies to writing Gothic romance novels "for refined young ladies" that had begun to generate good sales.

Still grieving for the death of her son Kyle, murdered at the hands of Doc Holliday, she had not written for a while. It was she, sitting by the fire, her hands folded in her lap, who saw Colonel Shamus O'Brien and a party of men draw rein outside her house.

Shamus, the heavy blackthorn stick across his saddle horn, called out, "James Start, come out and show yourself, man!"

Behind the colonel were Jacob, Samuel, Patrick, and Ironside. Four vaqueros flanked the Dromore men, two on each side.

Five men had stepped out of the bunkhouse when the Dromore men arrived. Four of them punchers, but it was the fifth man who attracted Jacob's attention. The tall, lanky form, still sporting a beaded Cheyenne band on his hat, was unmistakable.

Wolf Hartmann was a gun for hire, one of the best there was. A couple years before, he and Jacob had guarded a gold shipment out of the Black Hills.

Hartmann's presence was bad news. A man who drew gun wages was always on the prod, hunting somebody to smoke up to justify the expense.

The ranch house door opened and James Stuart stepped outside. A light fall of snow was coming straight down in the cold, windless morning. He wore a gun and a sour expression. "You interrupted my breakfast, Shamus O'Brien. Declare your intentions and be damned to ye."

"I have two questions for you, James Stuart, and you will answer them on your honor. Did you steal my Black Angus bull? That, sir, is one. The second is did you have a hand in the murder of one of my vaqueros, Quique Ortega by name?"

Stuart's face flushed with anger, and he opened his mouth to speak.

But Shamus held up a silencing hand. "No, don't answer me yet." He swung stiffly out of the saddle. Blackthorn stick in hand, his face like stone, he advanced on Stuart. The old saber scar on his cheek stood out like a livid streak of lightning.

Stuart seemed alarmed.

Hartmann's hand dropped to his gun as he looked quickly at his boss seeking a sign.

Jacob noticed the move and called, "Wolf."

Hartmann's eyes darted to Jacob, then recognition dawned on his face.

Jacob shook his head, a slow, slight movement.

Hartmann's hand moved away from his gun.

Shamus stopped in front of Stuart, holding the blackthorn stick in both hands. "I'll have my answers soon, James Stuart."

"Aye, and I'll give them to you."

Shamus moved quickly. He used the stick to draw a circle in the muddy ground around Stuart, who watched him in puzzled amazement. "What the hell are you doing?"

"James Stuart, don't take a step out of that circle until you are willing to give me truthful answers to my questions as a Southern gentleman should," Shamus said. "If you refuse, then by God you'll die in that ring I scribed, circled by your own disgrace."

Stuart's face was black with anger. "Damn you Shamus O'Brien. I never in my life told a lie to any man."

"Do you swear it?"

"Aye, I swear it as a Southern gentleman who bears a king's name. And I swear it to God, and I swear it on the soul of my dead son, and I swear it by the reformed religion of the Presbyterian Church of

Scotland of which I am a member that my answers will be truthful."

"It is benighted you are, James Stuart, cast adrift from Holy Mother Church with the stain of excommunication on you like the mark of Cain, but you've sworn a powerful oath and I will listen to you."

"Then hear me well, Shamus O'Brien, and know that from this day forth there will be only enmity and the mailed fist between us."

Stuart angrily kicked away all trace of the circle that surrounded him and then moved closer to Shamus until their noses were almost touching. "I did not steal your black bull, Shamus O'Brien, and I had no hand in the murder of your vaquero. Such is not the way of me and mine. And this I say to you, if you do not release the murderer Holliday to me soon, you'll find me at your front door, gun in hand and then, by God, we'll have it out."

"You have made your intentions clear and you have sworn a mighty oath that you tell the truth," Shamus said. "I do not doubt you on either. So do your worst, James Stuart, and be damned to you, I say."

The ranch house door opened and Alice Stuart sat her wheelchair in the doorway. A tall, good-looking young man with reckless blue eyes stood behind her.

Finnean Stuart was twenty that winter and he had a wild streak, but Patrick O'Brien who knew him quite well had nothing bad to say about him. Nothing good, either.

"James," Alice called out, "it's a cold morning.

Invite the gentlemen inside. I have coffee on the stove and hot biscuits."

James Stuart's face fell. Suddenly, a prisoner of the manners of the South and the open hospitality of his Scottish culture, he looked like a hunted deer trapped in a thicket.

Shamus, the devil in him, decided to enjoy this. He stared at Stuart and, smiling, his left eyebrow rose in a question.

"James," Alice yelled, "please do as I say." She directed her attention to Shamus. "Colonel O'Brien, I have salt butter and honey for the biscuits. You will come inside now before you all perish from cold."

Stuart's voice sounded like a freight wagon on a potholed road. "My wife has invited you into my home, Colonel."

Shamus looked past the other man, swept off his hat and gave a little bow. "I'd be delighted, Mrs. Stuart. You do me great honor."

# Chapter Twenty-two

It is easy for a man who doesn't sleep to get up early.

Doc Holliday rolled out of bed and stood open-mouthed in the chill air of his bedroom while his rotted lungs battled to keep him breathing. His nightgown flapping around his skinny legs, he stepped to the window and looked outside.

The snow had stopped, but the night had not yet shaded into morning and beyond the window panes he saw nothing but darkness.

He knew it would come, violent, bloody, and racking, and he took a chair beside the cold fireplace, a clean white rectangle of cloth in his hands.

It came, worse than he ever remembered, the dreadful cough that pounded his chest like a sledgehammer and sent jolts of pain slamming through his frail body.

When it was over the cloth was scarlet as a bullfighter's cape and Doc lay back on the chair struggling for breath, exhausted.

After a few minutes, he felt strong enough to struggle to his feet and pick up the whiskey bottle beside his bed. He drank deep and the bourbon soothed him, warming him like a visit from an old friend. He carried the bottle with him back to the window.

Four vaqueros, wrapped to the eyes in heavy mufflers, walked saddled horses to the front of the house and Doc knew he had no time to lose.

He dressed hurriedly, dropped his Colt into the pocket of his overcoat and then settled his bowler hat on his head. Like the vaqueros, he wrapped a long scarf around his neck, the fringed ends hanging to his knees. He stepped to the window and again glanced outside.

Shamus O'Brien was already in the saddle, three of his sons and the vaqueros with him.

Doc smiled. Good. He wasn't going to miss any of the fun.

After the O'Briens rode away, Doc made his way downstairs. He met no one. The household servants had not yet started their tasks and everyone else, including the snooty Englishman and his daughter, were still abed.

When Doc stepped outside the icy air knifed into his lungs and made him gasp. But he continued to walk purposely toward the stable. His face was ashen, his nose red with a pendulous drip at the end.

If there was to be a gunfight, he didn't want to miss a moment of it. Doc was ready to start chiseling

the first words of the epitaph that would adorn the
fine marble tombstone he'd no doubt deserve.


The O'Briens were riding south.

Doc Holliday followed at a fair distance. His little
mustang seemed eager for the trail, but Doc kept
him at a walk. With snow and mud underfoot, he
had no fear of raising dust, but the O'Briens were
the kind to check their back trail carefully and often.

After a couple miles riding into a cold wind, Doc
felt the familiar bumping in his chest that always
gave warning of a coughing fit. He tried to ignore
it, hoping it would go away.

It didn't.

The cough started slow and rumbling deep in his
chest, then moved higher, thickened with bloody
phlegm. Doc's thin body reeled in the saddle as the
full, hacking force of the fit hammered at him.

Alarmed, the mustang lifted its forelegs off the
ground and Doc tumbled out of the saddle. He hit
the ground hard, then struggled to his feet and
staggered to a patch of snow near a stand of mixed
pine and spruce.

He lost his footing and fell on his face, the raking
coughs tearing at his lungs. Doc buried his face in
snow that soon turned crimson.

He pounded his fist again and again into the
ground, angry and knowing it was how the last spasm
of coughing would be. The one that would kill him.

Only it would be worse, much worse, beyond anything he could imagine even in his nightmares.

Finally the cough eased and he could breathe again. But barely. He felt like a man dying of thirst who can take only a tiny sip of water at a time.

His shredded lungs were giving up the battle and Doc Holliday realized his time was shorter than he'd imagined. He was fast running out of space on the dance floor.

His cough had laid it out for him.

Doc had trained the ugly little mustang to stand and it grazed close by. He grabbed a low pine branch and pulled himself to his feet.

He grabbed a handful of snow, let it melt in his mouth and then spat it out. It splashed pink onto the ground. He did it again, trying to get the taste of blood out of his mouth, then again and again until finally his spit was clear.

He looked up to judge how far he had to go to make it to the horse and stumbled to him. For a few moments, he rested against the mustang's flank, then climbed into the saddle.

He had lost time and the gunfight might already be over, but he dared not kick his mount into a run for fear of falling again. He walked the horse forward and prayed he would not be too late.

Damn it. He had to die with a gun in his hand, his booted feet planted firmly on the ground.

But, lurking unseen in the shadows, fate had a different plan for Doc Holliday . . . a different road to travel.

\* \* \*

It was snowing again, just a handful of flakes tumbling in the rising wind, when Doc saw the abandoned surrey. Only when he rode closer did he notice the dead man in the seat.

He drew rein and studied the body. The man was old, white-haired and he'd been shot and probably robbed. Certainly his ring finger was missing and his horse had been taken.

The bullet splintered the air next to Doc's head, followed a split second later by the flat statement of a rifle.

He didn't bolt for cover, but turned in the direction of the shot.

Two men sat their horses about a hundred yards away, one of them with a rifle in his hands, the other leading a paint pony.

It seemed the rifleman was satisfied with taking just one warning shot, because he and the other rider turned and vanished into the pines.

Normally, Doc would have reckoned that the murder of an old man was none of his business. But the fact that some lowlife had taken a pot at him changed his attitude quickly. It was a grave insult and one a gentleman of breeding could not ignore.

Doc swung his horse and headed for the pines.

He was unfamiliar with the lay of the land, but directly to his south were the shallow mesas of the White Bluffs, almost lost under a weight of black cloud. Ahead of him, forested high country was cut through by deep, mysterious arroyos.

Wary of crossing the open meadow between him and the pines, Doc swung wide and followed the tree line.

When he heard voices and a man laugh, he dismounted and hung onto the saddle horn until his breathing settled. After a few moments, he walked into the trees, his light feet making no sound. He had his gun in his hand, holding it behind the tails of his coat.

Two men, dressed in mackinaws and wool pants tucked into tooled boots, stood in a clearing, one of them holding a wallet in his hand, fingering through the bills inside.

"Fifty-fifty you said, Bud."

"That's right. We split seventy dollars." Bud continued counting the money in the wallet.

"Hey, what about the gold watch?"

They were totally oblivious to Doc until he coughed, something that came easily to him.

"What the hell are you?" Bud said, turning.

"Hell, it's the old man we done come back to haunt us." The other man's eyes grew wide.

"Shut your damned trap, Lou. This ain't no boogerman. He's just another old-timer lost in the woods."

"Hell, gun him, Bud," Lou said. "We'll have us another wallet and watch. The old geezer looks like he's well-heeled."

"How does that set with you, pops?" Bud smiled

like a man preparing to enjoy himself. "You got a wallet and watch you don't need anymore?"

"Are you the damned ruffian who just took a pot at me?" Doc said, ignoring that.

"Yeah, I did. Warning you off, like. You got something to say about that?"

"I don't like people taking shots at me," Doc said. "It scares me and when I'm scared bad things happen."

"Is that a fact?" Bud said. "Bad things happen, huh?"

"Indeed they do, my thuggish, knuckle-dragging friend."

"You got anything else to say before I put a bullet in your brisket, old man?" Bud's hand dropped to his gun.

"Only this." Doc's Colt flashed from behind his back and he fired.

Bud took the bullet in the center of his chest and his half-drawn gun dropped from his hand. He went down on his knees, his mouth agape, stunned at the manner of his death.

Doc ignored him, aware that he'd scored a kill, and swung his Colt on Lou, a loose-geared man who used a cross-draw holster. Lou's gun cleared the leather fast, but he didn't get off a shot. Doc pumped two bullets into him, both in the belly, and the man dropped.

The pain hit Lou like a massive punch to the gut and he screamed.

As is the habit of all gunfighting men, Doc punched out the three spent cartridges and reloaded. He dropped the gun back into his pocket and looked around at the carnage he'd wrought. One man dead, the second dying, but little glory in this fight.

"Mister, get me to a doctor, please," Lou wailed, his teeth clenched against an agony that went far beyond what any man should be asked to endure.

"It's too late for doctors," Doc said. "Best you take your medicine and make your peace with God." He shook his head. "By the way, I never did see a cross draw that was worth a damn in a close fight."

As Lou continued to groan in mortal agony, Doc saw the glint of gold chain hanging out of Bud's pants pocket. He stooped and pulled on the chain and found it was attached to an expensive gold watch. Partial to watches, Doc slipped it into his pocket. He turned and made to step out of the clearing to recover his horse.

Behind him Lou moaned, "Don't leave me, mister. I'm hurting bad here."

"Sorry, I have to go," Doc said. "Life goes on, you know."

Lou clutched at his belly, his hands slick with blood. "I knew it would come to this pass. Last night I dreamed the black bull crawled out of the devil's shoe." He grimaced, holding back the pain. "That was a bad omen. That's why I lie here gutshot and dying."

Doc was surprised. "You have the black bull? Where the hell is it?"

But Lou was beyond talking. He kicked his legs and moaned, beyond speech, beyond thought, intense pain the core of his being.

"Ah well, it doesn't matter," Doc said. "I'll leave you to die in peace."

"Kill me. . . ." Lou gasped. Snow crusted his ashen face.

Doc looked down at the man, his body strangely misshapen as he contorted himself around the bullets in his belly. "Damn it. That will cost me fifteen cents," Doc said. "Cartridges don't come cheap, you know."

"Kill . . . kill . . . me. . . ."

"Oh, all right," Doc said. "It's a charitable act so to hell with the expense, right? I mean, it's my Christian duty."

He pulled his Colt and fired a bullet into the top of Lou's head.

"There," Doc said, as snow and gun smoke coiled around him. "Now are you satisfied?"

But the only sound was the wind in the trees. The dead were silent.

# Chapter Twenty-three

"Well that was awkward. To say the least," Patrick O'Brien said.

Luther Ironside grinned. "Alice Stuart makes good biscuits, though."

Shamus was riding in front with Samuel and he turned. "Did you see James Stuart's face, all down in the mouth? 'Twas a sad sight that would bring tears to a glass eye in a jar."

"It was strange, us bunched on one side of the kitchen, Stuart's men on the other," Patrick said. "Not the most sociable breakfast I ever ate."

The flat bulk of Glorieta Mesa loomed in the distance. The windblown peaks of snow on its top made it look like an unmade bed.

The air was crystal clear and cold.

"I will say this," Shamus said, "James Stuart told the truth when he said he didn't steal the Angus bull or murder my vaquero. He is not a man to lie."

"Then who did, Pa?" Samuel asked.

"Son, if I knew that, we'd be riding in the direction of the thieves and not Dromore."

Shamus turned in the saddle so he could see Jacob. "That man you were talking with, the one with the Indian hat band. Who is he?"

"He's a hired gun by the name of Wolf Hartmann," Jacob said. "The last couple years he's been operating out of Dallas, Texas. I was surprised to see him this far north, way off his home range."

"How good is he, Jake?" Ironside asked.

"Good enough. He's fast on the draw."

"Why would James Stuart hire a gunfighter?" Shamus said.

"If shooting starts between us and Stuart, Wolf is a handy man to have around," Jacob said. "He's fast on the draw and he'll stand, no matter what."

Ironside grinned. "Hell, you can shade him any day of the week, Jake."

"Probably, but I don't like drawing down on people I like."

"You like this man Hartmann?" Shamus asked. "Although I don't know why I should find that surprising."

Jacob's horse tossed its head, jangling the bit.

"He and I guarded a gold shipment out of the Black Hills a few years back," Jacob said. "Wolf pulls his weight, is as steady as a rock, and doesn't scare worth a damn. He sings almost as well as Shawn and makes good coffee on the trail, so I took to liking him."

"His kind of man can be a handful," Ironside said. "If it comes to shootin', like any other dead wolf, I won't trust him until he's skun."

Shamus shook his head. "Luther, you take the most roundabout ways to say a thing."

Patrick smiled. "What's your opinion of Stuart, Luther?"

"Well, he's a good Presbyterian like me, so in my book he can't be all bad."

"What did you say, Luther?" Shamus frowned.

"Nothing, Colonel. I didn't say nothing."

"I should hope not. Luther, you're not a good Presbyterian, you're a bad Presbyterian. When did you last say a prayer?"

"I don't know, Colonel. I haven't bucked the tiger in quite a spell, so prayin' hasn't entered into my thinkin' real recent."

Shamus shook his head. "Luther, I'm not going to chide you because you don't know any better. But when we get back to Dromore I will give you instruction on the benefits of fasting, prayer, and abstinence from gambling and strong drink as laid down by the doctrines of the Holy Mother Church."

Ironside bent his head and whispered something to Jacob about strong drink, fasting, and kiss my ass.

"What did you whisper, Luther?" Shamus glared.

"Nothing, Colonel."

"I should hope not. Remember that the whisper of temptation can be louder than the most triumphant call to our holy duties."

Ironside nodded. "I'll keep that in mind."

"See you do," Shamus said.

"Something up ahead," Samuel said, his eyes

staring into distance. "Hey, isn't that old Doc Lloyd's surrey?"

"Sure looks like it." Without another word, Shamus urged his horse forward and the others followed.

The old man lay sprawled on the seat, the front of his coat covered in blood. The coat had been ripped open and the gold watch and chain that Matt Lloyd always wore was missing, as was his wallet. His left ring finger had been cut off to get at his wedding band and the robbers had taken his mare from the traces.

After a single glance at the body, Jacob and Ironside were already casting around, looking for tracks and not finding any because it was snowing again.

"Looks like they just rode up on him and cut loose," Samuel said.

Patrick shook his head. "Who would do this to Doc Lloyd? He was the gentlest, kindliest old man that ever was."

"He was all of that," Shamus said. "And more."

Doc Lloyd had retired and lived with his widowed sister in a cabin north of Glorieta Mesa, but he still delivered babies and treated cuts, bruises, and broken limbs when needed. He had likely been answering such a call when he was waylaid and murdered.

"Jacob, Luther, did you find anything?" Shamus yelled, his voice pitched louder by the shock of what he'd seen.

"Nothing so far, Colonel," Luther answered. "But we're still lookin'."

"Pa, how long do you figure Doc's been dead?" Samuel asked.

"A couple hours, looks like. Patrick, what do you think?"

"His body is ice cold. Two hours, maybe more."

"We can't lay this murder on James Stuart," Samuel said.

"Samuel, please don't state the obvious," Shamus said, irritated. He'd been fond of Matt Lloyd and his murder disturbed him deeply.

"It could have been anybody, a couple drifters trying to make a fast buck," Patrick said.

"Why do you say, 'a couple,' Patrick?" Shamus asked. "Why not one?"

"I don't know why I said a couple. It just feels to me that there was more than one man involved."

"Interesting," Shamus said, but his mind was no longer on Patrick. Jacob had called Ironside over and both of them had dismounted and were checking the ground.

"What do you see?" Shamus hollered. "Tell me what you see."

Jacob rose from a kneeling position and cupped his hands to his mouth. "It looks like tracks."

Shamus swung into the saddle again, stiffly. The healed wound in his back still punished him in cold weather. He rode to Jacob and Ironside and dismounted. After studying the ground he said, "They're horse tracks all right, heading west is my guess."

"It will have to be a guess, Colonel," Jacob said.

"It's been snowing off and on for hours and the ground is hard. I don't think we'll find more."

The three men stood still in thought, snow drifting around them.

"Jacob, terrible things are happening and I have no understanding of them," Shamus said. "It's as though the world is passing me by at a tremendous rate."

"I'm just as confused as you are, Pa. There must be a connection. Our bull is stolen, then a vaquero is bushwhacked and cattle are rustled . . . and now this, the death of an old doctor who never harmed a living soul in his life."

"Suppose we call a meeting of all the ranchers in the area," Ironside said.

"Why?" Shamus asked.

"Well, to get their opinions on what's happening around here."

"Getting them together in one place at one time is tough enough," Shamus said. "Now with winter cracking down hard, it will be even more difficult."

"What would happen anyway?" Jacob asked. "As usual, they'd drink our whiskey and then poke holes in the air with their fingers and demand more law for this part of the territory."

"Jacob is right, Luther," Shamus said. "Finding the killers of my vaquero and Doc Lloyd is something Dromore will do alone."

"Talkin' of docs, all this trouble started with the arrival of Doc Holliday," Ironside said. "Strange that, ain't it?"

"Do you think Holliday is involved in this in some way?" Shamus asked.

"No, I reckon I don't," Ironside said. "I was just sayin' that it's mighty queer."

Shamus brushed snow off his saddle with a gloved hand and mounted. "Luther, we'll take Doc Lloyd's body back to his sister, a thing I do with a heavy heart. Neither of our horses will cotton to pulling a surrey so you'll need to put Doc up behind you."

"I don't mind. Doc Lloyd was always good company."

# Chapter Twenty-four

Doc Holliday made it back to Dromore before Shamus O'Brien and the others returned. The cough, aggravated by altitude and cold, didn't hit again until he was in his bedroom.

Doc had laid his gun and the gold watch on a table by the window and had removed his damp coat when his chest exploded in a violent, bloody eruption. He fell on the bed and within seconds his pillow turned scarlet. His frail body racked, he lay on his belly, helpless and battling for a breath that refused to come.

Shawn O'Brien found him in that position. "My God, Doc, I heard you all the way downstairs."

Unable to answer, Doc coughed . . . and coughed . . . as though he'd never stop. Like the gutshot man back at the clearing, he foresaw only death at the end of this nightmare of blood, phlegm, and pain.

The harsh, kettledrum racket of the raking coughs

filled the room and brought Lorena to the door. She stuck her head inside.

Shawn said, "Don't come in, Lorena. I'll take care of it."

Her face registering shock, Lorena left and Shawn could only stand and watch and listen, unable to help, no words of comfort coming to him.

After what seemed an endless time, the coughing subsided a little.

Doc rolled off the bed, his head leaving a pillow that could only be thrown away. He staggered to the window. With a movement of a thin hand he indicated to Shawn that he should open it.

Shawn, weakened himself, tried to lift the window, failed and tried again. He brushed against the table which tipped over, spilling Doc's gun and the gold watch to the floor, then lifted the window, allowing a blast of icy air inside.

Doc stood at the window and fought for breath, his narrow chest rising and falling from the effort.

"Breathe deep, Doc," Shawn said. "Just take it slow and easy."

As Doc fought his never-ending battle to get air into his lacy lungs, Shawn bent to pick up the watch and revolver. The fall had opened the back of the watch and revealed the tinted portrait of a middle-aged woman.

Shawn recognized her immediately—she was Daisy Clark, Dr. Matt Lloyd's widowed sister. An impossible suspicion nagging at him, Shawn sniffed the muzzle of Doc's Colt. It had been fired recently, so recent that sooty powder residue blackened the barrel and cylinder.

Doc was still at the window, his back turned.

Shawn felt his coat. It was damp and the pants Doc wore were wet around the bottom. He'd been out somewhere and Shawn was willing to bet his horse would show signs of being ridden recently.

Even as he snapped the watch shut and stood, Shawn told himself that his suspicions were preposterous.

But how much did he really know about Doc Holliday? The answer was—very little. Was the man truly capable of murdering a much-loved old doctor for his watch?

Shawn had no answer to that question, a fact that disturbed him greatly.

"How is Doc?" Jacob O'Brien asked.

"After what you've just told me about finding Matt Lloyd, I'd say he's in a heap of trouble," Shawn said.

Jacob's face asked a question and Shawn told him about the watch and Doc's recently fired Colt.

When his brother finished, Jacob said, "Doc had no reason to kill Lloyd."

"Maybe he wanted his watch," Shawn said.

"Doc Holliday is a scoundrel, but he wouldn't murder a man for a gold watch."

"Then how did he come by it, Jake? And why had he fired his gun? Answer me that."

"I don't know. But I aim to find out."

"You asked me how he is, well he's failing fast.

The consumption is far gone. When I was up there he had a fit of coughing that covered his bed with blood. It took the maids an hour to get his room cleaned up, and that was with Lorena and Judith helping."

"Against my better judgment," Shamus said. "Lorena shouldn't be around Holliday and expose her son to tuberculosis."

Jacob smiled. "It's useless to tell Lorena not to do a thing."

"And that also goes for Judith." Sir James grimaced. "She feels sorry for Holliday. Calls him a poor thing."

"He's not a poor thing if he killed Doc Lloyd," Shawn said.

"No, then he's a murderer," Jacob said.

"In England we hang murderers," Sir James said.

"And we hang them right here at Dromore," Jacob said.

"Jake, you'd better talk to Doc before the colonel and Luther get back," Shawn said. "You know how those two feel about him, especially after taking Matt Lloyd's body to his sister. They're liable to stretch Doc's neck just on the evidence of the watch."

"I'll talk with him," Jacob said. "I don't think he killed Matt, but if he did, I'll hang him myself."

Doc Holliday sat by the fire, shivering in his shawl, a glass of whiskey in his hand. He looked like a skeletal wraith and his blue eyes were fevered. He made a striking contrast to the tall, muscular Jacob, dramatic as a pale poet standing next to a blacksmith.

"Well, 'pon my soul, Jacob, to what do I owe this honor?" Doc asked.

Jacob was not in the mood for small talk. "I may have to hang you, Doc.

"For what, pray? I swear, I only pushed your maneating cat out of my room, and visited no violence upon her. She's a pretty calico to be sure. Nice white teeth."

Jacob ignored that. "Where did you get Dr. Matt Lloyd's watch?"

"Was that the dead man's name? Ah, and a physician to boot."

"You have his watch and your gun was fired recently, Doc. Explain all that to me."

"Jake, after all the time we've known each other do you really think I'd murder an old man for a watch, and a gold-plated one at that?"

"How did you get it?"

"If I tell you will you believe me?"

"I don't know. Give it a try. And Doc, make it good."

Doc refilled his glass. "It's a depressing little tale, and I know how prone you are to dark moods."

"Let me hear it, anyway."

Doc took a gulp of whiskey then told how he'd found the body in the surrey and had been fired upon by two men that he later killed. "As for the watch, the gentleman who had it in his possession had no further need for it, so I took it. My own watch is old and doesn't keep good time."

"Then the bodies will still be there," Jacob said.

"Yes, unless dead men can walk."

Jacob stepped to the window and looked outside. The snow had stopped and there were still a few hours of daylight left. He made up his mind. "I'm going to look for the bodies, Doc, and they'd better be there."

"I imagine they still are."

Jacob moved toward the door, but Doc's voice stopped him. "One of the low persons I killed mentioned something about a black bull. He might've been talking about the one you mislaid."

"What did he say?" Jacob asked.

"He said the bull was an animal of ill-omen, and that's why he got shot." Doc shrugged. "He was quite wrong. In point of fact, he got shot for taking a pot at me."

"Did he tell you anything more?"

"No, that was it. If it's any help, those boys weren't passing through. They'd no bedrolls, so I have the feeling they were close to their home range."

"What else can you tell me about them?"

Doc shrugged his thin shoulders. "Nothing else, Jake. They were young and wore expensive boots. That's about it."

Jacob was about to say, "Thank you," but he didn't. He wasn't in the mood to be polite to Doc Holliday.

\* \* \*

The surrey was where Jacob and the others had left it, but it was shrouded with snow, as though prepared to take a skeletal bride to her wedding.

Doc had described the forested area where he'd had his gunfight and Jacob rode into the trees and scouted around for several minutes, working back and forth along the tree line.

He found no bodies.

High country heavy with pines, it was a scattered growth in some places and thick stands in others. Higher on the ridges, aspen and a few spruce grew. If a man wanted to hide bodies, this was the place. On the other hand, if he wanted to find them, then he had his work cut out for him.

Jacob dismounted and led his horse back to the clearing that he'd figured was the one Doc had talked about. He studied the ground more closely and cast around in the brush.

After fifteen minutes of searching, he found splashes of dried blood and three spent .45 cartridge cases. It seemed that Doc had been there all right, but where were the bodies?

Jacob realized that further search would be futile. He gathered up the reins of his horse when heard footsteps behind him and froze.

"Don't be alarmed none, Jake. It's only me, ol' Nathan Cox as ever was."

Jacob turned and smiled. Cox was one of the old gold prospectors who roamed that part of the territory and he was rumored to have earned and spent several fortunes, a liking for gambling, whiskey, and sporting women his undoing.

"What the hell are you doing here, Nathan?" Jacob asked. "Don't you always sleep away winter in a hollow log somewhere?"

"Usually, Jake, but I found me some color down Cougar Mountain way an' I've got enough in my poke to hole up in Santa Fe 'til spring."

"Still got old Polly, I see.

"Sure do," Cox said, patting the little animal's neck. "Best damn burro a man ever had."

"You been watching me for a spell, Nathan?"

"Not long. Heard you trompin' around in the woods is more like. I figgered the grizz was back."

"What grizz?"

"The one that took them two bodies you're lookin' fer, I reckon."

"He carried them away?"

"That's exactly what he done." Cox scratched his long white beard. "Ol' Ephraim ain't partic'lar what he eats in winter."

"I thought grizzlies hibernated like you, Nathan."

"That's what a lot of folks think, but a b'ar can wake up hungry fer a snack, just like me or anybody else."

"Did you see where the grizz took those two dead men?"

"Nope, just seen him carry one away, then come back for t'other. Me an' Polly watched for a spell, but we didn't come close." Cox jerked a thumb over his shoulder. "Somebody left a good-looking surrey over that way. Did it belong to them two?"

Jacob didn't feel like going into it. "No. No it didn't."

Cox raised a hand. "Got to be on my way, Jake. Nice talking to you again. How long since I seen you in Silver City that time?"

"It's been a spell, Nathan."

"Yup, a long time, seems like." Cox raised his hand again. "Well, so long, Jake. Take care."

"You too, Nathan. Take care."


Night was cracking down fast as Jacob headed back to Dromore.

Doc was in the clear as far as the Lloyd murder was concerned, but the mystery remained of why one of the men he'd killed had mentioned the black bull. Was it just the raving of a gutshot man? Or had the man helped steal, or at least seen the Aberdeen Angus? And where?

More questions without answers.

Jacob kicked his horse into a canter.

No doubt Doc Holliday deserved to be strung up for the many crimes he did commit. But Jacob had no wish to see him hung for one he didn't.

# Chapter Twenty-five

"The place is a damned dump," Black Tom Church said. "And it stinks."

"Tom, be reasonable. Look at the potential of the place," Morgan Rowlett said. "A few improvements and in a couple years this ranch will be worth five times what you paid for it."

Black Tom glanced out the ranch house window into the gray day and then directed his attention to Johnny Sligo, who was sitting with his back to the fireplace wall.

"What's that, Rowlett?" Black Tom said, nodding in Sligo's direction.

"Why, Tom, that's—"

"I can speak for myself," Sligo said, his face ugly. "The name is Johnny Sligo, and if you ain't heard it before, Church, you should've."

"Hell," Black Tom said. "If I had to keep track of the names of every snot-nosed kid with a gun I've met, I'd need to keep a book."

Johnny Sligo rose to his feet, death in his eyes. "Don't ever put me in your book, mister."

For a moment Black Tom was taken aback, then he laughed. "Johnny, I like the cut o' your jib. I reckon you and me will get along just fine."

"See, Johnny, didn't I tell you that ol' Tom was true blue?" Rowlett said. "Now get yourself a drink and simmer down while he and I talk business."

"Just so long as he never calls me a snot-nosed kid again," Sligo said.

"I won't Johnny, I swear it," Black Tom said. "Once I own this ranch you and me are gonna cut a wide path in this territory. Now how about giving ol' Tom a whiskey, huh?"

To Rowlett's surprise, Sligo did just that, and all the prod seemed to have left him.

"So, Tom, you got the fifty thousand?" Rowlett asked.

"Right here in my saddlebags, Morg. Fifty and a shade more."

"Then I'll make you out a bill of sale and we're done."

"Let me see your own bill of sale for the place first."

Rowlett retrieved the bill of sale that the murdered rancher Tom Johnson had signed and handed it to Black Tom. "There you go, all legal and above board."

Black Tom scanned the paper and threw it on the table. "This one-loop spread ain't worth fifty dollars, let alone fifty thousand. How many cattle you got?"

"I don't know, Tom. I haven't counted them yet."

Rowlett felt a twinge of unease in his gut. This wasn't going to be as straightforward as he'd thought.

"How big is the spread?"

"I don't know that, either."

"Don't know much, do you, Morg?"

"I know this. The bull in the pen outside is worth five, six thousand if it's worth a dime. That's a good start, Tom."

"It's only one bull. I want to know how many other cattle go with it. You catch my drift?"

"I'll find out, Tom. I'll have the boys do it right away."

"No you won't, Morg," Black Tom said. "I got the sneaking suspicion you got something else in mind. So first of all, I don't have the money with me."

Rowlett's eyes popped and his chin dropped to his chest. "Tom . . . what . . . I mean, what the hell?"

Black Tom laughed. "Morg, you didn't think I'd walk into a den of thieves with fifty thousand dollars in my poke, did you?"

"But where is the money?"

"In a carpetbag I stashed in a hole before I rode in."

This wasn't going as planned and Rowlett tried to salvage something out of the ruins. "Tom . . . I'm hurt that you don't trust me. I was all set to deal fair and square with you and all I got in return is a slap in the face."

"You wasn't gonna deal on the square, Morg. Oh sure, you'd give me a bill of sale for this place, then shoot me in the back like the cowardly, treacherous dog you are."

Rowlett opened his mouth to speak, but Black

Tom held up a silencing hand. "After I was dead, you'd tear up the bill of sale and peddle this place again and again. Hell, you'd get rich selling one, worthless dump."

"That's not the way it was to be, Tom," Rowlett said. "I swear to you, I—"

He didn't say another word. Black Tom Church shot him right between the eyes, then swung his gun on Johnny Sligo.

The young gunman sat in his chair grinning at him. "Looks like I've got myself a new partner.

"You ain't taking a set against me because of this, Johnny?"

"Hell no, Tom. Morg was an idiot. He dreamed big, but he didn't have the brains to make them dreams come true. For some men it's too late to get wise the day they was born."

"And I got the brains, huh?"

"That's the way I see it."

"Then you're seeing it right," Black Tom said. "And I say good for you."

The door burst open and a couple men charged inside, guns in their hands.

"Put away the iron, boys," Sligo said. "We got ourselves a new boss."

One of the gunmen, a short, stocky youngster with freckles across his pug nose spoke first. "What happened here, Johnny?"

"Well, this here is Black Tom Church and Morg tried to draw down on him. It was the worst mistake he ever made."

The youngster looked confused. "Lay it out for me, Johnny, real slow." He kept the gun in his hand.

"I guess that goes for the rest of us, too," the man with him said.

"It ain't difficult," Sligo said. "We got ourselves a new boss, but the deal stays the same."

"And that means that I'm paying top gun wages, twice what Rowlett was paying you, and every man jack of you will see a bonus come Christmas," Black Tom said. "Now I ask you boys, can I say any fairer than that?"

The freckle-faced man named Ben had lowered his gun, but he still needed convincing. "State your intentions, Mr. Church. You paying gun wages for us to go on lifting cattle?"

"How many have you lifted so far?" Black Tom asked.

"The bull out there, and maybe another dozen white-faced cows," Ben said.

"And we shot us a puncher," the other man said. "Some kind of Mex."

"Well, you ain't stealing cows no more," Black Tom said. "I've got other plans. What's the biggest spread around here, anyhow?"

The two gunmen looked blank, but Sligo offered the information. "It's called Dromore, over to the east of here somewhere. That's all I know about it."

"Big place?" Black Tom asked.

"I don't know," Sligo said. "But I reckon it is."

"I'm looking for a place like that. Somewhere I can retire to, put my feet up, and get respectable. Hell, I even like the name, whatever it means."

"Get respectable and rich," Sligo said. "Don't forget the rich part."

"We're all gonna get rich, Johnny," Black Tom said. "You can depend on it."

"Ol' Morg made us that same promise," Sligo said.

"Ol' Morg was an idiot. That's why I'm setting here drinking his whiskey and he's got his beard in the dirt."

The man called Ben holstered his gun. "Well, you can count me in."

"Goes double for me," the other man said.

Black Tom nodded. "That sets up just fine." He pointed to the body on the floor. "Now get that out of here. Dump it someplace and let the coyotes have at it."

Once Rowlett's body was dragged away, Johnny Sligo said, "We've lost four men in the past couple weeks. It's troubling me."

"How did you lose them? Did they get gunned?"

"No, I reckon they just lit out. Didn't like the way things were going around here, maybe."

"Well, all that's gonna change now the boys know who's in charge." Black Tom's face changed— became angry. "You let them know that if anyone else tries to quit, I'll hunt him down and skin him alive. Johnny, you let them know that."

Sligo grinned. "I sure will. You're the boss."

"Yeah, Johnny I am. And soon, I'll be the boss of a big chunk of this whole damned territory." Big, vital and in command, Black Tom held up his whiskey glass for a refill. "What was the name of that big ranch again?"

# Chapter Twenty-six

The Excelsior Hotel lay in open brush country a mile west of the ancient pueblo village of Galisteo. It was the only structure for miles around, a three-story white elephant that had been waiting patiently for the railroad since the end of the War Between the States.

The rails had never arrived, but the Excelsior remained, rundown, weather beaten, and barely alive. It once boasted sixteen rooms, but now only a couple were habitable, used occasionally by an overnighting miner or a too-drunk-to-ride cowboy. It maintained a bar and a bacon and beans restaurant, and on Friday nights attracted a fair clientele of miners, punchers, drifters, soldiers, and faded girls from Santa Fe who were on a downward career slope.

The current owner of the hotel was a man named Phillips, a Boston native who told all who would listen that the Excelsior was making him broke and giving him gray hair.

It was to this place that Johnny Sligo rode through

snow on a Friday night to drink and show off his guns. He was not in the best of moods.

For the past week, Black Tom Church had done nothing but sit on his fat ass and drink whiskey. If the man had a plan of action he sure wasn't working on it. He seemed to grow lazier with every passing day and even his ambitions seemed to have fled since he didn't mention them anymore.

The remaining gun hands were getting restless.

A dozen horses were looped to the hitching rail and Sligo made room for his own mount. He glanced up at the grand façade of the Excelsior. The wood was an ashy gray, but here and there streaks of ancient white paint still clung to the warped timbers. Bullet holes pockmarked the entire building, especially around the door and windows, relics of an 1875 battle between a party of buffalo hunters and raiding Comanche.

The owner proudly recounted that three white men fell in the fray, but the Comanche carried off sixteen dead, the exact number of rooms in the hotel and wasn't that a real strange coincidence?

Johnny Sligo mounted the steps to the porch and walked inside to the lobby. His spurs chiming, he stepped into the saloon . . . and saw the man he'd kill that night.

Sligo ordered whiskey and glanced around him. The saloon was busy by Excelsior standards, maybe two dozen men—mostly miners and ranch hands— and three women. A fiddler and a banjo player picked out their version of "Please Write to Mother, Billy," and over by the window a drunk tinpan spoke earnestly and endlessly, jabbing his finger at someone who wasn't there.

Johnny Sligo didn't like the raw whiskey, he didn't like the sweaty, smelly crowd, and he particularly didn't like the big, blond farm boy who sat at a table, tugging at the breast of a bored saloon girl with a heart of lead.

The youngster was dressed in denim overalls and a ragged mackinaw and wore a gunbelt, an old cap and ball Army Colt in the holster. The gal had the sodbuster's battered hat on her curly head and her left hand moved down at his crotch.

Sligo knew the kid was harmless, but he was in a foul mood, and when Johnny Sligo was in a foul mood bad things happened.

"Another?" The bartender was a plump, pleasant-looking man with clean fingernails and an emerald stickpin in his cravat.

Sligo nodded to his glass and then said, "Who is the rube?"

The bartender poured the shot, then followed Sligo's eyes. "Him, with Tracy? I don't know. He drifted in earlier."

"I don't like him."

"He isn't doing you any harm." Whiskey bottle still in his hand, the bartender looked into Sligo's snake eyes and was shocked at what he saw—the gleam of triumph and the urge to kill. "He's only an overgrown kid. Emptied his pa's moneybox and ran away from home, probably."

"I don't like him."

"Mister, I don't argue with a man on the prod who

wears two guns and looks like he knows how to use them, but go do your killing somewhere else," the plump man said. "You'll prove nothing here."

"You got a scattergun back there?" Sligo asked.

"Yeah, I got me one."

"Well my friend, if you don't shut your damned trap you better get ready to go for it."

The bartender put the bottle back on the bar. "I've had my say."

Sligo ignored him, drained his glass, then stepped into the floor. A couple miners were dancing with the girls, but when they noticed Sligo they moved aside, watching him.

The saloon had been noisy, but it gradually went quiet and even the poker players at a table under a smoking oil lamp looked up from their cards.

"You, farm boy. Get away from my woman." In the taut silence, Sligo's words dropped like rocks into a tin bucket.

The rube was either stupid or too drunk to scare. He jumped up from the table and grabbed one of the girls on the dance floor and grinned. "Come on, fellows, play," he said to the musicians who had gone quiet."

"She's my woman, too," Sligo said. "Get your filthy paws off her."

The youngster let go of the girl. "Mister, is there a woman in here that ain't yours?"

"You trying to be funny? You trying to make me look small in front of my women?"

"Nope, just askin'," the kid said. "I'll take the one you don't want."

"Yeah, well I claim all three of them. Now what are you going to do about it?"

The farm boy looked confused. Nothing like this had ever happened before and he'd no idea where it was leading. That it would be his death, he hadn't the slightest inclination.

The kid gave Sligo a snaggle-toothed grin that lit up his whole face. "Well, do I have your go-right-ahead to dance with one o' your women, mister, huh?"

Sligo knew he had to push it. He was starting to look bad. "I told you, they're all mine." His hands dropped to his guns. "You calling me a liar?"

A man's voice from the back of the room cut through the scared, expectant silence. "That's enough, Johnny. Let the boy be."

Sligo's head moved like a striking rattler in the direction of the speaker, his eyes ugly. Then he saw who it was.

Dave Chaney, the gambler who'd been in the saloon the night Doc Holliday shot Kyle Stuart, stood up from the card table and walked into the middle of the floor, the ring of his spurs loud in the room. "You already have a rep, Johnny. Killing this boy won't add to it. In fact, I'll make damn sure it doesn't."

Sligo looked the gambler over. Chaney wasn't wearing a gunbelt and never did, but he'd have a hideaway somewhere. He'd be fast and would hit what he aimed at. He had a reputation of a man who never sought a fight, but if one was pushed on him, he was a hundred different kinds of hell.

Bracing a raw farm boy was one thing, Dave Chaney was quite another.

"A fair piece off your home range, ain't you, Dave?" Suddenly, all the fight had gone out of Sligo.

"Trying to outrun a losing streak, Johnny. What brings you to the end of the world?"

"Oh, this and that. Nothing much."

Sligo felt eyes on him. Everybody in the room, from the punchers and miners to the saloon girls, realized he was backing down.

That angered him. He knew he could shade Chaney, but would take lead doing it. That was no part of Johnny Sligo's plans, not when fifty thousand dollars was at stake. "I was only joshing the rube, trying to scare him. Welcome him to the bright lights."

"Yeah, Johnny, I figured that was the case. Hey, boy, come here," Chaney said without turning.

The kid stepped to his side. "You mean me?"

"Yeah, I mean you. What's your name, boy?"

"It's Stanley. Stanley Clements."

"Well, Stanley Clements, get yourself a woman, go upstairs, and do what you have to do, then sleep it off. You catch my drift?"

The gal named Tracy took the boy's arm. "You come me with me, Stanley, and have yourself a gallop around the pasture."

Chaney smiled. "Just don't use your spurs, boy."

"I don't have spurs, mister," Stanley said, his red-cheeked face puzzled.

"No, you surely don't," Chaney said.

After Tracy dragged the boy away, the musicians

struck up with "Mother's Out Praying" and Chaney said, "Can I buy you a drink, Johnny?"

"No, I'm leaving. I wore out my welcome."

Chaney's eyes were the color of smoke and Sligo felt that they looked right through him, all the way to the pus underneath.

"I've took a notion to like that farm boy, Johnny," Chaney said. "If anything happens to him I'd take it hard."

Anger flared in Sligo. "Don't threaten me, Dave. I can shade you any day of the week."

"I know, Johnny. But you know that I'll be the one standing when the smoke clears."

*Mist*, Sligo decided. Chaney's eyes were the color of mist, not smoke, and dangerous things lurked in mist. Everybody knew that.

He turned and walked out of the saloon. Behind him, one of the girls laughed, and Johnny Sligo wanted to kill her real bad.

Dave Chaney seldom acted on impulse, but he stepped out of the saloon onto the porch and watched Johnny Sligo leave.

An owl glided through the falling snow and disappeared like a gray ghost into the gloom where Johnny Sligo rode. From somewhere close, coyotes yipped and hunted for squeaking things.

The door behind Chaney opened and one of the girls stepped outside and hung his coat over his shoulders. "I want to thank you for saving the farm boy's life."

Chaney nodded, but said nothing.

"I just wanted to tell you that." She turned and

walked back into the saloon, her high-heeled ankle boots thudding on the wood floor.

Dave Chaney was disturbed. Johnny Sligo was a pestilence, an infestation, a man who killed for the pleasure of killing. He blighted and brought death and decay to everything and everyone around him, human and animal . . . even to the very earth. He was an animal of towns, dark alleys, and dingy saloons where he and the cockroaches scuttled and bustled. The wide open spaces and clean air held no appeal for him.

So what was he doing in the part of the New Mexico Territory where settlements were few and far between and opportunities limited for a man of his talents?

Something had drawn him there and it could only be money. Big money.

Chaney was drifting, endlessly visiting places where no one was glad at his coming or sad at his leaving. His cobwebbed room at the Excelsior Hotel was just one more dreary stop on a road to nowhere. He felt no loyalty toward the territory nor had he any affection for its wild, beautiful land.

But Johnny Sligo was there and Chaney felt that he should tell someone. Warn them more like. Not Phillips the hotel owner, a man of little account, but someone of substance, a landowner perhaps.

Chaney lit a cigar and watched the snow fall on the land like a blessing. He had some thinking to do and some questions to ask.

# Chapter Twenty-seven

"I have a question to ask," Patrick O'Brien said.

"The fences look good and the ponds aren't iced over," Jacob O'Brien said, his breath smoking in the cold air. "There's still good grass in the hollows and with the hay, I reckon we haven't lost a single cow."

"You weren't listening to me."

"Sure I was. What's your question, Pat?"

"It's about those two men Doc Holliday shot."

"What about them?"

"Before he died, one of them said something about a black bull. Does that mean it's around here someplace?"

Jacob nodded. "I've been studying on that my ownself. According to Doc, those boys weren't drifting, so it seems like." He pointed to the truncated cone shape of Starvation Peak to their east as he and Patrick rode the high country just south of the Pecos River. "Legend has it that a bunch of settlers on the old Santa Fe Trail were attacked by Apaches and took refuge on top of the peak. The Apaches surrounded the place and starved them all to death."

"Is that a fact?" Patrick had heard the story before.

"I don't know if it's a natural fact, but that's what folks say."

"I read that it happened in 1712 and it was Spaniards who died up there," Patrick said.

Jacob smiled. "If it was in one of your books, then that's the truth of it."

"Unless nobody starved. It would take a lot of Apaches to surround a mountain."

"I don't know about that," Jacob said. "But there's ghosts up on the top."

"You've seen them?"

"No, but one night, oh, maybe twenty years ago, Luther and a vaquero did."

"Had they been drinking?"

"Probably."

"Then the only spirits they saw that night were the ones that came out a tequila bottle."

Jacob shook his head. "Oh ye of little faith, Pat. Hell, I believe every word Luther says."

They rode west under a cold, climbing sun then looped around Hurrado Mesa and swung north again through piñon and mesquite country. The cattle they passed look sleek enough and a few early calves were on the ground. But it was doubtful if they'd survive the winter.

By noon, the O'Brien brothers were fifteen miles south of Dromore House in the arroyo country when Patrick said, "Rider to the west."

Jacob angled his head a little. "I know. I've been watching him for the past ten minutes."

"Who'd be out riding in freezing cold weather if he didn't have to?"

"Beats me. But we'll soon be able to ask him because he's angling toward us."

"Coming on like kinfolk, isn't he?" Patrick pointed out.

"Coming on like something." Jacob unbuttoned his mackinaw and slid his holster nearer to hand. "Hell, I had my mind on frijoles, beef, and tortillas, not gunfighting. It's too damn cold for that."

"He's got a Winchester under his knee and he's wearing a long coat," Patrick said, peering through his glasses like an owl. "Nothing gun-handy about any of that."

"We'll see."

The horseman reined up when he was ten feet from Jacob. He was a tall, slender man who stood on the threshold of middle-age. He had an open face and gray eyes and by his duds—once expensive, but very much in need of repair—Jacob pegged him for a gambler/gunfighter, a rapidly vanishing breed that was rare to begin with.

"Good afternoon, gentlemen," the rider said. "A cold day."

Jacob nodded, his eyes wary. "What can we do for you?"

"Well, nothing really, unless you can get the cards to once again fall my way."

"I'm the unluckiest gambler in the world, so that isn't going to happen." Jacob said.

The man smiled and it was a good, warm smile. "Ah, that's indeed a pity, on both our counts. My name is Dave Chaney, and I'm passing through. Well, not really. I intend to spend a few days at the Excelsior Hotel."

"I thought that place was all closed up," Patrick said. "It's in the middle of nowhere, isn't it, built for railroad passengers that will never arrive?"

"The establishment is still open, more or less," Chaney said. "But you're right. It's at the edge of the world."

"And you need a grubstake," Jacob said. "No offense."

"None taken. Will you put out your name, sir, or do you prefer not to?"

"I'm Jacob O'Brien and this is my brother Patrick."

"Of Dromore," Patrick added.

"I'm pleased to meet you," Chaney said. "As for the grubstake, I'm not yet down on my uppers, though I suspect it's only a matter of time. However, I was on my way to Dromore to impart some information."

"Well, impart away. We're of Dromore," Jacob said.

"Are you the owner of the ranch, Mr. O'Brien?"

"Part owner. My father is still the boss."

"Then I will talk with him, if it's all the same to you."

"Suit yourself, we're headed home anyway."

Patrick said to Chaney, "Does your information involve an Aberdeen Angus bull?"

"Pat, if the man says he wants to talk with the colonel, then let him talk with the colonel."

"Anything you say, little brother. I was just asking."

Patrick pulled his horse next to Chaney. "Tell me, Mr. Chaney, have you any interest in butterflies? It's a most fascinating subject. Take the Dotted Checkerspot, Latin name *Poladryas minuta*, that's found around these parts. . . ."

Jacob groaned, but Chaney smiled and at least pretended an interest.

"Jacob, you're always interested in these matters," Shamus O'Brien said. "Have you heard of this . . . Johnny Sligo person?"

"I've heard he's fast with a gun and a man to step around. I don't know if that's true or just talk."

"It's true all right," Dave Chaney said. "Johnny likes to kill and he's done more than his share."

"How do you know so much about him?" Luther Ironside asked.

"I'm a professional gambler and I drift from town to town," Chaney said. "I've met Johnny Sligo a couple times here and there and a heap of wanna-be Johnny Sligos. None of them was a patch on the original."

No one spoke and Chaney took it as a sign they wanted him to talk more. "Johnny got his start with Bill Bonney and that hard crowd over to Lincoln County way. Next he drifted up north of the Picketwire and got involved in a range war, working for a cattleman called McGraw, at least I think that's what he was called. He was only there a week when he killed a local gunman by the name of Ed Grove and that established his reputation as a fast draw.

Johnny's been selling his gun ever since, and there are some who say he's killed a dozen men. If that's the case he'd pegged the farm kid I told you about as number thirteen."

Luther Ironside glanced out the parlor window. The snow had stopped and cool sunlight gilded the land all the way to the mesa. Shawn, a tall, handsome figure stood with Judith Lovell under a pine, their bodies close, the girl's face upturned to his. Ironside read the sign of a budding romance, for good or bad he couldn't tell, but he turned his attention to the matter at hand. "Colonel, you reckon James Stuart's got himself another gun?"

"Why would he do that?" Jacob asked. "He already has Wolf Hartmann on the payroll. He doesn't need anyone else."

"Wolf Hartmann out of Dallas?" Chaney asked.

"Until recently," Jacob said. "Now he's signed on for gun wages with a local rancher named Stuart."

Chaney smiled. "If he comes up against Sligo, he'll earn every penny of those wages."

"Wolf is no slouch. He's fast on the shoot."

"I know. But even on his best day he isn't Johnny Sligo."

Patrick shoved his glasses higher on his nose and entered the conversation. "Here's how I analyze this situation. The missing bull, the death of our vaquero, and the presence of Johnny Sligo here in the territory are all interconnected."

"Pat, it doesn't take a genius to figure that much," Samuel O'Brien said.

"Samuel, let please Patrick finish," Lorena said. "He may be getting to the heart of the matter."

"Unfortunately, I've nothing else to say." Patrick frowned. "I don't know the why of the thing. And of course, there's the complication of Doc Holliday living, or rather dying, here at Dromore."

Chaney was surprised. "Holliday is here?"

"He's an old saddle pard of Jake's." Ironside grinned, pleased at the barb on his hook.

Jacob didn't let it go unnoticed. "Thank you, Luther. I appreciate that."

"Have you known Doc long, Mr. Chaney?" Lorena asked.

"No, ma'am. I first met him the night he shot a man in a dugout saloon north of Santa Fe."

"That man was Kyle Stuart, Colonel James Stuart's son," Shamus said.

"I don't blame Doc for that shooting," Chaney said. "Kyle would've killed him. He wanted to beat Doc to death with his bare hands."

"Kyle could've done it, all right," Samuel said. "He was a mean one."

Shamus rose to his feet. "Mr. Chaney, our troubles are not yours. Thank you for the warning about Johnny Sligo and now I'm sure you're anxious to be on your way before dark."

Chaney placed his empty glass on the table beside him and stood. "I just hope my warning was of some use, Colonel."

"Time will tell, Mr. Chaney," Shamus said. "God willing, we'll just have to wait and see how things play out around here."

"Colonel, one thing more. Johnny Sligo is a scourge, a pestilence. Wherever his shadow falls, it brings death and destruction, to people, to towns. Even the land around him ceases to bloom and it withers and dies. He is evil and the devil rides with him."

Shamus hurriedly crossed himself. "Jesus, Mary and Joseph, and all the saints in Heaven, help and protect us. Is he such a demon?"

"Yes, he is, and worse than I can ever describe."


That night, Shamus found Jacob in the kitchen, the parts of his disassembled Colt spread out in front of him. "Shouldn't you be in bed, son?"

"Soon, Pa."

"But why so late?"

"I'm getting ready." Jacob pointed to the clock on the kitchen wall. "Hear that tick, Colonel?"

"I hear it."

"You know what it means? It means time is running out." Jacob had the Irish gift and he saw shadows that other men didn't.

Shamus felt a sudden pang of fear. "For Dromore?"

"For all of us."

# Chapter Twenty-eight

Dave Chaney rode west through a day shading into evening. Around him the snow-covered land was deep into its winter sleep and there was no sound but the steady thud of his horse's hooves, the creak of saddle leather, and the frosty sigh of the wind. Gunmetal clouds gathered again and swelled low, threatening snow to come.

He passed a number of Herefords with the Dromore D brand on their flanks and spotted a lobo wolf disappear into a stand of piñon like a fleeting shadow. Feeling the effects of Colonel O'Brien's excellent brandy, he felt relaxed and drowsy. His eyelids drooped, despite the cold wind and his bay's rough gait.

He dozed in the saddle. When the first bullet crashed into his back and severed the spine between his shoulder blades, Dave Chaney woke from shock and sudden pain. The second bullet, a solid hit to the back of his head, killed him.

* * *

Johnny Sligo stood over Dave Chaney's body and was well pleased.

It had been a long wait among rocks and trees, but it had been worth it. He'd followed Chaney from the hotel that morning and would've killed him earlier if the gambler hadn't met two other men and ridden off to the big plantation house near the mesa.

Sligo had watched and waited near the house and when Chaney appeared he'd followed. Rifle shots carry far and he'd tracked the gambler until he was far enough away from the house to gun him without others hearing.

Sligo was not a forgiving man and he vented his rage on Chaney by kicking his ugly face into a pulp. He shot the bay out of spite that the horse had carried an enemy, then swung into the saddle again and headed west.

His revenge was not yet complete.


For some reason the Excelsior Hotel disturbed Johnny Sligo. It shouldn't be there, alone in a flat, bleak wilderness, like a single headstone in an abandoned graveyard. The hotel was out of the norm, and the very sight of it curdled Sligo's blood as though it marked the spot of his own death.

He sat his horse outside for a long while and stared at the place, wondering why it haunted him so. He glanced at the dark sky and the eye of lilac light that marked the position of the hidden moon.

It was cold, distant, threatening, and for a moment he thought about riding away.

But only for a moment.

Johnny Sligo grinned, remembering who he was and what he was, and swung out of the saddle. His was the only horse at the hitching rail. Good, because he had an uppity rube to kill.

His worries about ha'ants and such forgotten, he walked into the hotel and then entered the saloon.

The same man was behind the bar, a couple miners played an unenthusiastic game at the card table . . . and the damned farm boy was still there, sitting sober at another table with the saloon girl called Tracy.

The tolling of Sligo's spurs made the boy look up. He smiled, half-shy, half-puzzled. "Howdy, again."

Sligo ignored that. "Whiskey," he said to the bartender.

"Mister, we want no trouble."

Sligo told him to shut the hell up.

Tracy, experienced in the ways of men, knew something bad was about to happen. "Stanley," she said, her eyes on Sligo, "go to your room. Go now and lock the door."

"But I love you Tracy," the boy said. "I want to be with you."

"Yeah, yeah. I love you too, and I'll come to your room. Now, get the hell out of here."

Johnny Sligo, a man who hated the weak and the innocent, smirked. "Do like your mama tells you, boy. Tracy and me got things to do."

Stanley rose to his feet, his slack-jawed face flushed.

"You leave her be, mister. Me an' Tracy is gonna be hitched real soon an' go back to my pa's farm."

"Beat it," Sligo said. "And leave the girl to me. Tracy, get over here."

"She ain't going with you, mister," the boy said. "Not now, not any time."

And, as Sligo knew he would, the stupid kid, nurtured on dime novels, drew.

His gun only halfway out of the leather, Stanley found himself looking at Sligo's drawn Colt. "Geez, I'm sorry, mister," he said, his pale blue eyes huge. "I shouldn't have done that."

"Sorry don't cut it, farm boy," Sligo said. "And you're right, you shouldn't."

He fired and the youngster took the bullet in the center of the breast pocket of his bib overalls. Stanley staggered back and stared down at the blood spreading across his chest. He looked up at Sligo, an unbelieving expression on his face. His knees buckled and he fell to the floor.

"Damn you!" Tracy shrieked. "You killed him!" She ran at Sligo, her long, scarlet fingernails coming at him like talons.

Sligo grinned and pushed the girl aside, but she lunged at him again and her nails raked his cheek, slashing three deep furrows that immediately welled blood.

No longer grinning, Sligo swung his gun on Tracy and fired. A small woman, the impact of the .45 sent her reeling back and Sligo shot her again.

Out of the corner of his eye, he saw the bartender throw a Greener to his shoulder.

For the benefit of the miners at the card table, Johnny Sligo made a grandstand play. He drew the Colt on his left hip, the motion almost too fast for the human eye, and fired. His bullet hit the scattergun's sideplate, whined viciously upward, and crashed into the bartender's face just under his right eyebrow.

For one horrific moment, blood and brains fanned above the man's head, then he hit the floor, his final death throes hidden behind the bar.

"Me, I'm Johnny Sligo!"

The two miners at the card table were startled, their scared stares on the wild-eyed gunman.

"Did you hear me?" Sligo yelled, blood trickling down his cheek. "Damn you tinpans, I'm Johnny Sligo. Remember that."

The older of the two miners had sand. He'd once stood his ground and stared down an enraged grizzly, but wanted no part of Johnny Sligo that day. "We'll remember. We ain't likely to forget."

Sligo holstered his guns, reached into the pocket of his coat, and spun a double eagle toward the miners. "Buy yourselves a drink on me, boys," he said as the coin hit the floor.

"Hell, mister, you done shot the bartender," the younger miner said.

"Then the drinks are on the house, ain't they?" Sligo turned and stepped out of the saloon, smiling, feeling just fine.

The ranch house was dying, Black Tom Church decided. The roof sagged, windows were broken or spider webbed with cracks. The place was filthy, smelling of vomit, piss, rotten food, stale sweat, and tobacco smoke. Outside, the barn had taken a decided tilt to one side and the corral was falling down board by board.

Even the willow and cottonwood trees around the place were skeletal, lifting white, skinny limbs toward the gray sky.

"Time to move on, Johnny," Black Tom said. "Find us new quarters."

Johnny Sligo leaned on a corral post and stared at the black bull. "You count the cattle on this place yet?"

"Hell, I don't know how to make a count."

"Use an abacus, I guess."

"I don't know how to use an abacus, either."

"There are hayricks all over the place. Shouldn't you be putting hay out for the cattle?" Sligo asked.

"Cows eat grass. They don't need anything else."

"It's winter. Not much grass on the ground."

"There's enough. Hell, look around you, Johnny, there's grass everywhere. Well, there was before it turned brown."

Sligo sighed and directed his attention to the bull again. "That animal is sick, Tom. Hell, he's skinny as a rail and he's got sores all over him."

"Yeah, well maybe I can find a buyer for the bull." Black Tom looked hard at Sligo. "Where the hell were you all day and what happened to your face?"

"I had some unfinished business to attend to and a woman gave me this." Sligo's fingers straying to his cheek. Then, to close the matter, he said, "I saw the Dromore place this morning."

"Is it a big ranch like we thought?"

"Big enough to have a plantation house, a school, a commissary, a bunkhouse, and plenty of other buildings. It's got white-painted fences and a lot of horses and cattle. Hell, it's even got a church of some kind. Looks like one of them Southern mansions from before the war."

"Any darkies?"

"I didn't see any."

"When I move into Dromore I want darkies. Give the place some class, know what I mean?"

"I'd say it's got plenty of class already."

A shot racketed into the waning day and Sligo and Black Tom hauled iron, looking around them.

The door of the ranch house crashed open and a man tumbled outside, blood on his chest. He staggered a few steps and fell on his face.

A moment later, another gunman appeared in the doorway, a smoking revolver in his hand. "He called me a liar." The man turned and went back inside.

Black Tom shook his head as he holstered his gun. "The boys are falling apart. I'm beginning to think this damned place is cursed."

# Chapter Twenty-nine

Sir James Lovell was so concerned he was seriously considering a return to England immediately. "That's how much I'm worried," he said to Lorena O'Brien.

"Judith could do a lot worse than Shawn, Sir James. He's a kind, considerate man and he'll be a loving husband and a good provider."

"A good provider for his wife and children, you mean?"

"Of course, what else would I mean?" Lorena and Sir James sat in the warmth of the kitchen, sharing a pot of Earl Grey tea that she loved, but that no one else in the O'Brien family would touch.

"He won't have children, Lorena," Sir James said.

"Shawn loves children. He adores my son and before he leaves the house he always fills his pockets with candy for the children of the vaqueros. They follow him everywhere." Lorena sipped her tea, then smiled. "Trust me, Sir James, Shawn will want children."

"But he won't have them, and that's what troubles me." The Englishman hesitated as though he knew his next words would be painful for him. "Judith can't have a child," he said finally. "I'm not a doctor, so I can't explain these things, but when Judith's husband was killed in India, the shock was so much that she lost the child she was carrying. She can never have another."

"Are you sure?" Lorena asked, her distress obvious.

"Queen Victoria's personal physician examined Judith and he was of the opinion that she can no longer conceive."

"Doctors can make mistakes, Sir James."

"Sir Edward Reid is the foremost physician in Europe. He would not make a mistake on such a serious matter."

Lorena lapsed into silence. Then she said, "Does Shawn know?"

"Yes. Judith told him."

"And he's still determined to marry her?"

"He says he is. But my question is why? Is it a genuine desire to make my daughter his bride or is he sticking by her out of a misplaced notion of chivalry?" Sir James smiled. "It's the British thing to do, as my countrymen say."

"If Shawn loves Judith and she loves him, a lack of children won't stand in their way. Sir James, there are many happy, childless marriages." Lorena poured more tea into the thin china cups she kept for such occasions. "Will you give the match your blessing?"

"With all my heart," Sir James said. "I will do everything in my power to see that my daughter is not hurt. She's had tragedy enough in her young life."

"It is a most singular dilemma, but I wish the couple well. I'm very sure they'll live happily together."

"What about Colonel O'Brien? Will he bless the union?"

"The colonel's dream since he left Texas all those years ago was to found a dynasty. Well, he's done that and in my son he already has an heir." Lorena smiled. "But I'm sure he wishes for a spare."

"Then he'll be against a marriage?"

"Not at all. Shawn is a grown man and the colonel won't stand in his way. Shamus seems rough and tough by times, but deep inside he's a kind, understanding man."

"Judith and Shawn wish to announce their engagement on Christmas Eve," Sir James said.

"Wonderful. It will be a fine Christmas present for all of us."

"Who's getting a Christmas present? You talking about me again, Lorena?" Luther Ironside, snow on the shoulders of his coat, stepped directly to the coffeepot on the stove, his spurs ringing across the kitchen's stone floor.

"Shawn and Judith are getting married," Lorena said. "They plan to announce their engagement at Christmas."

"Good. It's about time that boy was hitched," Ironside said. "I've taught him all he knows about women an' sich so he'll make a good husband."

"Have you ever been married, Luther?" Sir James asked.

"Hell no. I never did take a notion to it." Ironside poured coffee into a tin cup. "Marry in haste, repent at leisure, the colonel says, and I reckon he's right."

He gulped his coffee and threw the cup in the sink. "Well, I got to go. The colonel's given me a list of chores to do."

"I've never known you to do chores, Luther," Lorena said.

"Well, Jake and Pat are doing the chores, but I'll be there to supervise in my capacity as segundo." Ironside stepped to the kitchen door, then stopped. "The course of true love never did run smooth, Lorena. You know who said that?"

"Shakespeare wasn't it?"

"Damn right it was. If Shawn and Judith really love each other, they'll let nothing stand in their way." Ironside smiled. "By the way, Jake's kitty cat is under the table right where you're sitting. Don't put your hand down there if you value your fingers."

After Ironside left, Sir James said, "Luther understands more than we give him credit for."

Lorena smiled. "He never ceases to surprise me."

# Chapter Thirty

The vaquero's name was Jaimenacho Rios and he had wandered off Dromore range in pursuit of a deer. The sight of six dead Herefords sprawled on the slope of a rise a couple miles west of Lone Mountain drew him closer. The horse he rode was a line-back dun, mountain-bred and tough and it took the slope at a canter.

When he reached the crest and drew rein he was shocked at what he saw.

Stretching across the range lay the carcasses of dead Herefords, a few live cows, thin and weak, grazing among them on sparse grass. The scene reminded him of a buffalo slaughter he'd seen on the Kansas plains when he was a younger man.

The hunt was forgotten as he stared at the carnage. The cattle were not getting hay and hadn't seen any for a long time. The heavier than usual snowfall had killed off about half the range grass and without hay even the Dromore cows would starve, including the hardy longhorns.

Fences were down and he saw couple ponds frozen over solid. No attempt had been made to smash holes in the ice for the cattle to drink.

Rios shook his head. Surely it was a situation to be investigated.

The man who owned the range was called Tom Johnson and his TJ Connected spread was the pride and purpose of his life. He was not a man to let his cattle starve for lack of feed.

As Rios rode deeper into the TJ range, finding more and more dead or emaciated cattle, he felt a growing sense of dread. Something was terribly wrong. Even the air seemed even colder, the clouds blacker, and around him was more dead grass than he'd seen elsewhere.

It was as though a terrible curse had settled on the land.

The thought disturbed Rios so greatly and brought with it such a sense of foreboding that he crossed himself, whispered a prayer to the Madonna of Guadalupe for her protection, and kissed her holy medal that he wore around his neck.

The cone of Lone Mountain passed on his right and Rios figured he was getting close to the Johnson ranch house. Situated on the bank of a dry wash under a dead cottonwood he happened on four ancient graves, probably of people who had tried to pioneer the harsh land and discovered that high desert brush flats don't take kindly to the plow.

One of the graves had been opened and the yellowed bones were scattered, including a delicate skull that hid in a clump of mesquite and grinned at him shyly.

Rios figured that the opened grave had been dug last and in haste. Coyotes, being what they were, had dug up the corpse.

It was another bad omen, in a range full of them, and Rios began to feel afraid. Even the rifle under his knee and the Colt on his hip offered no reassurance.

What use were lead bullets against evil?

It seemed the closer he got to the ranch house, the more afflicted the land became . . . as though the Four Horsemen had passed this way and left death and destruction in their wake.

He crossed himself again. *Madre de Dios!* That was not a thought that should enter a man's head, especially one growing gray like his.

Thirty minutes after he passed Lone Mountain Rios saw smoke rise straight as a string in the distance, a smear of black almost invisible against a blacker sky. Snow fell again and the vaquero pulled the collar of his mackinaw higher up his neck. The air was cold and thin and he suddenly found it hard to breathe. Only after a few moments did he realize it was caused by his terrible dread.

Rios had first gone up the trail when he was fourteen and not yet man grown. Later, he'd been tempered by the hard ways of an unforgiving land. He was strong by necessity, for the New Mexico Territory, like the Apaches it once nurtured, had no place for the weak, indecisive, or timid and killed them without conscience.

The clouds above where he judged the Johnson place to be gave Rios pause. He drew rein and studied the sky, his mouth dry as mummy dust.

Deeply superstitious as any homespun Texas cowboy, the vaquero studied the cloud formation. Black ramparts piled one on top of the other. The massive colossus looked like a crouching beast that might suddenly spring upon the land and envelop it in darkness all the way to the Mexican border.

Snow drifting over him, Rios was very afraid of the sky and of the threatened land. He decided to turn back, and then decided again—to see the powerful mystery through to the end.

His grandmother had once told him, "Jaimenacho, in years to come, the manner in which you respond to evil will be the measure of yourself as a man."

Well, his grandmother would not find him lacking. Not this day. Besides, the colonel, his patron, would no doubt say to him on his return, "Jaimenacho Rios, my bravest vaquero, give me a full description of the great catastrophe that has befallen the TJ Connected."

Afterward, who could say? Might not the colonel, a gallant soldier, pin a gold medal on his chest and then might not his own wife swell with pride and the wives of the other vaqueros look on her with envy?

With such thoughts spinning through Jaimenacho's head, he urged his horse forward and rode through the falling snow under the fearsome sky.

He had it to do.

* * *

Rios seldom thought about dying, but knew he would one day, like all mortal men. Thus, as he rode deeper into the stricken land, he was well aware that death owed him no favors and that he could die very soon, within the hour. Maybe so.

Ay, ay, ay . . . it was a terrible thought and one not to be borne for too long.

Close enough to the ranch house, he could smell the smoke from the fire. He'd never smelled smoke so rank, like the fires of hell, and he felt his courage drain from him again.

But he kept to his path, afraid to be afraid.

Less than half a mile ahead rose a brush-covered hogback, not high, but perhaps tall enough that it overlooked the Johnson place. He had no desire to ride up to the front door and announce, "It is I, Jaimenacho the vaquero."

No, that was not the way. God only knew what horrors might lurk inside.

When he was close to the hogback, Rios swung out of the saddle and tethered his dun to a mesquite.

He slid his Winchester from the boot and climbed the rise, covering the last few feet on his belly. He found cover in some brush and peered over.

Damnation! He had the wrong place. It wasn't the Johnson house.

But it was.

He'd been there before, usually accompanying one of the patrons, since the colonel now and then did cattle business with Tom Johnson.

Rios blinked, looked, blinked again.

The house seemed abandoned, lifeless, yet there

were horses in the corral and the rancid smoke rose from the chimney. The windows, many of them broken, were frosted and Rios couldn't see inside.

But it was the house itself that caught his attention. The once sturdy roof was swaybacked and some of the wooden shingles had slid off and were scattered on the muddy ground. The front door had been pulled off its top hinge and hung askew and the brass handle that had fascinated Rios on his last visit because of its brightness was green with mildew.

Nothing grew around the house, not a weed nor a blade of grass, and the snow, still falling, was nowhere white but had turned to black mud.

An air of decay hung about the place as though the house had suddenly been stricken by a terrible disease, had died and was rotting.

A lumpy black shadow in a pen set away from the house caught Rios's attention. It looked like an animal was lying down in the deep mud, but it wasn't moving. Surely it was dead. But what kind of an animal? A horse or—

The front door pushed open and a man stepped outside. He wore tight pants tucked into fine boots, a white shirt and two guns in crossed belts. His hair was yellow as straw and even from where Rios lay on the hill he noticed the green of the man's eyes, glowing strangely in the gloom of the day.

He was not Tom Johnson's son or one of his riders. He was not a vaquero of any kind. The man was a *pistolero*. He could be nothing else.

Rios froze, fear spiking at him.

The yellow-haired man lifted his head and his

eyes swept the hilltop, lingering at the brush where Rios was hidden. The vaquero ducked out of sight— he hoped. He was good with a rifle but to aim and fire he'd need to expose a part of his body to the man with two guns . . . and that would mean certain death.

This Rios knew with terrible certainty. He'd seen the man's eyes and they were not human . . . the eyes of an animal.

After a few moments, he removed his hat and looked down at the house again. The gunman was no longer there.

Rios remained where he was, waiting until the hammering of his heart grew less. A man like the one he'd seen could hear a thudding heartbeat because he was not of this world. He was a demon of some kind, a devil who dwelled in the body of a man. And he'd brought plague and death to this house and to the land and cattle around.

Rios was certain Tom Johnson was dead, and his family with him.

He had to ride for Dromore and tell the patron what he'd seen and what he'd felt.

He slid down the hill on his belly, rising to his feet when he reached the bottom.

The man with green eyes stood there watching him, a smile on his lips. "What the hell are you doing here, Pancho?"

Rios was very afraid, but he was glad to hear that his voice was steady. "I'm hunting a wounded deer, senor. I'm sure it came this way."

The pistolero shook his head. "There's no wounded animal around here."

Rios managed a smile. "Ah, then I was mistaken, senor."

"You're right. You made a big mistake."

"Please don't kill me, senor," Rios said. "I have a wife and she will be brokenhearted if I am killed."

"Who do you work for, Pancho?" the green-eyed man asked.

"Colonel O'Brien at Dromore. I am one of his vaqueros."

"Were, Pancho. You *were* one of his vaqueros. Best you start talking in the past tense."

"Then you will kill me?"

"I can't leave you alive. Maybe you'll talk too much."

"No, senor, I will not talk. Jaimenacho Rios can keep a secret very well."

"That ain't your name. Your name is Pancho. All you damned greasers are called Pancho."

Rios sighed. "Then you have made up your mind and all I can do is fight. Is that not so?"

He went for his gun, but Johnny Sligo killed him right where he stood.

# Chapter Thirty-one

Lilia Rios had never been in the big house before and her knees knocked as she stood in the foyer and awaited the arrival of the patron.

She'd been told by one of the other wives that the colonel was a very busy man and would not spare time to search for a lowly vaquero like her Jaimenacho. Besides, maybe her husband had found another woman. Such things happened, you know.

It was therefore with great trepidation that Lilia stood in a corner of the marble foyer and tried to make herself as small as possible. The colonel was a great and rich man and she a poor vaquero's wife and he'd surely send her packing, perhaps even kick her.

A door opened to the right of the grand staircase and the patron emerged. After a while, he saw her in the corner, smiled, and walked toward her.

Lilia saw that the colonel did not walk very well. Jaimenacho told her it was because he'd been wounded by Apaches and the scar on his face was from another wound he had received in the war.

"Good evening, senora," the patron said. "Forgive me, my memory is not what it was. You are?"

"My name is Lilia, patron, the wife of Jaimenacho Rios the vaquero."

"Ah yes, a good man," Shamus said.

In fact, he'd never heard the name before. Since Samuel had taken over the running of the ranch, the colonel had little contact with the vaqueros, though Luther still worked with them now and then when he felt like it.

"What can I do for you, Senora Rios?"

The woman explained that her husband had left early that morning planning to kill a deer, but he had not yet returned, though it was already growing dark.

"He has never done this before, patron," Lilia said. "I worry that he may be lost or injured."

It was cold in the foyer. The woman shivered and pulled her shawl closer around her.

"Please, Senora Rios, come into the parlor and we'll talk there. You can sit by the fire."

"Oh no, patron, I cannot intrude on—"

Shamus smiled. "You're not intruding in the least, dear lady."

The butler was hovering nearby and the colonel said, "Please ask my sons and Mr. Ironside to join me in the parlor."

After the man left, Shamus gestured toward the hallway. "This way, Senora Rios."

"He might've got th'owed an' broke his neck," Luther Ironside said. "I seen that happen plenty before."

"Please, Luther, try not to alarm Senora Rios further," Shamus said. "I'm sure there's another explanation."

The huge fireside chair shrank the woman to the size of a china doll. She had a glass of wine in her hands, but had hardly touched it.

"Senora, it's too late to mount a search tonight," Samuel said. "But if Jaimenacho is not back by morning, we'll go looking for him."

"You are very gracious, patron," Lilia said.

"Did he tell you in which direction he was headed?" Samuel asked.

The woman shook her head. "No. I do not know. What man tells his wife such things?"

"Does your husband have a saint he prays to, senora?" Shamus asked pointedly.

"*Sí*, patron. He prays to the Madonna of Guadalupe. She hears Jaimenacho's prayers sometimes and answers them. She is a very fine Madonna."

"Then tonight I will say a rosary to the Madonna of Guadalupe that your husband returns home safely."

"Yeah, that's sure gonna help him if his neck's broke," Ironside muttered.

"What did you say, Luther?" Shamus said, looking stern.

"Nothin', Colonel. I didn't say nothin'."

"I should hope not. Our Blessed Mother helps those who approach her devoutly and with reverence and she adopts them as her needful children. Saying a rosary or two would do you no harm."

Ironside looked at Jacob and winked. "That'll be the day," he whispered.

"What did you say, Luther?" Shamus asked once more.

"I said we'll search better in the day, Colonel. That's what I said."

"I hope that's what you said." Shamus scowled.

"That was it word for word, Pa." Jacob grinned.

"God help us, one heathen vouching for another." Shamus threw up his hands. "Now I've heard it all."

Patrick realized his father was just getting warmed up about Luther and Jacob's piety, or lack thereof. "I'm sure your husband is just fine, Senora Rios. No doubt he was held up by the snow and has camped for the night."

The woman smiled her appreciation, and Shamus added, "That's a more likely reason than others I've heard tonight, senora. But if your husband doesn't come home in the morning, we'll find him, never fear."

Lilia rose, placed her glass on the table beside her and gave a little bow. "Thank you, patron, and thank you for your prayers. I will spend the night in the chapel and pray for Jaimenacho's safe return. He is a good husband."

Patrick got to his feet. "Allow me to escort you to the chapel, Senora Rios. It's dark outside and slippery underfoot."

"Take a gun, Pat," Jacob said.

His father and brothers looked at him in amazement, and even the warlike Luther Ironside seemed surprised.

# Chapter Thirty-two

"Who the hell was he?" Black Tom Church asked.

"A greaser who said he worked for Dromore," Johnny Sligo said.

"Did he say what he was doing out here, off his home range?"

"Deer hunting."

"Deer hunting?"

"That's what he said."

"I don't hold with hunting," Black Tom said. "It's cruel to helpless animals."

The black bull was dead and so were a third of Church's cattle. That was cruelty enough, but Sligo figured it wasn't a good time to mention that.

"Hell, Johnny, why did you kill the man? We could've got information about this Dromore spread and found out what we're up against."

"I don't like greasers, especially when they're snooping around spying on me."

Black Tom smiled. "Do you like anybody, Johnny?"

"I like you, Tom."

"Yeah, sure you do. If you thought you could profit from it you'd put a bullet in my back."

"I can't do that until you tell me where the fifty thousand is hidden," Sligo said.

"I know. That's why you haven't tried to kill me yet."

The stench in the house was intolerable. The floor was littered with rotting scraps of food and empty bottles, and dung and mud had been trekked inside on boots. The oil lamps cast dim, yellow orbs of light and smoked as much as they reeked.

Black Tom wallowed in the filth. His clothes were food stained and stank of stale sweat. Watching him, Sligo reckoned the man hadn't bathed in years.

Like the house, like the land, Black Tom was festering.

"Here's what you do, Johnny," the big man said. "Find out as much as you can about this Dromore place. Who owns it, how much money he's worth, stuff like that."

"How much grass, how many cattle and horses, maybe?" Sligo said.

"Yeah, that too. I'm gonna retire there, Johnny. I can see myself in the big mansion, servants looking after me and"—he grinned—"pretty maids all in a row."

"Suppose the owner doesn't want to sell?" Sligo asked.

"Hell, Johnny, I ain't buying. I'm taking."

"I'll see what I can find out. This part of the territory is still pretty wild and he could have gun hands."

"If the greaser you shot is an example, we got nothing to worry about. Hell, me and you could take on all the guns he's likely to have. I mean, once I start to feel better, Johnny. I feel like I'm coming down with something. I sweat all the time, damn it."

"Where is the money, Tom?"

The big man shook his head. "The money is my ace in the hole, Johnny. Maybe when I'm settled at Dromore, I'll tell you and then we can share it."

"You don't trust me.

"You're damn right about that, Johnny. I don't trust anybody, especially you."

When Johnny Sligo walked his mount to the barn, he got a shock. All the horses were gone, including Black Tom's buckskin.

It looked like the gun hands had lit a shuck, taking with them whatever they could steal.

Sligo shook his head. No, that was impossible. Probably they'd headed for the Excelsior Hotel and its saloon. If that was the case, he'd bust a few heads when they got back, just to keep those boys honest.

The bunkhouse told a different story.

The door hung wide open on a long, spacious room with cots along each side, a couple tables and chairs, and heated by a wood stove that was cold. Usually, the place was packed with damp mackinaws, spare slickers, dirty clothing, and the odds and ends drifting men accumulated.

But the bunkhouse was stripped clean, not even a dirty sock left on the floor.

Sligo's lips tightened. There was no getting around it . . . the gun hands had called it quits.

\* \* \*

"You mean you didn't see them go?" Johnny Sligo asked impatiently.

"Hell no, I didn't see them go," Black Tom said. "I was right here sleeping off whatever it is that ails me. They snuck out on me, is what they did, damn them."

"They took your horse," Sligo said.

Black Tom's face purpled with rage. "The hell they did!"

"Yeah, it's gone. Too bad."

Black Tom got to his feet. "I'm taking yours and going after them . . . them traitors."

"I'll go after them. That's what you're paying me for. That is, if you ever get around to paying me."

"Damn, I've got a bellyache and my gum still hurts from where I had a tooth yanked." Black Tom sat again. "Yeah, Johnny, you go find them and don't bother bringing any of them back."

"You want those boys dead?"

"All of them. I could never trust them again, the damned trash."

"Be dark soon," Sligo said. "I don't have much time."

"Then get the hell out of here and get 'er done." Black Tom reached for a bottle. He was sweating like a pig.

A month after Johnny Sligo rode after the fleeing gunmen, a young Texan by the name of Bill Claybrook told a newspaper reporter in Santa Fe what had happened that day. "Made me hang up my guns and quit the owlhoot trail forever. Hell, I'm working in Anderson's feed lot so that should tell you something."

The reporter, a man named Quinn, prompted, "How did it happen, Bill?"

"Well, how it came up, I was only but nineteen when I figured I could throw a Colt with the best of them, so about then I started to work for gun wages. Then I hooked up with Black Tom Church up in the New Mexico Territory."

"Church was a mankiller from way back, so how did that work out?" Quinn asked quickly.

"All right at first, when there was still nearly ten of us hired guns. But then we lost, I think it was four, maybe five men, and Johnny Sligo took charge."

"Black Tom let him do that?"

"Yeah, Tom said he was done with the outlaw profession and he let Johnny run the show. Besides, he took real sick. Well, after that, a few more men lit a shuck and then the rest of us did. That's when Johnny Sligo came after us."

"You took Church's horse, I understand."

"Yeah, we figgered he owed us something. You got to remember that by then the ranch was ruined. It was like a plague had descended on the damned place. Cattle died all over the range and a black bull that was worth more than I could earn in a three-year died of starvation in its pen."

"How did that happen, Bill?"

"Hell, Black Tom didn't know how to run a ranch and the rest of us were gun hands, not punchers. What the hell did we know, or care?"

"I see."

"No you don't see, damn you. It was Johnny Sligo. He brought the damned plague or whatever you want to call it to the ranch. The man was death walking. Look what happened to Black Tom for God's sake. He went from being a true blue outlaw and a named gunfighter to a stinking drunk, lying like an animal in his own piss and vomit."

"How many of you ran, Bill?"

"Five of us, but I split off from the rest, figuring we were too much of a crowd," Claybrook said. "We agreed to meet up again in Santa Fe and look for gun work, even for the law if that's all there was to hand."

"And then what happened?"

"I seen it with my own two eyes."

"Go on. What happened, Bill?"

"Well, we crossed a frozen creek—it was snowin' mind—and I headed for some hills to the west where there was plenty of timber to keep a man hidden if'n he had a mind to."

"And the others?"

"Kept heading north. From where I was on a low ridge among some juniper I seen Johnny Sligo catch up to them other boys. One o' them was Ransom Miller. Ever heard of him?"

Quinn shook his head. "No, I haven't."

"Well, Rance was out of Kansas somewhere and by his own reckoning he'd killed five white men. He was fast on the draw and shoot, and nobody considered him a bargain. You see what I'm doing here? I'm laying it out to you so you know that them four boys were no pilgrims."

"I catch your drift, Bill. Please go on."

"Well, I got off my hoss and hid in the trees and watched what was going on below me. Johnny Sligo dismounted, and that was something them boys should never have allowed. See, he could get to his guns easier, them being low on his hips and all."

"Did he start shooting after that?"

"No, him and the boys got to cussin' and discussin', then Johnny drew down on them. All four of them, mind, and them real slick with the iron."

Quinn opened his mouth to speak, but Claybrook said, "Clap your hands, boy. Just once. Go on, do it."

The reporter did and Claybrook said, "That's how long it took Johnny Sligo to get off four shots. Hell, I didn't even know a Colt's revolver could work that fast."

"He killed them all"—the reporter clapped his hands again—"that fast?"

"Yeah, I never seen the like and I hope I never to again."

"What happened after that, Bill?"

"Johnny gathered up Black Tom's hoss and rode away."

"That winds it up for me," Quinn said. "I already know what came afterward."

"Then you know more than I do," Claybrook said. "Now buy me the bottle you promised and get away from me."

"A pleasure talking to you, Bill."

"Go to hell."

# Chapter Thirty-three

Jacob O'Brien kneeled in the chapel his father had built for himself, the vaqueros, and their families. The familiar odors of incense and candle smoke did nothing to lift his mood. Depression was on him, filling his mind and body with blackness.

In a pew closest to the altar, Lilia Rios kneeled in prayer, head bowed, her red coral rosary beads clicking through her fingers.

The sacristy lamp was lit, casting a red glow at the side of the altar. A few dripping candles spread a pale yellow light that served only to darken the shadows in the corners where the silent spiders spun their silk.

Jacob told himself he didn't know why he'd come. But he did. The chapel was a safe haven, a place where he could commune with himself without fear of interruption. He couldn't think his way out of depression, but could sometimes outlast it and will the pain away.

Above the altar, a tormented Jesus hung on the

cross and stared down at him with painted eyes. The crucifix had been made from copal wood by a Mexican, a race that understood suffering very well. The artist had carved all the agonies of his people into the bloody, writhing figure of Christ crucified.

The only sounds in the chapel were the thin whisper of Lilia's prayers and the occasional sputter of a candle flame.

Depression, that sense of nothingness, of meaningless existence, overwhelmed Jacob and he found it hard to breathe. The racked and scourged Jesus gazed at him, but made no effort to offer comfort.

The chapel door opened, allowing entrance to an icy blast of wind that made the candle flames shiver and Lilia to turn her head in hope, then bowed it again in bitter disappointment.

Jacob's hand pushed inside his mackinaw and dropped to the Colt in his waistband.

"Don't shoot, Jake, it's only me." Doc Holliday pushed into the pew and took a seat beside Jacob. "I'm not a kneeler, so forgive me if I sit."

"What are you doing here?" Jacob said, in that hoarse whisper a man uses in church.

"Saw you walk out into the snow and figured you were going one of two places, to visit a senorita or more likely, here."

"I don't want to talk to you, Doc," Jacob said. "Get away from me."

"You don't want to talk to anybody because you can feel it, can't you?"

"I don't know what you're talking about."

"Yes you do. You can feel the evil. Remember in

*Macbeth* . . . 'Something wicked this way comes.' Well, Jake my boy, it's coming."

"What is it?" Jacob asked quietly.

"I don't know. Why are you carrying a gun in church if you don't sense danger?"

Jacob was silent for a few moments then said, "You're right, Doc. I feel it."

"Sure you do." Doc looked around him. "Nice place God's got for Himself here."

"Doc, what do you know of a fast gun by the name of Johnny Sligo?"

"To sum up . . . not a thing."

"He drifted into the territory a few weeks ago and I think he could be mixed up in the murder of one of our vaqueros and the theft of the Angus bull." Jacob nodded in the direction of Lilia. "Now that woman's husband is missing, another vaquero."

"Could this Sligo feller be the source of the evil we both feel?" Doc asked.

"I don't know. Maybe."

"Who is he working for?"

"I don't know that either, but I intend to find out."

"Maybe that Scottish feller. What's his name?"

"James Stuart. Yes, it could be him, but somehow I doubt it."

"Jake"—Doc looked around him—"I hesitate to say something like this in church, but do you want me to call out Johnny Sligo and get rid of him for you permanently?"

Jacob smiled. "Doc, from what I've heard, you'd be more than a sight overmatched."

"Maybe, but what have I got to lose? My life?"

That last brought a brief, bleak smile to Jacob's lips. "Let's see how it plays out, Doc."

Doc's eyes wandered to the cross above the altar. After studying it for a while he said, "You up there tonight, Jake?"

"Something like that, Doc. Unlike him, I'm nailed to a cross of my own making though."

"You're going to do one of two things, Jake. You'll either kill yourself or become a monk."

"Those are my only choices?"

"Yes, the way I see it."

"I've killed too many men, spilled too much blood to be a monk."

"Have you ever read *Le Morte d'Arthur*?" Doc asked.

"Yeah, Patrick had me read it when I was a boy. It was a fair story as I recollect."

"Remember Sir Lancelot? He did more than his share of cuttin' and skull-splittin' yet he became a monk."

"Because he lost his Guinevere. I don't have a Guinevere."

"No," Doc said, "you aren't exactly cut out to be a great lover."

"I'm not going to kill myself," Jacob said. "Does that come as a disappointment to you?"

"No, it doesn't. Then you'll be a monk."

"I won't be that either, so let it go."

Doc took a dark brown bottle from his pocket and took a long swig of the contents. "Laudanum. It's helping me less and less, but I'm afraid to stop taking it."

Jacob turned his head and stared at Doc. "You

lied to me before. Now tell me the truth—what do you know about Johnny Sligo?"

"I didn't—"

"Doc, I know when a man is hiding the truth. Tell me."

"You sure you want to know, Jake? Sometimes the truth can hurt a man."

"Tell me, Doc."

"He's the best with a gun there is or ever will be. Heard enough?"

"What manner of man is he?"

"A devil. A demon. Satan in disguise. I've heard him called all those things. But I believe Johnny Sligo is just a mean, homicidal monster, the kind history throws up every hundred years or so."

"Doc, is he better than me?" Jacob spoke quietly.

"He's the best there is, Jake. Do I have to draw you a picture?"

Jacob fell silent. An errant breeze guttered a candle flame that collapsed into the wax, sputtered out, and sent up a thin ribbon of smoke. Suddenly, the chapel became a darker place.

"That's the way it is, Jake. I'm sorry."

"We're all sorry. You, me, Senora Rios, the Christ on the cross up there. One way or another, we're all sorry about something." Jacob gathered up his hat and rose to his feet. "Let's get out of here.

"Maybe," Doc said as he and Jacob stepped to the door, "Johnny Sligo will drift and it will be all over."

"You know what I think," Jacob said as they stepped outside into windblown snow. "I think it won't be over until I kill him."

"A lot of men who are now dead in the grave have thought that way about Johnny Sligo. Don't become one of them, Jake."

The windblown snow that shrouded Jacob O'Brien and Doc Holliday as they walked away from the chapel also fell on Johnny Sligo as he sat his horse outside the Excelsior Hotel.

The building was dark, shuttered, empty, and dead.

After the massacre in the saloon the owner had lost heart, packed his bags, and headed east, vowing never to return.

Sligo had no idea what had drawn him back to the place again, but it held a certain fascination for him and its death and decay pleased him. It was like looking on the rotten, stinking corpse of a man he'd killed weeks before and saying, "See, I did that. It was me, Johnny Sligo."

The Excelsior was a rectangular obelisk of blackness against the lesser darkness of the night. It was silent as a tomb yet seemed to call out to Sligo, inviting him inside. His green eyes wary, he swung out of the saddle and stepped onto the porch, a slender whip of a man whose spurs rang loud in the quiet.

A couple blue tiles slid from the hotel's steeply pitched roof and smashed into pieces on the porch boards. The building creaked and groaned as though it mourned losing yet another piece of itself.

Johnny Sligo walked to the door and tried the handle. It turned and the door creaked open a few inches. "Is anybody there?" he called.

Silence. As far as he could see, the interior was empty and black as sin.

Wary as a snake that's just shed its skin, Sligo pushed on the door and let it creak open. "Is anybody to home?" he said, aware of how strange that sounded.

The only answer was the hollow echo of his voice.

He stepped into the hotel foyer, his gaze trying to pierce the darkness. The stale air smelled of dampness, decay, and the odor of people gone from the place.

But there was something else . . . a gossamer scent in the air, delicate, fleeting, haunting.

The smell of candle smoke.

And something else, sweeter . . . the musky scent of incense that reminded him of a Chinese opium joint he'd once frequented along San Francisco's Barbary Coast.

He was alarmed enough to draw a gun and his cat's eyes probed the darkness as the candle smell grew stronger. "Damn you, is there anybody there?"

He heard an edge of panic in his voice and that troubled him.

Warily, one slow step at a time, he backed toward the front door again then stopped as his right boot heel crunched on something hard.

Johnny Sligo looked down and saw the twisted figure of a silver man on a wooden cross. He picked up the crucifix and stared at it. He'd seen such a thing before. The Mexicans set great store by the cross and hung it on walls in their homes and cantinas.

The air in the dark hotel thinned and Sligo felt

his breath catch in his throat. The odor of burning candles, smoke, and hot wax was very strong.

Phillips, in his haste to vacate the Excelsior must have dropped the cross, Sligo told himself.

He threw the thing away and heard it thump onto the floor and skitter across the oak boards until it hit a wall.

Johnny Sligo was done with the place. He walked quickly outside and swung into the saddle.

The building watched him go with blank eyes and Sligo experienced an emotion he'd never felt before. He recognized it as fear. Setting spurs to his horse, he galloped into a night that had turned dark, damp, and cold as the grave.

# Chapter Thirty-four

Shawn O'Brien declared himself well enough to ride and that, despite being nursed by Judith and Lorena, he was tired of loafing around the house. He was a welcome addition to the three separate search parties that set out from Dromore at first light in the hunt for Jaimenacho Rios.

The vaquero's wife, supported by a couple other wives, was there to see them leave. "You will bring my husband home, patron?" Lilia Rios said to Samuel.

"We'll find him Senora Rios." Samuel smiled. "You look tired, Lilia. Why don't you get some coffee and a bite to eat?"

The woman ignored that. "If you find Jaimenacho dead, bring his body home that I may wash him and say prayers for his poor soul."

Like the other wives, Lilia was dressed in black and Samuel knew that many Mexican women also had the Irish gift.

He tried to keep his voice light. "Don't worry. We'll bring him home alive and well."

The woman's eyes, black as midnight ponds, met his and at that moment he knew what Lilia knew.

"Sam, we ready to ride?" There were dark shadows under Jacob's eyes and the hollows of his cheeks as though he hadn't slept.

Samuel tried to muster enthusiasm for what he suddenly realized was a lost cause. "Yes. Jake, you and Luther ride south. I'll head west with three of the vaqueros and Shawn and Patrick will take the other two and push north."

Jacob nodded. "Then let's get it done."

Snow lay on the ground and the air smelled and tasted like steel. Crows flapped above the roof of Dromore, scraps of black against the slate-colored sky.

Shamus stood at the door and watched the searchers leave, the icy weather doing no favors for his back. To Lorena and Judith he said, "Take those women into the house and get them some coffee and food. They'll freeze to death out there."

And then he wished he hadn't used the word *death*. Like the crows quarreling above his head, it was a bad omen.


An hour after leaving Dromore, Jacob and Ironside found Dave Chaney. The gambler had been shot dead and by someone who knew how.

Ironside took a knee beside the body and brushed snow from Chaney's face. "It's him all right and it looks like he's been dead for quite a while."

Jacob looked at the bleak landscape around him. "The coyotes left him alone, seems like."

"Yeah, not that it makes much difference to him," Ironside said.

"Shot in the back. His gun is still in the shoulder holster."

Ironside nodded. "Somebody got the drop on him, sure enough."

"Well, what do you reckon, Luther? Do we take him back to Dromore or go on with the search?"

"I think we'd give that little Mexican gal a shock if we ride in with a dead man. And he ain't even her husband."

Jacob nodded. "You're right. Mark the place and we'll pick him up on the way back."

"Just so long as he doesn't ride with me," Ironside said.

"Dead men scare you, Luther?"

"Only the ones I didn't shoot my ownself."

"Mark this spot. He can ride with me."

"Who do you figure done for him, Jake?"

"Johnny Sligo, maybe. Chaney was talking to the colonel about him, remember." Jacob's smile was bleak, his face drawn into haggard lines. "It seems like recently we pin everything bad on Johnny Sligo."

"Maybe that's because he's the one that does everything bad."

"Could be, Luther. Could be."

Ironside watched Jacob swing into the saddle, tiredness in his every movement, and then he too mounted. "What's eatin' you, boy?"

Jacob considered that, and then said, "Nothing, Luther, nothing at all."

"Jake, you're a damned liar. Is the black dog a-settin' on your chest again?"

"Yeah, Luther, I guess so. Doc Holliday says that one of these days I'll kill myself or become a monk."

"Hell, what does Holliday know? Nothin'. And you ever tell me you're becoming a monk I'll shoot you my ownself."

"The colonel might like it if one of his sons entered holy orders."

"Holy orders my ass. The colonel's mind is all jumbled by popery and priests an' sich."

"Want me to tell him you said that, Luther?"

"You can, but I'll just deny it. One thing you ain't ever . . . *ever* . . . gonna be as long as I'm alive is some pale, puny, prattling prelate."

Despite his black mood Jacob laughed. "That was good, Luther. Pale, puny, prattling prelate."

Ironside grinned. "Pat teached me to talk like that. He called it ill . . . illit . . ."

"Alliteration."

"Yeah, that's it. It's a good way to talk if the occasion to talk like that ever comes up when you're talkin'. Pat said that."

"Well, I'm sure he said something like that."

"What do you mean?"

"No one can mangle the language like you, Luther."

"Damn right. That's how come I speak such good American."

\* \* \*

Jacob and Ironside headed due south into broken country where mule deer and antelope often gathered among stands of piñon and juniper in the winter months.

They quartered back and forth for several hours and startled a number of deer and once a hunting cougar, but there was no sign of the missing vaquero.

The day grew colder, the sullen clouds darker, and Jacob saw by Ironside's stiffness in the saddle that his rheumatisms were acting up.

"I'm about ready to quit and see what the others have found," Jacob said.

"I can go on for a spell yet, Jake." Ironside blinked away what Jacob supposed was the ache in his hips and knees. "But you young 'uns do get tired, so I guess we'll call it a day."

"Be dark soon anyway," Jacob said, easing Luther's way. "I don't much like night riding."

"Damn right. Me neither."

Jacob stared at Ironside with sudden alarm. "Luther, are you all right?"

"Sure, I'm fine."

"You look . . . hell, Luther, you look kinda gray, white almost."

"Naw, I'm just fine, Jake. It's the cold air getting' to my lungs."

"You don't look fine, Luther. We're resting up for a spell."

Ironside grimaced. "Well, maybe that's a good idea, boy. But only for a short spell, mind."

"Damn it, Luther, you're getting too old for this."

"Don't you sass me, boy. You ain't so old an' tough that I can't take a willow switch to you."

"There's a ruined hacienda a mile to the north of Mule Mesa. We'll head there," Jacob said.

"I can make it to Dromore, Jake."

"No you can't, so let's ride." Jacob swung his horse to the south and Ironside followed.

"Luther, are you in pain? Hell, Luther, you look like you're hurting."

Ironside made his fist of his gloved right hand and tapped his chest. "Yeah, right there."

"Is it bad?"

"Bad enough."

"Maybe I should come up with you and help you stay in the saddle," Jacob said.

Ironside's blue eyes flared. "You try that, Jake, an' I'll shoot you right off'n that damned pony."

Jacob smiled. "You're a terrible, violent man, Luther."

"Damn right I am."


The hacienda had been destroyed by Apaches many years before and all that was left of the main structure were piles of mud bricks and a few charred timbers. But, built for defense, most of the arched entrance still stood and roofed an area about the size of a small cabin.

Jacob knew better than to help Ironside out of the saddle and stood aside until Luther stepped under the arch, sat wearily on the granite flagstones, and fetched his back against the wall.

"Damn it, Jake. I'm all in," Ironside said. "I never felt this tired afore."

"Maybe you're coming down with something, Luther. A bad cold, maybe."

Ironside shook his head. "I think what you think, Jake, and I think it's my ticker. It's paining me some and my left arm feels kinda numb."

"You just lie still, Luther. I'll light a fire and we got coffee and grub in the saddlebags."

"No grub, Jake, but I could sure use a cup o' coffee." Ironside opened his sheepskin and clumsily unbuckled his gunbelt. "Here, take this. I'm gonna bend my damned iron sittin' on it."

Wood was easier to find than Jacob had anticipated. Many of the charred timbers had plenty of unburned areas and those hidden under tumbled bricks were still dry. He also found a packrat's nest that flamed well as a fire starter.

The kitchen maids had packed beef sandwiches, coffee, and a small coffeepot.

Ironside had dozed for ten minutes when he opened his eyes and grimaced. "How's that coffee coming, boy?"

"It's about done, Luther."

"Bile it some more, Jake. I can't abide the swill the womenfolk make us drink at Dromore. Toss a silver dollar into the pot. If it floats, she's done."

"How are you feeling, Luther?"

"Like I've got a hundred different kinds of miseries. How the hell are you?"

"I'm fine. Just sit there and save your strength."

"It's gonna be a cold one tonight, Jake. I can feel the chill already."

Jacob untied the bedrolls and spread Ironside's blankets over him. "That better?"

Ironside nodded, then his eyes took on a faraway look. "Jake, if I cash out—"

"You aren't going to cash out, Luther," Jacob said. "You're too damned ornery for that."

"Well, anyway, I want to make my last will and testament just in case."

Jacob poured coffee for them both, then sat beside Ironside and lit a cigarette. Deciding to humor the old timer, he said, "All right, Luther, let's hear it."

"You'll honor it, Jake? I mean be true blue as ever was?"

"Depend on it. I'll see that your last wishes are carried out."

"Good. Get out your tally book and write this down." Ironside tested his coffee. "Swill." He took a deep breath. "Being of sound mind, I bestow my Colt gun and my Winchester rifle on Jake O'Brien, because I know he'll put them to good use."

Jacob suppressed a smile. "Very generous, Luther."

"Damn it, boy, I ain't finished yet." He glared at Jacob. "Are you taking this down?"

Jacob held up his stub of pencil. "Getting every word, Luther."

"Then we'll continue. Damn, my chest hurts. To Pat O'Brien I bequeath my saber an' cavalry guidon, even though it be torn by shot and shell. Pat has an interest in such old things."

"Yes, he does, Luther. You're not in too much pain, are you?"

"If I am, there's nothin' you can do about it, boy, so write. Now where was I? Oh, I remember. To Shawn O'Brien, I leave the ten double eagles he'll find in a tin box under my bed. It's my wedding present to him and his intended. To Sam O'Brien I leave my medals so he can pass them down to little Shamus when he's old enough. The boy should know that once upon a time me and his grandfather fought for the Confederacy and states' rights and I hope he'll be proud."

"He'll be proud, Luther."

"To Colonel Shamus O'Brien I leave my silver watch that I received from the hand of General Robert E. Lee himself and also my King James Bible that he may read God's word without taint of popery."

Jacob smiled. "He'll love that, Luther."

Ironside grinned like a mischievous imp. "Yeah, won't he though?"

He closed his eyes and for a moment Jacob thought he was asleep. But then he said, "All my other traps—chaps, boots, belts, spurs and the like— dispose of them as you see fit, Jake, since you're the executor of my will. Didn't think I knew that word *executor* did you?"

"It's a fine, impressive word, Luther. Rolls right off the tongue."

But Luther Ironside had closed his eyes again and was really asleep.

Jacob gently removed the coffee cup from the old man's hand and kissed his leathery cheek. "Don't die on me, Luther. Please don't die on me."

# Chapter Thirty-five

"The doctor says Luther had a mild heart attack," Lorena said. "He's in no danger, but he needs rest."

"How do you plan to keep the stubborn old coot in bed?" Jacob asked.

"The colonel came up with a solution. He had a cot set up in the parlor and says he'll make sure Luther stays in it—at gunpoint, if necessary."

Jacob and Patrick had just returned from another unsuccessful search for Jaimenacho Rios, and hope was fading that the vaquero was still alive.

Lorena asked about that. "What could have happened to him, Jacob?"

"This is a hard land and it can kill a man a hundred different ways, Lorena. So the answer to your question is that I don't know."

Lorena shook her head. "Poor Lilia Rios. She spends all her time in the chapel, praying for her husband's safe return. I feel so sorry for her."

Jacob helped himself to coffee from the pot on

the kitchen stove, and then Patrick did the same. "Jake, what do you reckon that smell in the wind was over to Lone Mountain?"

"Death and decay, Pat. That's what it smelled like to me."

"Oh my God," Lorena said. "It's not—"

"It was too strong a stink to be caused by one body, Lorena," Patrick said. "I think it's more like there's been a big cattle die-off somewhere."

"Tom Johnson's spread is out that way." Jacob took a drink of the coffee. "He's not a man to lose cattle to winter."

"Maybe we should ride out that way and take a look." Patrick took a cookie from the jar on the counter.

"The colonel says we'll call off the search after one more day," Jacob said. "Then I guess we can go pay Tom a visit."

"Probably dead deer, anyway," Patrick said with his mouth full.

"It would have to be a lot of them." Jacob drained his cup. "Let's see how Luther is doing."


"Hell, Jake, how did you get me back home?" Ironside asked, sitting up on his cot in the parlor. "I was out of it most of the time."

"You rode, Luther. You wouldn't let me take you up in front of me."

"Damn right I wouldn't. How about Dave Chaney's body?"

"It's still out there. The vaqueros will take a

buckboard and pick it up later today." Shamus O'Brien shook his head. "There seems to me a lot of misfortune surrounding Dromore. One vaquero dead, another missing, Dave Chaney dead, Luther ill. Where will it end?"

"It all started when Holliday arrived," Ironside said. "He's the damned cause of it."

"Or when Johnny Sligo appeared," Jacob said. "He's a bearer of misfortune, if we can believe what Chaney told us."

"He's a man needs killing by the sound of it," Ironside said. "And Holliday is another."

"Don't get yourself worked up, Luther," Shamus said. "You know what the doctor told you."

"When I think of Holliday above my head a-lyin' in bed and drinking your whiskey, Colonel, how can I do anythin' else but get worked up?"

"Did I hear my name mentioned?" Doc Holliday stood at the parlor door, dressed in a nightshirt, slippers, a shawl wrapped around his shoulders. He looked gray and old and sick.

"Yeah, you did," Ironside said. "It's time for you to get the hell out of Dromore . . . and out of the damned territory come to that."

"How are you feeling, Luther?" Doc asked. "Nothing serious, I hope. The only people I talk to are the housemaids and they don't tell me anything."

"What the hell is it to you how I feel?" Ironside grumbled.

"I like you, Luther. You are the sort of man I always wanted to be and couldn't."

Ironside, his face belligerent, opened his mouth

to speak again, but Doc held up a silencing hand. "I have good news. So I'm very glad the whole family is gathered to hear it." He waited for effect.

Shamus said heatedly, "Spill it. We need some good news around here."

"I feel that I've worn out my welcome at Dromore, so I'm leaving," Doc said. "It's in my mind to head for pastures new."

"About time," Ironside mumbled.

"Why this sudden change of heart, Dr. Holliday?" Lorena asked.

"Ah, a good question, ma'am. An excellent question. May I take a seat? Perhaps on the corner of your bed, Luther?"

"Try that an' I'll shoot ya."

"Sit on the sofa by the fire," Shamus said. "I'm sure Patrick and Samuel will make room for you."

"And a whiskey, perhaps?" Doc asked. "To keep out the winter chill."

"Patrick, do the honors," Shamus said.

After he was settled, a glass in hand, Doc said, "Now where was I?"

"You were tellin' us why you decided to leave Dromore—finally," Ironside said.

"I always regretted being born, but I found that dying is a long, tedious business and therefore I tried to expedite it—"

"What does that mean?" Ironside said, scowling his suspicion.

"It means to make a thing go more quickly, Luther," Patrick said.

"Exactly," Doc said. "And so I engaged in many a

perilous escapade, many a desperate encounter, hoping to meet the man who would be a daisy and end my miserable existence."

"A most singular ambition, I must say," Judith Lovell said. "And not one that inspires a person."

Sir James shook his head at his daughter and she flushed and looked down at her hands.

"Yes, young lady, as you say, it was indeed a most singular ambition and for many years I considered it of the greatest moment," Doc said. "But now I've decided that I must prolong my life, at least for a few more years, and inspiration is in fact my motive."

"What about going out in a blaze of glory, Doc?" Patrick said, a statement that drew an irritated look from the colonel.

"Ah yes, my final act before the curtain fell"—Doc closed his eyes—"gun in hand, ending it all in one hell-firing moment of scarlet-streaked violence. That was the legacy Doc Holliday wanted leave for posterity."

"So what changed your mind?" Ironside asked, caught up in Doc's tale. "If it ain't too much to ask."

Doc opened his eyes again and extended his glass to Patrick. "Please fill it this time."

"Well?" Ironside said. "We're listenin'."

"In a word . . . well, in two words . . . my memoirs."

This was rewarded by silence.

Doc looked around the room at each person gathered there. "What better legacy than a personal account of my many and exciting, and may I say, sometimes noble, Western adventures? The New York publishers will go wild for such a journal."

"I'd buy that book," Patrick said. "It sounds like it could be crackerjack."

"Yeah, well if I was you, Holliday, I'd learn to write real fast," Ironside said. "You don't have much time."

"Luther, may I remind you that we don't abuse a guest in our home," Shamus said.

"Nonetheless, Colonel, Luther's is an astute observation, and one I haven't yet addressed," Doc said. "Tomorrow I will leave to take the waters at Glenwood Springs in Colorado. I was told that the sulfur in the springs does wonders for consumptives. All I need is two more years to complete my memoirs and see them published. After that, the devil can take me any time he feels like it."

"How do you plan to get out of the territory, Doc?" Jacob said. "James Stuart may have men watching Dromore."

"That is a possibility to be sure," Shamus said.

"I've eluded posses before," Doc said. "But I was younger then. What I had in mind is an escort to Santa Fe where I can catch a train and be out of your hair."

"Hell, I'll do—"

"You'll do nothing of the kind, Luther," Shamus interrupted. "You need bed rest and plenty of it. And before anyone else volunteers, I need Samuel here to look after the range, Shawn is still recovering, and Patrick is . . . well, he's not suited to such a task. And I will not risk the lives of my vaqueros. This was none of their doing."

Jacob smiled. "So that leaves me, Pa."

"Indeed it does not. I want you here, Jacob. The

business with that Johnny Sligo person has made me uneasy and you're the only one I trust to handle him."

"Then who, Pa?" Samuel looked at his father in confusion.

"Me," Shamus said. "I'll escort Doc to Santa Fe and see that he gets on a train. I doubt very much that James Stuart would shoot me down."

"Colonel, it's the middle of winter and you're not fit for such a ride," Lorena said.

"Daughter-in-law, this is my home, Dr. Holliday is my guest, and it's my responsibility to see him safely to his destination. And contrary to what you may think, I'm not yet so decrepit that I can't ride fifteen miles to Santa Fe and back."

"Sam, talk to your father." When Lorena got no reaction from her husband, she said, "Jacob, please."

Jacob shook his head. "When the colonel has his mind set on a thing, nothing I can say will change it."

"I should hope not," Shamus said. "What was that you said, Luther?"

"Nothin', Colonel. I didn't say nothin'."

"I'm sure I heard foul and angry words directed at Dr. Holliday. May I refer you to Proverbs 29:11, that 'a fool gives full vent to his anger, but a wise man keeps himself under control.'"

"Damn, my chest hurts," Ironside said, lying back in bed and doing his best to look languid.

"Yes, you are ill, Luther, and that is why I will not chide you further."

"Thank'ee, Colonel," Ironside said. "I am feeling mighty low."

Shamus directed cold words to Doc. "We leave at first light tomorrow. Are you sure you can make it to Santa Fe?"

Doc nodded. "I can make it. My memoirs are going to keep me alive."

"Then let us hope that is the case," Shamus said.

# Chapter Thirty-six

Wolf Hartmann rode into the tiny Mexican village in the upper Pecos Valley as he had every Friday night for the past several weeks. As settlements in the New Mexico Territory went, El Cerrito was at the backend of nowhere, a cluster of adobe peasant hovels, each with a chicken coop attached, and a fair-sized church where services were conducted every Sunday, even when no visiting priest was present.

The village had a cantina that served good mescal and in winter, cold beer, and Hartmann enjoyed the ambience of the place. Its adobe walls were hung with colorful rugs and logs blazed in the huge open fireplace.

The girl who served tables was young and pretty and Hartmann engaged in some harmless flirting before she brought him his usual order of mescal and a beer.

"Not many customers tonight," the girl said. "Who wants to come to El Cerrito in such cold weather?"

"Only me," Hartmann said, "and those two gents at the bar. Miners by the look of them."

"They say there are rumors of a gold strike at Apache Mesa to the east, but no one in El Cerrito has heard of such a thing."

Hartmann smiled, showing good teeth. "Gold miners lie to each other all the time. Keeps rivals away from their own hole in the ground."

"This is so, senor. We talk with many of them who pass through our village and they tell tall tales about lost gold mines."

The girl left and Hartmann took a drink of the beer, the alcohol relaxing him. He built then lit a cigarette, listening idly to the miners' conversation. A name was uttered that made him sit upright in his chair.

"Johnny Sligo, that was his handle, Jeptha. I swear, you ain't got a memory fer nothin'."

"Yeah, well maybe so, but that's a name I'd sooner forget, if'n it's all the same to you, Ben."

Hartman leaned toward the bar. "Excuse me, gentlemen, would you care to join me? I don't like to drink alone."

His face deeply wrinkled by weather, the man called Ben had candid blue eyes and the hair that showed under his hat was touched with gray. However he looked at Hartmann with some suspicion, noting his gun and expensive handmade boots and silver spurs. "You another o' them Texas draw fighters, mister? If'n you are sich, we seen enough of your kind recent."

"I heard you mention the name Johnny Sligo," Hartmann said. "It interested me."

"You know him?"

"I know of him." Hartmann smiled. "And to set your mind at rest, I'm not one of his kind."

"Hell, Ben, the gent's buying drinks." Jeptha knuckled his forehead, a gesture that marked him as a former seaman. We take that most kindly, cap'n, us being a mite short of the actual."

"Then sit down and join me," Hartmann said. "I'm paying tonight."

After the miners ordered mescal, Ben said, "I didn't mean to be unsociable, mister, but that Johnny Sligo feller left us afeared of men who wear guns like they were born to them."

"Like your good self, cap'n, and no offense meant, lay to that," Jeptha said.

"None taken," Hartman said. "Where did you boys meet up with Johnny Sligo?"

Ben scratched his head. "Well, how it come up is there's an old Indian pueblo village by the name of Galisteo up there in the Arroyo San Cristobal brush country, catch my drift?"

"No, but go ahead," Hartmann encouraged.

"Now, about a mile to the west of the pueblo there's a hotel called The Excelsior, just stands there in the middle of nowhere, waiting for the railroad that ain't ever gonna come because—"

"And that's where you met Johnny Sligo." Hartmann cut short what he reckoned was going to be a long story.

"Exactly, cap'n. We seen him in the hotel saloon and the very devil was in him that night," Jeptha said.

"So what happened?"

"He killed three people in the time it would take you to light a cigar, is what happened," Jeptha said.

A north wind explored ways to enter the cantina and the log in the fireplace shifted, sending up a cascade of sparks. Somewhere in the village a baby cried and then fell silent.

"First one Johnny Sligo killed was a farm boy," Ben said.

"Maybe a poor Swede boy," Jeptha said. "But I'm not sure about that."

"Yeah, maybe so, Jeptha. Well anyhoo, Johnny shot him."

"Why?" Hartmann asked.

Ben drained his glass. "For messing with his saloon girl, Johnny said. But that warn't the reason. He just wanted to kill somebody that night. It was wrote plain on his face for all to see. He looked like a demon right out of hell."

"And then what happened?" Hartmann pushed.

"What came down was that the gal who was planning to get hitched to the—"

"Poor Swede boy," Jeptha jumped in again.

"Yeah, that's right, Jeptha," Ben said. "Anyway the gal attacked Johnny and scratched him up real bad, and he shot her."

"Then the bartender came up with a scattergun and Johnny shot him as well," Jeptha said. "The bartender died hard. He didn't deserve that kind of end."

"No man does, Jeptha." Ben sipped his drink and laid the glass back on the table. "Strange thing was, Johnny told us his name, said we should remember it. It was like he was real proud of what he'd done and how he done it."

Hartmann raised his hand and ordered more mescal. "You boys are lucky you're still alive. Johnny Sligo is a killer and he's better with a gun than anybody I know."

"Including you, cap'n?" Jeptha asked.

Hartmann nodded. "Better than anybody." He tried his mescal and it didn't taste as good as it had before. "You boys have any idea where he is?"

The miners looked at each other and then at Hartmann, their faces blank. "He could be anywhere," Jeptha said finally. "I just don't want to see him walk through the door over there."

"Amen to that," Ben said. "The gent just ain't human."

# Chapter Thirty-seven

Johnny Sligo haunted the darkness, drawn again to the Excelsior Hotel like a hellish moth to a black flame. A rising wind slammed a door open and shut inside the building and its echoes thudded like a muffled drum.

The clouds had parted and a sickle moon spread tarnished silver light.

"Why are we here?" Black Tom Church was ill, his face bloated and gray. His mighty chin hung slack and the light had fled his eyes.

Quiet as a mouse, Johnny Sligo watched the sky. The flat country was a lake of mist and tendrils coiled around the house like gray snakes.

"Why are we here?" Black Tom asked again. "Why did you bring me to this place?"

Johnny Sligo broke his silence. "I was born at midnight on All Hallow's Eve. Did you know that? It's why I have the power to talk with the dead."

"Is that why we're here?" Black Tom pulled up the

collar of his mackinaw against the chill. "To talk with the dead?"

"We're here because it's Friday night and people are having a good time."

"Where? I don't see any damned people. The hotel is empty, abandoned."

"Ah, that's the whole point, Tom. It's the damned people who are having a good time. They're drawn to this place, just as I am."

"Are you feeling all right, Johnny? You're talking strange, like a crazy preacher."

"Here's a lark," Sligo said. "Let's go inside and dance with the dead." An owl hooted from somewhere nearby. "Hear that? We're being invited to the shindig."

Black Tom was alarmed. He always figured that Johnny Sligo had a fragile grasp on sanity, but tonight the man was mighty weird. "There's nobody there. The place is dark and it's as quiet"—he was about to say *as a tomb*, but changed his mind—"as an empty house, which it is."

"It's not empty, Tom. Listen to the fiddle music. . . ."

Black Tom opened his mouth to speak, but Sligo hushed him into silence and sang in a whisper, "Buffalo gals won't you come out tonight, come out tonight, come out tonight. Buffalo gals won't you come out tonight and dance by the light of the moon."

He smiled into Black Tom's face. "Can't you hear it? It's the music of the dead, Tom."

"I don't hear a thing. Only the wind and the clouds scraping across the sky."

Sligo scowled. "You're spoiling the party, Tom. Make sure you don't get shot for being such a cranky ol' sourpuss." He swung out of the saddle. "Come inside, Tom. I want to show you something."

"Show me what?"

"You'll find out when we get inside among the folks."

"Johnny, you are crazy. I'm heading back to the ranch. Now mount up and come with me. Hell, Johnny, I'm burning up with a fever so hot my bowels are melting."

"What's this? Oh, look, Tom, it's a gun in my hand and it's pointed right at your fat gut."

Black Tom saw the Colt all right. Moonlight gleamed on its blue barrel and madness gleamed just as bright in Johnny Sligo's eyes.

"Will you join me, Tom? Oh, please tell me you'll join me. Hell, we might drink champagne out of the devil's slipper. You'd like that, Tom, wouldn't you?"

"Anything you say, Johnny," Black Tom said, dismounting. "Any damned thing you say."

He realized then that he'd have to kill Johnny Sligo. The man had become too dangerous to keep alive. *God, I'm hot, burning up.*

"Follow me, Tom. Just watch your step. It's so dark out here they really should light a lamp, make it nice for the folks."

Clouds passed over the arc of the moon and walking into the hotel was like stepping into blue-black ink.

Sligo's boots sounded on the floor then stopped. He chuckled softly and called out, "Hey, Tom, they're all here, everybody I ever killed. Only my pa isn't too happy because he's got no head. I cut it off him with an ax when I caught him in bed doing stuff with my ma. Your head bounced all over the floor . . . bump . . . bump . . . bump . . . didn't it, Pa? Remember that, huh?"

Black Tom stood in the darkness, gun in hand. *Keep talking, Johnny boy. Just keep talking.*

Sligo walked to the bar. "Tom, this here is the bartender I shot the other night. You got no hard feelings, do you? No, I thought not. Bartending ain't much of a life anyhow, old fellow."

Despite the cold, Black Tom's gun hand sweated and he wiped it on his mackinaw. He couldn't decide if it was fear or because he was so sick. He looked into the darkness.

Where was Sligo? He'd have to keep the man talking and fire at the sound of his voice. He'd only get one shot because the flash would blind him. If he missed there wouldn't be time for a second. He had to be sure.

A sudden silence had fallen in the room, but from somewhere in the hotel a door banged with maddening insistence, setting Black Tom's nerves on edge. Sweat beaded all over his face and under his coat his armpits were soaked.

"I found what I was looking for, Tom!" Sligo yelled. "Damned farm boy I shot broke it. I got a good mind to kill him all over again."

The voice was to Black Tom's left. No, to his right. No, straight ahead.

Where the hell was he?

Black Tom decided he couldn't take a chance.

He'd wait, bide his time. There would be better opportunities to kill Johnny Sligo. He holstered his gun. "What did you find, Johnny?" he said, talking rationally as though the man was sane.

"I'll show you, Tom."

Sligo's ringing spurs crossed the floor, and now and then he said, "Excuse me," to people who existed only in his shattered mind.

When he was within seeing distance, Sligo held up something. "What's this?"

The big man took a step closer for a better look. "It's a cross. It's Jesus on the cross."

"I stepped on it. It wasn't the stupid farm boy over there talking with his whore, it was me. See there, I broke the arm off, Tom."

"It was just an accident, Johnny. Hell, it's only a pot metal Jesus."

"No, now I'm cursed. The man on the cross will kill me."

"Throw it away, Johnny, and forget about it. Don't talk about such things."

Sligo turned and threw the cross into the dark room. "Take it!" he yelled. "All of you! I don't want the damned thing."

"What the hell?" Black Tom's voice was ragged with fear.

"I gave it back to them," Sligo said.

"Damn it, I'm talking about that sound."

"Oh, the dead are coming toward us, shuffling their feet. They don't walk too well, dead things."

"It's the wind!" Black Tom was almost hysterical. "I'm hearing the wind."

"The dead aren't silent, like folks think, Tom. They sound like the wind and their souls are the color of storm clouds. Did you know that?"

The shuffling came closer . . . a rustle . . . a harsh whisper . . . like dry leaves blowing across the floor of a marble tomb. . . .

Black Tom shrieked, then turned and ran outside . . . into the falling snow and the welcoming cold.

The clock on the mantel said two-sixteen, but it had been claiming that was the time for days since no one had troubled to wind it. Black Tom Church watched a huge rat make its way along the mantel then perch on top of the clock and regard him with sly, black eyes.

Fevered and sick, Black Tom sat in a chair by the fire, a shotgun across the armrests. The acrid stench in the ranch house was unbearable, but, sunk in his own filth and too ill to care, he didn't notice.

An hour after his return from the abandoned hotel, the door opened and Johnny Sligo stepped inside.

Black Tom reacted by grabbing the scattergun, but he found himself looking into the muzzle of Sligo's Colt.

"What the hell are you doing?" Sligo said. "I could've drilled you for sure." He stepped to the chair, yanked the shotgun away from Black Tom. and threw it into a corner.

"Damn you, Johnny. Did you bring them with you?" Black Tom asked.

"Bring who with me?"

"Them dead people at the hotel."

Sligo looked puzzled. "What the hell are you talking about?"

Sweat beaded on Black Tom's forehead and he took a swig of whiskey before he answered. The rat on the mantel was joined by another and then they scurried away, squeaking.

"You know what I'm talking about, Johnny. You were there. You showed me the Jesus on the cross you broke and you said you were cursed. You talked to dead people, all the folks you've ever killed in your life. Remember that?"

Black Tom took another drink. "You told me how you killed your own pa with an ax because you caught him in bed humping your mother. His head bounced across the floor. You said that, Johnny."

"My pa was hung for a horse thief by the Texas Rangers and Ma died giving me birth. The fever's got you crazy as a loon, Tom. You're imagining things."

"The dead people chased me, Johnny. I heard them come after me and their souls were the color of storm clouds like you said they'd be."

"So that's why your horse is lathered up. You rode to the Excelsior Hotel tonight." Sligo shook his head. "You knew about the man on the cross because I told you about him and the story about the kid who murdered his pa must have been in one of them dime novels you read. You're fevered, Tom, out of your damned head. You heard those dead people at the hotel because you invented them in your mind."

Black Tom's red, bloated face revealed uncertainty. "You weren't there?"

"I was in the bunkhouse all night. I can't stand the stink in this place."

"Then I rode to the hotel by myself, when I was crazy with the fever?"

"You're a sick man, Tom. Half the time you don't know what you're saying or doing."

"Tomorrow . . . listen, Johnny . . . tomorrow we'll make a count of the cattle. We'll put this place up for sale and we'll buy that Dromore place with the big house, buy it cheap. That's a good plan, Johnny, a fine plan, ain't it?"

"The cattle are all dead or scattered, and in your state of health you can't take on a big outfit like Dromore."

"I know I'm real sick, Johnny, and I need a doctor's care. Tell me what to do. I was gonna kill you, but I've changed my mind because I need you, Johnny. You see how it is with me? I need you real bad."

Sligo smiled. "You're right. The fever and whatever is eating away at your bowels will kill you soon enough, if you don't listen to me."

"Tell me, Johnny. I feel like I'm sitting on top of a Fourth of July bonfire here, and I'll do anything you say."

"Where is the money you hid, Tom? The fifty thousand dollars?"

"In a safe place, Johnny."

"Where?"

"I can't tell you."

"Then I'll leave you here to die in your own filth when your guts explode. It doesn't matter a damn to me."

"You don't trust me, Johnny."

"And you don't trust me either. We're two of a kind."

Black Tom frowned. "What are we? What are we, Johnny?"

"The darkness at midnight. The dirt that fills the grave. Nothing else."

"No, that's not us, Johnny. We'll be rich. When a man's rich, he's somebody. I don't want to be nothing, a nobody."

"Then we need the money, damn you."

"I'll take you to it, Johnny. And then you'll help me get to a doctor, huh?"

"Sure I will, Tom. I'll sure as hell cure what ails you."


"It's close, Johnny," Black Tom Church said. "Not far now."

The night was bitter cold and Johnny Sligo lifted the lantern and watched Black Tom stagger across the numb ground. The man was on his last legs and Sligo fretted that he wouldn't live long enough to recover the money.

A blustering wind rushed through the pines with a sound like distant surf and clouds scudded across the horned moon. Shadows, black as fog, pooled around the two men as their boot heels thumped on the icy earth.

"We'll see a dead tree soon, Johnny. Then we'll know that we're close." The big man stopped then stepped to a snowdrift between the trees. He picked up a handful of snow and ate a few bites. Then he rubbed the rest over his face. "The sun's hot, Johnny." Melted snow dripped from his unshaven jowls. "We got to find us some shade."

"Yeah, sure, Tom, sure. Right after we get the fifty thousand."

"We'll find it, never fear," Black Tom said. "I know where it is."

After ten minutes of walking, following the huge lurching figure of his companion, Sligo saw a crack of moonlight slant across a dry wash and shine white on the ancient bones of a downed cottonwood. "Is that the dead tree?"

Black Tom nodded. "It's the tree. See, I pushed it over. The roots were rotten and I pushed it real easy."

The big man led the way to the uprooted cottonwood and got down on his knees, his hands digging in the dirt. After a couple minutes of digging, he pulled out a large carpetbag and beat loose the dirt from its sides.

"Is that it?" Sligo said, his eyes glittering. "Damn, is that the fifty thousand?"

"Yes, it's the money, Johnny, all of it," Black Tom said. "Now we can go back and get our horses and head for Albuquerque. They got good doctors there who'll make me feel better."

"Tom, I got a good doctor right here," Sligo said. "A certain cure for all ills."

Black Tom lifted his head, saw the gun in Sligo's fist, and knew he was a dead man. The last few grains of sand were dripping through his hourglass.

But he tried.

His hand dropped for his Colt and Sligo shot him. He shot him again and again, pounding bullets into Black Tom like a man nailing shut a packing case.

Gunsmoke drifted around Sligo as he stepped over the dead man's body. His hands shaking in anticipation, he undid the straps of the carpet bag. He looked inside, then tilted back his head. With his face turned to the uncaring sky, he screamed out his terrible rage.

# Chapter Thirty-eight

Colonel Shamus O'Brien and Doc Holliday rode away from Dromore just before dawn under a lowering sky that threatened snow.

No one saw them go or wished them a safe journey. That was the colonel's order.

In his long coat, Doc sat hunched in the saddle, the brim of his bowler hat pulled low over his eyes. He'd coughed his lungs up in bloody gobs in the barn and he looked weak, used up, a dead man riding.

Shamus was uncomfortably aware that he was responsible for the man. "How do you feel, Doc?"

Holliday turned his head, his eyes red as a sunset. "I'll be fine when I get to Glenwood Springs and pick up my pen."

It was a good three-hour ride to Santa Fe, and maybe longer if the weather didn't hold. Shamus was prepared to be sociable to pass the time. "What are you going to call your memoirs, if I may ask?"

"Certainly you may ask, Colonel. I plan to call the

work *Bucking the Tiger: My Life and Times on the Wild Frontier*, by Dr. John Henry Holliday."

"That'll do," Shamus said, smiling.

"I sincerely hope so, but posterity will be the judge."

"I look forward to reading it." It was a small lie and the colonel was prepared to live with it.

"Good, then I'll send you a signed copy," Doc said. "Consider it a little thank-you for all the trouble I've caused."

Shamus was about to say, *You were no trouble*, but he didn't. He wasn't that much of a hypocrite. "I look forward to reading it," he said again.

Doc nodded. "It will be a fine book. I've had many adventures and met a lot of interesting people." He smiled. "Including yourself, Colonel O'Brien."

"I'm honored," Shamus said. But he didn't really mean it.

When they rode into the high timber country south of Shaggy Mountain, snow started to fall. At first only a few flakes tossed in the wind, then it came down thicker, as though the ancient mountain gods were shaking out a gigantic feather mattress.

Shamus and Doc were quickly transformed into snowmen on white horses. The colonel was shocked to see Doc's face turning blue as his breathing became more labored.

"Doc, we'd better hole up until this blows over," Shamus yelled over the rising wind. "You need to rest a spell."

Unable to speak, Doc merely nodded.

About a hundred yards ahead of them, Shamus saw a break in the trees and beyond that what looked to be a hanging meadow about ten acres in extent, its grass streaked by drifts of snow. The colonel figured that shelter could be found there if the clearing was enclosed by mountain ridges or stands of timber thick enough to break the force of the wind. He grabbed Doc's reins and rode at a walk in that direction.

To his joy, he'd been right about the meadow. To the north rose a high ridge topped by aspen, but what caught Shamus's attention was a narrow crack in the rock that promised a recess where the impact of wind and snow would be less.

He'd no way of knowing how wide the gap was until he got closer, but even if it provided a refuge for Doc it would be enough.

His head bent against wind and snow, hauling on the reins of Doc's reluctant horse, Shamus pushed across the meadow toward the ridge.

Then behind him he heard Doc Holliday shriek in terror.

The black bear charged out of the trees to Shamus's left and hit Doc's mount with tremendous impact. Screaming, the eight-hundred pound mustang went down under a vicious predator that weighed only a couple hundred pounds less.

Doc was thrown from the saddle, hit the hard ground hard, and lay still.

Shamus, trying to control his wildly rearing horse, could do nothing.

Within seconds the bear tore out the mustang's throat and its scarlet, glistening muzzle lifted as Doc slowly got up on one knee, his head hanging.

The bear roared and slashed at the mustang's head and neck with its curved claws. But then it stopped and headed for the helpless human.

Shamus was unable to stay with his bucking horse. The terrified animal finally threw him and galloped away, its stirrups flying. The colonel slammed into the hard ground with a thick thud, giving the bear pause.

It swung its huge head in Shamus's direction and roared, its piggy little eyes black with rage.

Shamus heard that terrible bellow and staggered to his feet, his hand scrambling for the Colt holstered under his sheepskin.

A moment later, after covering the ground between them almost as fast as a quarter horse at full gallop, the bear slammed into the colonel and brought him down.

Luckily for Shamus, the bear's attack was so violent the impact spun him around so that he fell on his front. Growling, the bear's claws pounded at him, slashing at his back. Despite the terrible, ripping pain and the taste of blood in his mouth, Shamus was aware enough to know that his only chance was to play dead.

Grizzlies and brown bears would occasionally fall for that ruse and walk away, but the black bear was less inclined to stop his attack for any reason. When he wanted you dead, he wanted you really dead.

The bear tore at Shamus, ripping apart his sheepskin, then tried to turn him over to get at his throat and belly. The colonel knew he was a goner, but tried to fight the bear . . . to buy enough time to say an Act of Contrition that his soul might be saved.

Then Shamus heard a shot, and another, and the crushing, six-hundred pound weight of the animal sank slowly on top of him. He groaned under the pressure, but managed to turn his head.

Doc Holliday stood close to him, a smoking Colt in his hand. "My first bear and the last chapter of my memoirs," Doc gasped, smiling slightly under his snow-covered mustache.

Shamus found it difficult to breathe and his inclination was to cuss out Doc for talking about his memoirs while a dead bear sprawled on top of him, its fangs only inches from his throat. Trying to keep his voice calm, he said, "Can you get this thing off me?"

Snow blowing around him, Doc looked like a scarecrow in a winter field. "I'm afraid not, Colonel." He shoved his revolver back in his coat pocket. "I can't be sure, but that damned animal must weigh half a ton."

Shamus arched his back and tried to push the bear off. It didn't budge.

Doc glanced at the black sky. "I suppose going for help is out of the question?"

"Doc, I swear, if I ever get out from under this thing, I'll put a bullet into you." Shamus tasted blood in his mouth and pain from his wounds hit him. "Of course it's out of the question. By the time you got back, me and this bear would be a single dead mound in the snow."

"What do you want me to do, Colonel?" Doc shivered. "God knows, I don't have the strength to do much."

"Go get my horse," Shamus said. "Can you manage that?"

Doc looked across the snow scourged meadow. "He's right over there, Colonel. Will he stand for me?"

"He'll stand. Now"—Shamus winced as his back punished him—"loop my rope around the animal's neck and—"

"I catch your drift, Colonel."

"Then do it, man," Shamus said. "I'm getting crushed to death here."

But Doc Holliday, betrayed by thin mountain air, lancing cold, and the fall he'd taken when his horse went down, was going nowhere.

He gasped. . . . The gasp became a throaty rasp. . . . The rasp progressed to hacking that hammered through his frail body . . . then to the full-blown hawking and whooping that did awful violence to Doc's lungs and triggered the eruption of phlegm, blood, and tissue that forced him to his hands and knees.

Blood stained the snow like red ink spilled on white paper and Doc's feeble body shuddered, each racking cough a sledgehammer blow that pounded him without mercy.

Shamus, pinned under the dead bear, could only watch helplessly, his lips moving in prayer . . . for himself, for Doc, and for a quick and painless death. Then the colonel witnessed something that would forever change his opinion of Doc Holliday . . . a miracle of sorts.

Despite his torment, Doc struggled to his feet and stood, swaying for a moment, snow swirling around him. He lifted his head, his bloodstained mouth twitching, and he staggered in the direction of Shamus's horse.

The colonel would later remember that the distance between Doc and the horse was no more than fifty yards and he'd say, "He fell eighteen times because I counted every one. But each time he'd get to his feet and stagger forward again, coughing up his lungs with every step."

Watching, Shamus caught a glimpse of the man Doc once was, or could have been, and never forgot it.

The injuries Shamus sustained in the bear attack were not as bad as he'd feared. His thick sheepskin coat had taken the brunt of the damage, but it was slashed to ribbons and was stained with blood.

Doc Holliday had recovered from his coughing fit. Weak and shivering, he stood beside Shamus in the narrow crack in the ridge wall.

"I'm taking you back to Dromore where you can rest, Doc," Shamus said. "You saved my life twice today and I owe you. Come with me back to Dromore."

Doc shook his head and smiled. "Your horse saved you, Colonel, when it pulled the bear off you.

Nonetheless, that was a kindly sentiment, but not one I care to act upon. I must get to Glenwood Springs and regain my strength there. My memoirs, you know."

"Then we will proceed to Santa Fe as we planned and I'll see you safely on a train. It's the least I can do. But I wish you'd change your mind and reconsider. You can spend Christmas with us as an honored guest and then head for Colorado."

"Once again, it's most kind of you, Colonel, but I prefer to stick with my original plan. As you probably gathered, time is not on my side."

Shamus left the meager shelter of the crevice and looked out into the meadow. "Snow's letting up a little. With luck and God's tender mercy we should be in Santa Fe for lunch."

"Will your horse carry both of us?" Doc asked.

Shamus nodded. "Yes, but if it's too much for him, you'll ride and I'll walk."

# Chapter Thirty-nine

When Shamus O'Brien and Doc Holliday rode away from Dromore, Johnny Sligo had already given up the search for Black Tom's hidden money.

He'd searched every likely hiding place around the ranch and had even torn the house apart, but had found nothing. All he had to show for his efforts was a carpetbag stuffed with torn-up newspapers.

His breath smoking in the early morning cold, he stood outside the ranch house and considered his options. They were few.

There was nothing to salvage from the ranch. Its range was covered in the bones of dead cattle and the house itself was falling down. It was as though it had given up the struggle and willed itself to die.

Then how to make a profit from this trip?

Sligo built a cigarette and stuck it between his thin lips. He lit the smoke and thought things through. He couldn't stay where he was, that was a given. Sooner or later somebody would come calling and ask questions about the dead cattle and the whereabouts of the rancher who once owned the place.

He decided he'd need to set himself up somewhere else, at least until spring, a remote location that no one would ever visit.

Then it came to him. The Excelsior Hotel was the obvious hideaway and Sligo was surprised he hadn't thought about it sooner.

Despite the emptiness of that part of the territory there were travelers on the trails, miners mostly, but sometimes a stage passed through. It would be easy enough to pull some holdups and keep himself in the ready until he headed south with the sun again.

Sligo dropped his cigarette butt in the mud and walked to the barn to get his horse. By then, he'd already dismissed the road agent idea. Why risk his life for a few miserable dollars here and there? What he needed was a big enough score that would net him enough money to last a couple months and longer if need be.

One thing he did know—damn it, he wasn't going back to Texas broke.

His mind made up, Johnny Sligo rode away from the ranch for the last time without a backward glance. He left a wasteland behind him.


Sligo spent most of the morning riding north in the direction of the Cerrillos Hills. He passed several Mexican villages, all of them too impoverished to support a bank, and, as the snow fell heavier, he was about to give up and leave his search for another day. If he did manage to find a bank to rob, there was always a chance of the rubes mounting a posse and he didn't want to stray too far from the Excelsior Hotel country.

Shortly after noon, he crested a low, treed saddleback and below him he saw a much more promising settlement. It was a white town, obvious by the timber buildings that lined its only street, a few of them boasting false fronts.

Sligo sat his saddle and studied the place. A railroad spur at the north end of town had a small station and a few cattle pens. East of the rails lay a scattering of cabins and a couple larger houses, the kind only the local merchants could afford. The place looked promising.

Sligo rode down the other side of the rise and took the wagon road into town, passing a painted board sign that proclaimed CEDAR CITY.

He rode the length of the street, seeing few people except a couple matrons carrying shopping baskets and a conversation outside a general store with a buckboard pulled up to the boardwalk. Snow had settled on the women's oilskin capes and had accumulated to a depth of an inch or two on the jutting bump of their bustles.

Keeping his horse to a slow walk, Sligo passed a few more stores, a false fronted saloon, a rod and gun shop, more stores, and then an assayer's office. Standing next to the assayer's, but separated by a narrow alley, was a low adobe building with a brass

plaque screwed to the door that said CEDAR CITY
BANK & TRUST.

Johnny Sligo's plan was simple, but it was a good
one that had worked for him before. Shoot the local
lawman, immediately rob the bank, and then light a
shuck before any organized resistance could form.

It was a plan that demanded speed and a cool
head, and Sligo set it in motion.

He dismounted and retraced his steps back to
the gossiping women. "Excuse me, ladies," he said,
touching his hat brim. "Is there an officer of the law
in town?"

The woman looked at him with questions on their
faces and Sligo said, "My seventeen-year-old sister
ran away from home and I've been sent by Ma and
Pa to look for her."

"Oh you poor man," one of the woman said. She
had a long, narrow face and looked like she lived on
scripture and prune juice.

"How did it happen?" the other woman asked.

*None of your damned business, you nosy old hag.*

Aloud, Sligo said, "She fell for the charms of a
traveling salesman and we fear he'll lead her into
evil ways because he is a man much given to gambling, strong drink, and loose women."

The woman clapped her hand to her mouth and
said from behind it, "Mercy me! You must be at your
wit's end."

"Indeed ma'am," Sligo said. "My poor ma is dis-
traught and has taken to her bed. That is why I must

speak to the local constabulary. Perhaps they've heard something."

The woman said, "I doubt that he's heard anything, because he would've told us, but John Clifford is our town sheriff. He owns the mercantile just down the street."

Sligo touched his hat again. "Much obliged."

"I hope you find her," the prune juice woman said to Sligo's retreating back.

The mercantile was a large building with a glass door, and when Sligo stepped inside a bell jangled above his head.

The man behind the counter, middle-aged and inclining to stoutness, looked up. "And what can I do you for?" He smiled. "For today and only today, I'm selling men's collarless shirts at cost."

"You John Clifford?" Sligo asked.

"I am indeed."

"That's all I wanted to know." Sligo drew and fired.

Clifford died with a puzzled look on his face and a bullet in his heart.

Sligo stepped quickly out of the store, mounted his horse, and rode at a walk toward the bank. People passed him on the street, running this way and that as they tried to determine where the shot came from.

Sligo tethered his horse at the hitching rail outside the bank and stepped inside. He stood for a moment shaking his head. What kind of burg was this? The bank didn't even have a grill, just an open counter, a balding clerk in an eyeshade standing behind it.

"Get a sack and fill it with money," Sligo said, his gun up and ready.

The man hesitated, frozen to the spot.

"Now!" Sligo yelled.

The clerk looked like a man just woken from a sound sleep. He grabbed a bag and began to stuff coins and notes into it. When Sligo figured it was full enough, he grabbed the sack and stepped quickly outside.

It was unfortunate for the bank clerk that he picked that day to be a hero.

Sligo had just mounted his horse when the man rushed outside. He pointed at Sligo and hollered, "Help! He robbed the bank!"

The clerk fell with two bullets in his chest, then Johnny Sligo rode back along the street, shooting at anyone who moved.

Back in open country, he headed south at a fast gallop.

Behind him, he left two men dead, another wounded, and a town that would never recover from the robbery and the killings. Many citizens were stripped of all they owned that day and they eventually lost heart and moved away.

Despite its railroad spur, Cedar City was abandoned and fell into decay as though a pestilence had descended on the place. The town finally turned to dust and blew away in the mountain winds.

# Chapter Forty

Shamus O'Brien, stripped to the waist, sat in a hard chair in the Dromore kitchen and his mood took a considerable turn for the worse. He was being fussed over by females, a thing he could not abide.

"You could've been killed, Colonel," Lorena said.

By Shamus's calculation it was the fourth time she'd said it that afternoon.

The maids glared at him with accusing eyes as though his failure to surrender to Lorena's administrations was a grievous fault.

"Don't fuss, daughter-in-law," Shamus said. "It's only scratches."

"Scratches!" Lorena said, throwing up her hands. "You've got deep cuts all over your back. How on earth did you manage to ride to Santa Fe and back? That's what I want to know."

"For most of the way there I walked." Shamus resigned himself to her ministrations. "Doc was feeling right poorly and I let him ride most of the time."

"Doc was feeling poorly! And you were not? After

getting nearly eaten by a wild bear?" Lorena dabbed more stinging stuff on Shamus's cuts and he winced.

"Why the change of heart about Doc, Pa?" Patrick said. "Kind of sudden, isn't it."

"If I could ever get rid of these infernal females, I'll tell you."

"Luther will want to hear this," Jacob said.

"Then we'll adjourn to the parlor," Shamus said.

"I'm not finished with you yet," Lorena said, a stern frown gathered between her eyes.

"Oh, yes you are," Shamus said. "It's a brandy I need, not . . . not female fussin'."

"Then upon your head be it, Colonel," Lorena said. "Those cuts could get infected, and that means a doctor."

The maids scowled their disapproval as Shamus said, "Jacob, for God's sake help me to the parlor away from this monstrous regiment of women."

Patrick beamed. "Very good, Pa. John Knox, the Scottish reformer said that about females."

"I know, Patrick, and those were the only wise words he ever uttered in his life."


"So that's the story," Shamus said. "Doc risked his own life to save mine. He's got sand and he proved it when he tackled that damned bear."

"Surprises the hell out of me," Luther Ironside said.

"Surprised me too, Luther," Shamus agreed.

"You got him on a train, Pa?" Jacob asked.

"Yes. By now, he's well on his way to Glendale Springs and his memoirs."

"Well, good luck to him," Ironside said.

"Amen to that," Shamus said.

The door opened and the butler stepped inside the parlor. "A gentleman to see Mr. Jacob. Mr. Wolf Hartmann presents his compliments."

The O'Briens exchanged puzzled glances, then Shamus said, "Show him in, please."

Ironside reached behind him and pulled his Colt from the gunbelt draped over the back of his cot. He shoved it under his blanket.

A few moments later, Hartmann entered, his hat held in front of him with both hands, well away from his gun.

Jacob rose to his feet, prepared to be friendly. "Good to see you again, Wolf. I believe you met the colonel and my brothers at the Stuart ranch."

Hartmann smiled. "Indeed I did, all biscuits, honey, and hostility as I recall."

"Take a seat, Wolf. Drink?"

Patrick made room on the couch and Hartmann sat. "Scotch if you have it, Jake. Bourbon if you don't."

"We have scotch and Irish, if that be to your taste," Shamus said.

"Then I'll try the Irish," Hartmann said.

The colonel waited until the gunfighter was seated, a glass in his hand, before he spoke again. "It's snowing outside. It must be an urgent message you bring from Colonel James Stuart. But be warned, be it peace or war, I care not which."

Hartmann tried his whiskey. "Very good, excellent, Colonel." His eyes ranged over Shamus's torn-up chest, but he said nothing as politeness demanded. If the colonel wanted him to know what happened, he'd tell him.

"I have no message from James Stuart," Hartmann said. "And there will be no war. Mrs. Stuart is keeping poorly and the colonel is beside himself with worry."

"You can tell James Stuart that Doc Holliday is no longer under my roof," Shamus said. "He won't doubt my word."

"I don't work for him any longer, Colonel. But he's allowing me to bunk with the hands until I'm ready to move on, so I'll let him know."

"You've caught us at a bad time, I'm afraid, Mr. Hartmann," Shamus said. "Luther was ill and is now recuperating and I was attacked by a bear. I will spare you the details of our miseries, but I will mention that Holliday saved my life. He shot the bear off me, though at the time he was much stricken by his disease."

"My best wishes to you and Luther for a speedy recovery, Colonel," Hartmann said. "As for Doc, he can usually be relied upon to do the indecent thing. I'm glad to hear that in this case, he acted like a gentleman."

"Doc's got sand, the colonel says," Ironside added.

"I won't argue that point," Hartmann said.

Jacob had enough of the small talk. "Wolf, you said you wanted to see me. Is it a private matter?"

"No, I guess not. I wanted to ask you if you knew the whereabouts of Johnny Sligo."

Jacob shook his head. "Your guess is as good as mine."

"What is your interest in the man, Mr. Hartmann?" Shamus asked. "His name keeps popping up here at Dromore."

"I reckon there's a bounty on him, Colonel, and I aim to collect it."

"Take him to the law, you mean?"

"Yes, maybe down to El Paso and hold him there until I can dig up his wanted dodgers."

Patrick said, "From what we hear, you won't take Johnny Sligo without a fight."

Hartmann smiled. "Then I'll pack his head in ice and take that to El Paso."

A silence followed this statement. Then Sir James Lovell said, "Good Lord, sir, that sounds barbaric."

"This is the frontier," Hartmann told the Englishman. "When it comes to men like Johnny Sligo, the normal rules of civilization don't apply."

"Don't try to shade him, Wolf," Jacob said. "I hear he's really fast."

Hartmann nodded his blond head. "You hear, Jake. I hear. This one hears, that one hears. Have you actually seen Sligo on the draw and shoot?"

"No, I haven't."

"Neither have I, and until I do, I won't pay heed to what people have heard about him." Hartmann rose to his feet. He was a tall man and solid, as though he'd be hard to kill. "Thank-you for your hospitality and drink, Colonel. From now on, I'll drink Irish whiskey."

"Your good taste does you credit, sir," Shamus said.

Jacob stood, too. "I'll see you to the door, Wolf."

Once they were into the foyer, Jacob said, "Don't brace Johnny Sligo, Wolf."

"Why, Jake? You have one of those bad feelings you get about stuff?"

"Yeah, maybe the worst in a while."

"Then I'll step careful."

"You don't even know where he is."

"I have an idea," Hartmann said. "Like you, I get hunches every now and then."

"Want me to ride with you for old times' sake?"

"No, Jake, this is my kind of work, remember? And when it comes to bounty hunting, I always go it alone."

Jacob extended his hand. "Well, good luck."

"And to you too, Jake. Good luck."

# Chapter Forty-one

Johnny Sligo was pleased with his haul. Eighteen thousand dollars, give or take, enough to keep him in some style for a couple years.

He was pleased, too, that the idiot owner of the Excelsior had quit in such a hurry he'd left behind most of his whiskey and a shelf of canned food in the kitchen. Hell, even a side of bacon hung from a rafter.

Sligo smiled. Life was good and he was ahead of the game.

He rose to his feet, whiskey in hand, and looked out the rear window of the saloon at the lightly falling snow. The day was shading into night and the coyotes were already calling.

He stepped back to the table, sat, and built and lit a cigarette. He tapped his fingers, hummed a tune, got to his feet again and went back to the window. The view hadn't changed. The night was just a little darker.

He sat, got up, sat, poured himself more whiskey.

Around him, over him, the building was never quiet. It creaked and groaned and welcomed inside the wind that banged doors and rustled in the corners. The air smelled of mildew and timber rot and more and more windows seemed broken, admitting silent flurries of snow.

Sligo restlessly tapped his fingers on the table again. *Damn!* The place was closing in on him. He tilted back his head and yelled, "Is anybody here?"

For a moment, he thought he heard a hush, as though the building was listening for the answer. But only for a moment and then the noises began once more.

"I'm here," Sligo yelled. "Johnny Sligo as ever was. How the hell do you do?"

There was no answering voice, just the death rattles of the dying hotel.

Sligo walked from the table to the piano in the corner, already spider-webbed. He lifted the lid, stretching the webs in gray strands, and exposed the keys. He tapped a key and the single note seemed very loud, echoing around the room.

Johnny Sligo tapped the key again . . . and again . . . and again. . . .

"Damn you!" he shrieked. He pounded both fists into the keyboard, smashing into ivory and ebony, filling the saloon with jarring jolts of jangled noise.

Then the building let out a deep-throated roar and the saloon shook so violently bottles and glasses fell off the shelves behind the bar and shattered.

Sligo ran a headlong charge out the front door and onto the porch. A moment later, an iron cot crashed on top of him and he collapsed under its sudden weight. More and more heavy debris plummeted onto the porch from the second floor and Sligo panicked. He pushed the cot away from him, staggered to his feet, and ran what he hoped was a safe distance from the hotel.

His forehead gashed, blood trickling down his face, he looked back at the Excelsior and was horrified at what he saw.

A large part of the roof had given way and most of the second floor had collapsed inward. Glass from burst windows still tinkled onto the porch. As he watched, a section of wall gave way and crashed to the ground, throwing up a thick cloud of sooty dust.

After the racketing roar of the stricken building, the ensuing silence was deafening.

His mouth hanging open, Sligo watched and wondered if the Excelsior Hotel had tried to kill him, blaming him for taking away the people that gave it life. The injustice of that and the viciousness of the wound to his head prodded him into a killing rage. "You mongrel!!" he screamed.

He drew both guns and emptied them into the open door of the hotel, then reloaded for good measure. He wanted to kill the place dead . . . dead . . . dead!

Just a mile away, camped in the shelter of pines, Wolf Hartmann heard Sligo's shots and wondered about them. He stood and stepped away from the fire and listened into the cold night. But he heard nothing else.

Except for broken glass on the floor and some panes shattered in the rear window, the saloon remained intact, as did the kitchen.

Johnny Sligo explored around the rest of the hotel and discovered that it was pretty much a ruin. A smell hung over it, the sickly, sweet stench of a decaying body.

Dead and rotten was the Excelsior Hotel, and Sligo was happy about that. The building had torn itself apart when it tried to kill him. And it had failed. All it could do was let wind, weather, and time bury it.

Sligo had no intention of leaving. The place was an even better hideout than before. Any passing lawman would look at the broken ruin and ride on, figuring that no white man could live in such a disgusting heap of rubble.

After lighting a lamp, Sligo picked a glass from the floor and filled it with whiskey. He ignored the tendrils of crusted blood on his face that felt tight as he smiled. Sure, he'd been scared for a spell, but not for long.

Johnny Sligo was back in charge and life was good again.

# Chapter Forty-two

After an uncomfortable night spent shivering in his blankets, Wolf Hartmann was grateful for the warmth of his fire and the hot coffee in his cup. The day was dawning cold, but the snow had stopped and there was no wind. He had it in his mind that he'd find Johnny Sligo and then take events as they came at him. The man was a killer and must have a price on his head, dead or alive.

One look at the scowling sky convinced Hartmann that the chilly weather would continue for a while. If he was forced to shoot Sligo and take the man's head, his features would still be recognizable when he reached El Paso.

He smiled, remembering the Englishman's horror at such a practice. Colonel O'Brien, on the other hand, took it in stride. And why not? Didn't the Irish have a history of head hunting back in the mists of time when tribal warfare was a way of life?

Hartmann poured more coffee and built a cigarette, his mind going back to the night before and the gunshots he'd heard. Rapid they were, the shots coming so fast they sounded like a burst from a Gatling gun.

But they were fired from revolvers.

There was probably only one man in the territory who could handle pistols with such rapidity . . . the man called Johnny Sligo.

Hartmann rose and stood once more at the spot where he'd listened into the night. He was sure the shots had come from the north. The two miners in the cantina had described the area to him, and he was convinced the Excelsior Hotel lay in that direction.

Was Sligo holed up there, close to a steady supply of whiskey and women?

Outlaws were creatures of habit, and if Sligo followed true to course, he'd do what other bad men did and find a cozy berth to pass the winter months. A hotel in the middle of nowhere would fit the bill nicely.

Hartmann was camped on a high mountain ridge, a place of bitter solitude that nevertheless gave him a view of the country for miles around. He saw no sign of the hotel, but beyond the tree line in the valley below stretched vast brush flats and if the miners were correct, it would come into view as soon as he reached level ground.

A man fast on the draw, he had killed eight men in gunfights. Johnny Sligo held no fear for him. The man was good, of that there was no doubt. But the question was how good?

Hartmann was determined to find the answer before the sun went down.

He squatted by the fire again and ate a small breakfast of sliced beef and tortillas packed for him by the Stuart ranch cook.

The swollen clouds had dropped lower and a fine mist hung over the valley below, hiding the brush flats from sight. As Hartmann finished his meal a young male cougar trotted past him and disappeared into a stand of aspen. His horse whinnied and acted up a little, but the sorrel quickly calmed down when he rose and patted its neck and whispered reassurances.

After throwing the last of the coffee on the fire, he saddled up and followed a switchback game trail down into the valley. The pines were sparser and yielded space to cedar, piñon, and sagebrush.

The grass on the valley floor petered out and gradually gave way to sandy soil, much of it streaked with snow. The only sound was the steady beat of the sorrel's hooves and the soft *thump, thump* of the booted Winchester against his inner left knee.

Because of the mist ahead of him there was as yet no sign of the Excelsior Hotel.


Johnny Sligo broke the thin shell of ice that had formed overnight on the horse trough at the back of the hotel. He splashed water on his face and wiped himself dry with his bandanna, the blue cloth staining rust red from the dried blood on his cheek.

He retied the bandanna and stepped into the kitchen. There was no fire in the stove and he didn't feel like starting one. He opened a can of meat, grabbed a fork, and walked back to the saloon.

The morning was graying into a gloomy dawn, but the saloon was still dark and Sligo lit the oil lamp. He ate from the can, but the meat was fatty and tasted spoiled. After a few bites, he threw it away and lit a cigarette.

He rose from the table and walked to the front window. Most of the panes were broken, probably when the building shook as the roof collapsed. There was little to see outside since a thin mist clung to the ground and the darkness had not yet lifted.

Sligo felt a sudden chill and his skin crawled. He sensed something was out there in the gloom . . . something dangerous.

Quickly, he stepped back to the table and retrieved his guns. He strapped them around his hips, returned to the window and stared outside. He saw only the mist . . . but felt the coming of an enemy.

Evil was wary. It picked its way carefully, and Johnny Sligo was not about to rush outside. He decided to wait where he was and let the danger, whatever it was, come to him.

He checked his guns and then slid the Colts back into the holsters, smiling. This was more like it, the action he craved. So much better than sitting in the dark bored to death.

Gunning a man before noon—it had to be a man out there—had always stimulated him and given him an appetite for lunch. Hell, even canned beef would taste good . . . so long as he had another kill under his belt.

\* \* \*

Johnny Sligo stood and waited at the window as the morning shaded into sullen light. With the patience of a predator, he remained perfectly still, his luminous green eyes staring.

He stood there for an hour without twitching a muscle and finally his face broke into a grin. . . .

A horseman was riding toward him through the mist.

# Chapter Forty-three

Johnny Sligo stepped back from the window into the murk of the saloon and studied the man as he rode closer.

The stranger was tall, well built, dressed in an expensive sheepskin and tight wool pants that were tucked into fancy Texas boots. He rode a good horse and his saddle and bridle were heavy with silver. The man himself was handsome and he sported a sweeping dragoon mustache that no doubt made female hearts flutter.

Whoever he was, he was a man worth killing, and that pleased Sligo immensely.

Wolf Hartmann cursed himself for figuring it wrong.

The Excelsior Hotel was a bleak ruin surrounded by dead land where not a blade of grass or a weed grew. It looked like the roof had collapsed and part of the wall was down, exposing a room with garish wallpaper and an overstuffed chair that lay on its side on the slanted floor. The ruin stank of decay and death.

He noticed that even the birds seemed to avoid the place. A flight of crows veered away at the last moment, cried out to each other in alarm, and then frantically flapped at the fetid air to gain height.

No one would choose to live in such a place, Hartmann decided, not even Edgar Alan Poe, the madman who wrote of such places.

Still, the bounty hunter had come this far and had to check the place out. He swung out of the saddle and walked toward the hotel.

Johnny Sligo stepped onto the porch and Hartmann knew he'd been right about one thing and wrong about another.

Yes, Sligo lived there. No, he didn't look like he'd inflated the gaudy carnival balloon of his reputation.

The man was a gunfighter. It was apparent in the way he stood—relaxed, ready, and confident—and in the green fire in his eyes. The thin, tight mouth under the sparse mustache was the mark of a killer.

"Are you Johnny Sligo?" Hartmann asked.

"Who the hell wants to know?" In the cold air, Sligo's breath smoked with every word.

"Name's Wolf Hartmann." He unbuttoned his sheepskin and pushed it away from his gun. "I'm taking you back to Texas, Johnny."

THE LAW OF VIOLENCE

Sligo was delighted. Wolf Hartmann was a named man, a gunfighter to be reckoned with.

"Fair piece off your home range, ain't you Hartmann?" Sligo asked. "I never heard of you riding this far north."

"I could say the same for you, Johnny. Never knew you to take a step outside the towns."

"Why take me back to Texas?"

"El Paso is close and I figure the law will have a dodger on you."

Sligo's face hardened. "Yeah, I have dodgers, a screed of them, but I don't like bounty hunters dogging my back trail."

"Can't say as I care for them myself, but it's a living."

"You ain't taking me anywhere, Hartmann." Sligo's his hands were close to his guns.

Hartmann shrugged. "Alive or dead, Johnny. The choice is yours. I ain't too particular one way or t'other."

"Sorry to hear that." Sligo's right hand dropped. Fast.

Only when a bullet slammed into his left shoulder and a second ripped across his ribs, did Wolf Hartmann realize that he wasn't in Johnny Sligo's class. He hauled iron quick enough, but fired way late.

Two things happened then.

For the first time since he'd buckled on a gun, Johnny Sligo got hit with a bullet . . . and Wolf Hartmann's life was saved by his horse.

Hartmann's shot burned across Sligo's left thigh,

just under the bottom of his holster, and the man yelped in pain and surprise like a whipped cur. Hartmann remounted and aimed, but had no time to fire again because the sorrel, already spooked by the cougar and made nervous by the firing, turned and bolted. All Hartmann could do was flatten himself over the horse's neck and hang on as the sorrel galloped into the flat, its eyes wild, hooves hammering on the icy hardpan.

Behind him, Sligo shrieked and danced on one leg, wailing his pain.

He limped into the saloon, howling and leaving a spattered blood trail behind him before he threw himself into a chair. He glanced at the growing scarlet blotch on his pants and screamed in horror. His clenched teeth looked like stained chips of ceramic in his mouth. "Oh my God!" he screeched. "I'm wounded! I'm going to die!"

Frantic, Sligo rose and hopped around the room, cursing the man who'd shot him and the mother that bore him.

He staggered to the saloon window and dropped his pants. In the light, he saw that he'd suffered a flesh wound, but it was raw and leaked blood.

Johnny Sligo squealed again and again, a series of panicked, high-pitched hoots and wails. He had taken a bullet and it was the worst thing that had ever happened to him. The worst thing that had ever happened to anybody.

"Damn Wolf Hartmann. Damn him to hell."

* * *

He'd seen enough gunshot wounds to know that he was hurt real bad.

The sorrel had finally exhausted itself and Wolf Hartmann drew rein at the edge of a tree line. He pulled his sheepskin away from his shoulder. As he already suspected, his shoulder was shattered and splintered fragments of bone showed white among the blood. The ribs on his left side were in no better shape and he had no way of telling how many were broken.

Several, he guessed.

He was losing blood and the nearest place he would find help was Dromore. If he could make it that far.

Hartmann kneed the sorrel into a walk and followed the timber east. Now that he was in no condition to fight, he checked his back trail often, fearing that Johnny Sligo would come after him. He saw nothing but a vast, empty distance and lightly falling snow.

Suddenly dead tired, his head swimming, Hartmann plodded on.

He thought he might have gotten a bullet into Sligo, but wasn't sure. Even if he had, it might not slow the man.

He looked back again, but as far as his eyes could see, there was no movement, no sign of life.

After riding around a boulder that blocked his path, Hartmann rode up a shallow bank and then dipped down into a small, ice-laced creek where cattle had watered recently, judging by the fresh tracks.

Painfully, slowly, he climbed down from the

saddle, drank a little and then splashed water onto his face. He stood again and looked around him.

How far to Dromore? A mile or two, no more than that. He could make it. Damn it, he had to make it.

Getting into the saddle again was an agonizing chore, but he managed to mount again and resume his ride.

Less than five minutes later, Hartmann was found by two vaqueros who rode, one on each side of him, all the way to Dromore.

# Chapter Forty-four

"We've sent for a doctor, Wolf," Jacob O'Brien said. "He should be here by tomorrow or the next day at the latest."

"How bad is it, Jake?"

Jacob looked from Lorena to Judith and read what he needed to know in their faces. "Do you want me to lie to you, Wolf?"

"No, I guess not."

"It's bad. Your shoulder is pretty much shot all to pieces and you've got three, maybe four broken ribs."

"Sum it up for me, Jake."

"To sum up, Mr. Hartmann," Judith said, pulling the sheet higher on the man's chest, "you won't be going anywhere for a while."

"That bad, huh?"

"Bad enough." Lorena looked at Jacob. "Suddenly Dromore is full of invalids—the colonel, Luther, and now Mr. Hartmann. Let's hope we have no more."

"Jake, I need to tell you something," Hartmann said. "It's pretty urgent."

Lorena vehemently shook her head and the smile left her face. "No, Mr. Hartmann. What you need until the doctor gets here is sleep, and plenty of it. You can talk later when you get your strength back."

"This is important, ma'am. Along with a doctor, you need the law down here in a hurry."

"Are you in pain, Wolf?" Jacob asked.

"So long as I don't move, it's not too bad."

"Then you can talk," Jacob said.

"Well, I'll have no part in this, Jacob O'Brien," Lorena said. "Come, Judith. We'll return with Mr. Hartmann's lunch later after Jacob decides his talking is done."

"Begging your pardon, ma'am, but I think you should stay and hear this," Hartmann said. "What I have to say involves everyone at Dromore."

"Can't it wait until later?" Judith asked.

"No, ma'am, I reckon it can't."

"Then we'll hear you out, Mr. Hartmann," Lorena said. "But at the first sign that you're tiring yourself, the conversation stops. Is that fair?"

"Sounds fair to me, ma'am."

The guest bedroom had a couch against one wall under the window, and the two women sat, hands in their laps and their mouths prim. Behind them snow drifted past the frosted panes.

"Jake, there's a ranch to the southwest of here, in mountain country cut through by deep arroyos,"

Hartmann said. "I don't know the lie of the land out there, so I can't describe it any better."

Jacob looked at Lorena. "Sounds like it could be Tom Johnson's place."

"It could well be." Lorena smiled at Hartmann. "He's a nice man, isn't he?"

"I don't know, ma'am, he wasn't there. Nobody was there. There's dead cattle all over the place and the ranch house is falling down." Hartmann waved Jacob closer. "Jake, there's a dead bull in a pen beside the house, a black bull."

Judith's hand flew to her throat. "Not the Prince!"

"I don't know his name, ma'am, but he was a fine-looking animal at one time."

"I know it's Bonnie Prince Charlie!" Judith said. "I just know it is."

"Wolf, you saw no sign of Tom Johnson and his son and daughter?" Jacob asked.

"No. Like I said, Jake, the place was abandoned. And the house was filthy inside. I mean, the worst stink you ever smelled."

"Tom Johnson never lived in filth," Lorena said. "He and his daughter kept their place as neat as a pin."

Jacob was silent for a while, then he said, his voice strangely toneless, "Lorena, if the ranch is in such bad shape then Tom Johnson is dead and so is his family."

It was Lorena's turn to be shocked. "But, Jacob, who . . . I mean . . ."

"If the rancher is dead, then my guess is that

Johnny Sligo had something to do with it," Hartmann said. "Why else would he be in the New Mexico Territory?"

"That name!" Lorena exclaimed. "If I hear it again, I think I'll scream."

"And so you should, ma'am," Hartmann said. "Sligo is a demon."

"Wolf, you reckon he's still there, at the Excelsior?" Jake asked.

"No. After he shot me I'm sure he moved on."

"Don't lie to me, Wolf," Jacob said.

"Jake, send for the law. Have them bring a bunch of deputies and let them handle it. I mean, we don't even know if Sligo killed Johnson."

"Is he still at the hotel?" Jacob asked again.

"You can't shade Johnny Sligo, Jake. Nobody can. He's got hell in him."

"Is he still at the hotel, Wolf?"

"Yes, he's still there. Maybe I put lead into him. I don't know."

"Hard times have come down on Dromore since we first heard the name Sligo," Jacob said. "It's high time that gentleman and I had a little talk."

"He'll kill you, Jake."

"I'll take my chances."

It was only then Jacob noticed that Lorena had left the room. She returned a few moments later with Shamus and the other O'Brien brothers.

"There he is, Colonel," Lorena said, waving a hand toward Jacob. "Perhaps you can talk some sense into him."

"Colonel, I want you to send a search party out to

Tom Johnson's ranch," Jacob said. "I think Johnny Sligo had a hand in killing Tom and his children and their bodies must be close. And you'll find the Black Angus in a pen by the house." He answered the question on Shamus's face. "The bull is dead."

"Who is Sligo working for, Jacob?" Shamus asked.

"I don't know, but I aim to find out. I'm going after him."

"You're the only one who can," Shamus said.

Lorena looked in confusion from Shamus to Jacob and back again. "Colonel, I want you to stop Jacob, not encourage him."

"It's this man Sligo who must be stopped, daughter-in-law. I believe he's the one who brought death to Dromore and he'll do it again."

"Then let the law stop him, as Mr. Hartmann suggested," Lorena said.

The colonel shook his head. "He has wronged us, and we must bring him to justice." He looked hard at Lorena. "Child, it must be Jacob. There is no one else."

"Pa, there's me," Shawn said.

"No, not you, Shawn," Judith said. "Must I get my heart broken again?"

Jacob said, "Shawn, you're good with the iron but Sligo will take a lot of killing. I'm the only one of us who has at least an even chance."

"Then we'll all go," Patrick said. "He can't shade all four of us."

"And how many O'Brien brothers would Pa mourn tonight?" Jacob asked him. "Do you really want to see Lorena and Judith hold all night vigil in the chapel for their dead menfolk?"

"There will be no further discussion on this matter," Shamus said. "Jacob, I will organize the Johnson ranch search party and then go to the chapel and pray until you return safely."

"Remember all the things I taught you, Jake. And take no chances with that man." Luther Ironside, tall and terrible, stood in the bedroom doorway, the incongruous, diminutive figure of Abe Grossman beside him, his bearded face worried.

"Do you hear me, boy?" Ironside wore his spurred boots, hat, and a nightshirt.

Jacob nodded. "I'll remember, Luther."

"Good, then go nail the jasper's hide to the wall," Ironside said. "You're the only one who can do it."

Shamus O'Brien stood in the early afternoon cold, his hand on the pommel of Jacob's saddle. "God help me, Jacob. Am I doing the right thing?"

"We're doing the right thing, Pa, you and me. Johnny Sligo brought a cancer to this land and he must be destroyed."

"We could wait for the law, Jacob, like Lorena wants."

"You know how wrong that would be, Colonel."

"I may be sending you to your death, with my blessing."

"I have it to do. There's no way around it."

"How many dead O'Briens, Jacob, if your brothers joined you and went after him?"

"Maybe all of us."

"I would not live long after that."

"No, you wouldn't, Pa."

"The law . . ."

Jacob smiled. "You're trying to drag this out."

"Yes, I am. I don't want to see you go."

"But you know I have to. There's only me this time."

"Yes, I know that."

Jacob took off his hat and leaned from the saddle. "Your blessing, Pa."

Shamus placed his hand on Jacob's unruly shock of black hair. "Go with God, my son, and may Jesus, Mary and Joseph, and all the saints in Heaven protect you."

Jacob replaced his hat and smiled. "Can't beat that for a blessing, Pa."

Shamus watched his son ride away until Jacob disappeared into distance and a lacy curtain of falling snow.

Unbidden, tears came to Shamus's eyes and he angrily dashed them away. Such an unmanly display must not be seen by his sons and the women of Dromore.

# Chapter Forty-five

Jacob O'Brien rode through the broad cattle country west of Dromore. Around him, the winter grass was nubbed down close, but the cattle were thriving and had not lost too much beef. The sky stretched iron gray to the mountains and a light snow fell, but the air was vibrant, the afternoon coming in clean.

Habitually sitting his horse like a ruptured farmer, he tried to analyze his emotions. He couldn't determine just how scared he was.

A little? A lot?

Thinking it through, he settled on a lot.

Johnny Sligo had shaded Wolf Hartmann, who was lightning fast on the draw. That was an inescapable fact, and it didn't do much for a man's confidence.

Jacob built a cigarette and was glad to see that his hands were steady.

Was the feeling that a garden rake was being

dragged across his guts really fear, or something else? Excitement maybe?

No, it was fear all right. He was scared, scared of Johnny Sligo and his flashing guns. Scared of dying. Scared of everything.

He dragged smoke deep into his lungs. Doc Holliday had told him that he'd either kill himself or become a monk.

"Well, Doc, you were right," Jacob said aloud. "Here I am, killing myself, just like you said."

Jacob rode into the little pueblo village of Galisteo. Somewhere in the distance ahead of him were the brush flats and the Excelsior Hotel.

In no hurry—why rush headlong to his death?—Jacob sat on the back step of a small cantina and drank coffee sweetened with condensed milk. The pulse of life ebbed and flowed around him, men performing a variety of tasks, their noses red from cold, women collecting eggs or hanging clothes that would freeze solid if left out overnight.

He watched a blue dog chase a cat and then have the ill fortune to catch it. The dog yelped and ran away with his tail between his legs and a red welt on his nose.

"Serves you right," Jacob said. "Chasing poor kitty like that."

A woman in a bright red skirt and glossy black hair to her waist must have felt the same way he did, because she chided the dog, then smiled at Jacob. He waved and she waved back.

Finally he got to his feet, left the coffee cup on the step, and climbed into the saddle.

No more time wasting. He needed to get it over with before he lost what remained of his courage.

Jacob had visited the Excelsior Hotel when it was prospering and the arrival of the railroad was still an exciting possibility. He was shocked at what he saw.

The roof had fallen and a large section of the front wall lay on the muddy ground. An iron cot lay on the porch and dozens of huge rats scurried around it, drawn by what, Jacob didn't even want to guess.

The hotel was dead, stank to high heaven, and the land around it was barren as though it had been smitten by a thing of terrible evil.

Jacob's smile was grim. The only person who fit that bill was Johnny Sligo.

Under a black sky, pummeled by an icy north wind, Jacob swung out of the saddle and stepped onto the hotel porch. The stench of death hung over the place and bustling, rustling rats were everywhere.

He walked into what had been the foyer, and remembered that the door to his right had led into the saloon. Jacob stood and listened to the silence. From behind the door, he heard a sound, soft, snuffling sobs followed by a despairing wail. Then it went quiet again.

He tried the door.

Locked.

"Johnny Sligo!" Jacob yelled.

There was no answer.

Jacob called Sligo's name again.

The man answered. "State your intentions."

"I intend to kill you, Johnny," Jacob said. "I'm a friend of Wolf Hartmann."

"He wounded me," Sligo wailed. "Nobody puts a bullet into me, nobody."

"Open up and we'll talk, Johnny. Wolf is still alive so maybe we can work something out."

He heard boots thud across the floor, one leg dragging, then a key turned in the lock.

Jacob waited until the steps receded again, then he opened the door slowly and stepped inside.

For a few moments, Jacob saw nothing but shadow, then as his eyes became accustomed to the dark he saw the figure of a man sitting at a table.

A chair scraped back, and the figure rose and lit the oil lamp. Johnny Sligo was no longer sobbing. "Hell, a puncher. Hartmann sent a thirty-a-month puncher."

"I'm his friend, Johnny," Jacob said. "Now make this easy on both of us. Unbuckle your guns and let them fall to the floor. Then I'll take you to a doctor and get that leg fixed up."

Sligo did something strange.

He inclined his head and said, "This is an insult, Johnny. You think so? Sure it is. It's a sign of disrespect. Give him a taste of hellfire, Johnny."

Sligo grinned at Jacob. "Hear that, cowboy?"

"You're crazy, Johnny," Jacob said. "Put your guns away and we'll talk."

"Hellfire!" Sligo yelled. "I'm going to give you a taste of hellfire."

Before Jacob could react, Sligo swept the lamp off the table and threw it onto the floor where burning oil spread like a crimson lake.

It was as though Sligo had opened the gates of hell. The ancient dry timber of the saloon burst into flame and it quickly spread to the walls.

Through the smoke and flame, Sligo advanced on Jacob, grinning like a demon.

Jacob went for his gun.

He froze, his gun still not clear of the leather, staring at Sligo's drawn Colts.

"Where do you want it, cowboy?" Sligo inclined his head. "You don't want to make a choice, huh? Well, I don't blame you. To make it easy on you, I'll put the first one right between your teeth."

A shotgun roared, the throaty *boom!* of two barrels fired at the same time.

The buckshot shredded Johnny Sligo's thin body and he turned to the rear window, his face shocked. "What the hell are you?"

From the outside the window, Abe Grossman hefted an expensive, beautifully engraved L.C. Smith shotgun. "Me? Am I not a poor Jewish peddler?"

His bloodied body matching the color of the fire that lapped around his feet, Sligo's guns dropped from his dying hands and he swung around and stared at Jacob in disbelief. "A peddler?"

Jacob nodded. "Yup, Johnny boy, and he's killed you."

Sligo found enough life left in him for one last, horrified shriek, then fell facedown on the floor where the eager flames found him.

"Mr. O'Brien, get out of there!" Grossman yelled.

Jacob saw what appeared to be a sack of money on the table and tried to reach it, but the flames beat him back. He turned and ran for the saloon door through thick smoke, dashing outside.

He grabbed the reins of his horse and walked it away from the burning building. Within minutes, the hotel was ablaze from gable to gable and soon nothing would be left but ashes and the blackened bones of Johnny Sligo.

Abe Grossman led his horse around the building and stood with Jacob, watching the hotel burn.

"You rode the colonel's favorite horse bareback?" Jacob asked without turning. "I thought you couldn't ride."

"Did I ever say that?" Grossman asked. "Did I not ride David Levy the greengrocer's horse when I was a boy?"

"And you said you didn't know about guns," Jacob said. "That's Pa's shotgun."

"I've seen other men use shotguns and don't the bullets go in one end and come out the other when the triggers are pulled?"

"They're called shells, Abe."

"So kiss my ass. What do I know from a gun?"

Jacob smiled. "You saved my life, Abe. That's something I won't ever forget."

"I told Luther that I wanted to go after you," Grossman said. "And he helped me put bullets in the gun and then get a horse."

"He should've been in bed."

"He was worried about you, and so was I. Don't I owe the O'Briens more than I can ever repay?"

"You arrived just in time, but Luther could've gotten you killed."

The Excelsior collapsed with a tremendous crash and flames and sparks flew into the air. A rising pillar of smoke got tangled in the north wind and smeared across the scowling face of the sky.

"With or without Luther, I would have followed you," Grossman said.

"I'm glad you did." Jacob shivered. "It's cold, Abe. Let's go home."

# Epilogue

Colonel Shamus O'Brien's Christmas celebrations went exactly as he planned, marred only by the discovery of the bodies of Tom Johnson and his family and their subsequent funeral.

Another body was found and the United States marshal Shamus had sent for said it might be that of Black Tom Church, but the corpse was torn up by animals and he couldn't be sure.

On Christmas Eve, Shawn and Judith announced their engagement. The happy couple were to be married in July, then honeymoon at Sir James's estate in England.

Colonel James Stuart didn't attend the celebrations because his wife was still not recovered, but he sent an ornate silver saddle to Shawn and Judith as a wedding present.

With the saddle, his ranch foreman delivered the news that Doc Holliday had died on November 8 in Glenwood Springs. As far as anyone knew, he had not written a single word of his memoirs.

Shamus said that the next time a priest visited Dromore he'd have him say a mass for Doc's soul.

Luther Ironside gained in strength and by Christmas Eve was well enough to drink whiskey and chase after the parlor maids with a sprig of mistletoe.

Shortly before midnight, Shamus announced to the assembled guests that he was making Luther a partner in Dromore and everyone cheered.

"Congratulations, Luther," Patrick said. "You deserve it."

"Damn right," Luther said.

But Shamus had yet another announcement to make. "Ladies and gentlemen, look around you at this brightly lit house and the happy faces you see everywhere. If it wasn't for my honored guest, Abraham Grossman, tonight Dromore would be a dark place indeed and filled with mourning."

Grossman, embarrassed, shrank against a wall and desperately tried to make himself invisible.

But Shamus took the little man's hand and pulled him into the middle of the floor. "Abe, you saved the life of my son Jacob, and I can never thank you enough."

Grossman smiled and bobbed his head, fervently wishing he was back in a dark corner.

"Now, if everyone would care to step outside for a moment, I have something to show you," Shamus said. "The night is chill, so bring your glass."

It took time for a hundred guests to file outside, but they had only to wait for a few moments before a vaquero drove a new Studebaker wagon to the front of the house, a fine Morgan mare in the traces.

"Abe, where is Abe?" Shamus shouted.

Grinning, Jacob pushed Grossman forward and Shamus put his arm around the little peddler's neck. "Abe, this is for you, a token of my thanks and appreciation."

Grossman was shocked. "Can such a fine wagon and horse be for me?"

"Indeed it can," Shamus said. "Now you can peddle your wares in style."

Much overcome, the little man tried to talk but couldn't. He stepped to the wagon and ran his hand over its painted woodwork, then he patted the Morgan's beautiful head.

"Three cheers for Abe!" Shamus cried.

After the huzzahs died away, Shamus lifted his glass. "A Merry Christmas to one and all, and may we see many more!"

"And God save the queen!" Sir James yelled, caught up in the moment.

"Yes," Shamus said. "Quite."

## A Little Bit of William W. Johnstone
### by J. A. Johnstone

William W. Johnstone was born in southern Missouri, the youngest of four children. He was raised with strong moral and family values by his minister father, and tutored by his schoolteacher mother. Despite this, he quit school at age fifteen.

"I have the highest respect for education," he says, "but such is the folly of youth, and wanting to see the world beyond the four walls and the blackboard." True to this vow, Bill attempted to enlist in the French Foreign Legion ("I saw Gary Cooper in *Beau Geste* when I was a kid and I thought the French Foreign Legion would be fun") but was rejected, thankfully, for being underage. Instead, he joined a traveling carnival and did all kinds of odd jobs. It was listening to the veteran carny folk, some of whom had been on the circuit since the late 1800s, telling amazing tales about their experiences which planted the storytelling seed in Bill's imagination.

"They were honest people, despite the bad reputation traveling carny shows had back then," Bill remembers. "Of course, there were exceptions.

There was one guy named Picky, who got that name because he was a master pickpocket. He could steal a man's socks right off his feet without him knowing. Believe me, Picky got us chased out of more than a few towns."

After a few months of this grueling existence, Bill returned home and finished high school. Next came stints as a deputy sheriff in the Tallulah, Louisiana, Sheriff's Department, followed by a hitch in the U.S. Army. Then he began a career in radio broadcasting at KTLD in Tallulah that would last sixteen years. It was here that he fine-tuned his storytelling skills. He turned to writing in 1970, but it wouldn't be until 1979 that his first novel, *The Devil's Kiss*, was published. Thus began the full-time writing career of William W. Johnstone.

He wrote horror (*The Uninvited*), thrillers (*The Last of the Dog Team*), even a romance novel or two. Then, in February 1983, *Out of the Ashes* was published. Searching for his missing family in the aftermath of a post-apocalyptic America, rebel mercenary and patriot Ben Raines is united with the civilians of the resistance forces and moves to the forefront of a revolution for the nation's future.

*Out of the Ashes* was a smash. The series would continue for the next twenty years, winning Bill three generations of fans all over the world. The series was often imitated but never duplicated. "We all tried to copy *The Ashes* series," said one publishing executive, "but Bill's uncanny ability, both then and now, to predict in which direction the political winds were blowing, brought a dead-on timeliness to the table no one else could capture." *The Ashes* series would end its run with more than thirty-four books and twenty million copies in print, making it one of the most successful men's action series in American book publishing. (*The Ashes* series also, Bill notes with a touch of pride, got him on the FBI's Watch List for its less than flattering portrayal of spineless politicians and the growing power of big government over our lives, among other things. "In that respect," says collaborator J. A. Johnstone, "Bill was years ahead of his time.")

Always steps ahead of the political curve, Bill's recent thrillers, written with J. A. Johnstone, include *Vengeance is Mine, Invasion USA, Border War, Jackknife, Remember the Alamo, Home Invasion, Phoenix Rising, The Blood of Patriots, The Bleeding Edge,* and the upcoming *Suicide Mission.*

It is with the Western, though, that Bill found his greatest success and propelled him onto both the *USA Today* and *New York Times* bestseller lists.

Bill's western series, coauthored by J. A. Johnstone, include *The Mountain Man, Matt Jensen the Last Mountain Man, Preacher, The Family Jensen, Luke Jensen Bounty Hunter, Eagles, MacCallister* (an *Eagles* spin-off), *Sidewinders, The Brothers O'Brien, Sixkiller, Blood Bond, The Last Gunfighter,* and the upcoming new series *Flintlock* and *The Trail West.* Coming in May 2013 is the hardcover western *Butch Cassidy, The Lost Years.*

"The Western," Bill says, "is one of the few true art

forms that is one hundred percent American. I liken the Western as America's version of England's Arthurian legends, like the Knights of the Round Table or Robin Hood and his Merry Men. Starting with the 1902 publication of *The Virginian* by Owen Wister, and followed by the greats like Zane Grey, Max Brand, Ernest Haycox, and of course Louis L'Amour, the Western has helped to shape the cultural landscape of America.

"I'm no goggle-eyed college academic, so when my fans ask me why the Western is as popular now as it was a century ago, I don't offer a 200-page thesis. Instead, I can only offer this: The Western is honest. In this great country, which is suffering under the yoke of political correctness, the Western harks back to an era when justice was sure and swift. Steal a man's horse, rustle his cattle, rob a bank, a stagecoach, or a train, you were hunted down and fitted with a hangman's noose. One size fit all.

"Sure, we westerners are prone to a little embellishment and exaggeration and, I admit it, occasionally play a little fast and loose with the facts. But we do so for a very good reason—to enhance the enjoyment of readers.

"It was Owen Wister, in *The Virginian*, who first coined the phrase *'When you call me that, smile.'* Legend has it that Wister actually heard those words spoken by a deputy sheriff in Medicine Bow, Wyoming, when another poker player called him a son-of-a-bitch.

"Did it really happen, or is it one of those myths

that have passed down from one generation to the next? I honestly don't know. But there's a line in one of my favorite Westerns of all time, *The Man Who Shot Liberty Valance*, where the newspaper editor tells the young reporter, 'When the truth becomes legend, print the legend.'

"These are the words I live by."

# TURN THE PAGE FOR AN EXCITING PREVIEW

The Jensen clan is William W. Johnstone's epic creation—God-fearing pioneers bound by blood on an untamed and beautiful land. Once more, Preacher, Smoke, and Matt are reunited in a clash of cultures and a brutal all-out fight for justice . . .

## HELL TO PAY

Smoke Jensen and his adopted son Matt are cooling their heels in Colorado when they are called to the Dakotas. Preacher, the legendary mountain man, is in the midst of a vicious struggle. Someone has kidnapped a proud Indian chief's daughter and grandchild. When the kidnapping turns to murder and Preacher vanishes after clashing with a ruthless Union colonel turned railroad king, Matt sets out to infiltrate the colonel's gang of killers, and Smoke seeks out the only honest citizens in the crooked town of Hammerhead. It will take brave men to blow Hammerhead wide open and force the Colonel and his gunmen on a hard ride into a killing ground.

### THE FAMILY JENSEN:
**Hard Ride to Hell**

by *USA TODAY* BESTSELLING AUTHORS
William W. Johnstone
*with J. A. Johnstone*

The Epic New Series
from the authors of *The Mountain Man*

ON SALE NOW,
WHEREVER PINNACLE BOOKS ARE SOLD

# Chapter One

The two men stood facing each other. One was red, the other white, but both were tall and lean, and the stiff, wary stance in which they held themselves belied their advanced years. They were both ready for trouble, and they didn't care who knew it.

Both wore buckskins, as well, and their faces were lined and leathery from long decades spent out in the weather. Silver and white streaked their hair.

The white man had a gun belt strapped around his waist, with a holstered Colt revolver riding on each hip. His thumbs were hooked in the belt close to each holster, and you could tell by looking at him that he was ready to hook and draw. Given the necessity, his hands would flash to the well-worn walnut butts of those guns with blinding speed, especially for a man of his age.

He wasn't the only one with a menacing attitude. The Indian had his hand near the tomahawk that was thrust behind the sash at his waist. To anyone watching, it would appear that both of these men were ready to try to kill each other.

Then a grin suddenly stretched across the whiskery face of the white man, and he said, "Two Bears, you old red heathen."

"Preacher, you pale-faced scoundrel," Two Bears replied. He smiled, too, and stepped forward. The two men clasped each other in a rough embrace and slapped each other on the back.

The large group of warriors standing nearby visibly relaxed at this display of affection between the two men. For the most part, the Assiniboine had been friendly with white men for many, many years. But even so, it wasn't that common for a white man to come riding boldly into their village as the one called Preacher had done.

Some of the men smiled now, because they had known all along what was coming. The legendary mountain man Preacher, who was famous—or in some cases infamous—from one end of the frontier to the other, had been friends with their chief Two Bears for more than three decades, and he had visited the village on occasion in the past.

The two men hadn't always been so cordial with each other. They had started out as rivals for the affections of the beautiful Assiniboine woman Raven's Wing. For Two Bears, that rivalry had escalated to the point of bitter hostility.

All that had been put aside when it became necessary for them to join forces to rescue Raven's Wing from a group of brutal kidnappers and gunrunners.* Since that long-ago time when they were forced to become allies, they had gradually become friends as well.

Preacher stepped back and rested his hands on Two Bears's shoulders.

"I hear that Raven's Wing has passed," he said solemnly.

"Yes, last winter," Two Bears replied with an equally grave nod. "It was her time. She left this world peacefully, with a smile on her face."

"That's good to hear," Preacher said. "I never knew a finer lady."

"I miss her. Every time the sun rises or sets, every time the wind blows, every time I hear a wolf howl or see a bird soaring through the sky, I long to be with her again. But when the day is done and we are to be together again, we will be. This I know in my heart. Until then . . ." Two Bears smiled again. "Until then I can still see her in the fine strong sons she bore me, and the daughters who have given me grandchildren." He nodded toward a young woman standing nearby, who stood with an infant in her arms. "You remember my youngest daughter, Wild-flower?"

"I do," Preacher said, "although the last time I saw her, I reckon she wasn't much bigger'n that sprout with her."

"My grandson," Two Bears said proudly. "Little Hawk."

*See the novel *Preacher's Fury*.

Preacher took off his battered, floppy-brimmed felt hat and nodded politely to the woman.

"Wildflower," he said. "It's good to see you again." He looked at the boy. "And howdy to you, too, Little Hawk."

The baby didn't respond to Preacher, of course, but he watched the mountain man with huge, dark eyes.

"He has not seen that many white men in his life," Two Bears said. "You look strange, even to one so young."

Preacher snorted and said, "If it wasn't for this beard of mine, I'd look just about as much like an Injun as any of you do."

Two Bears half-turned and motioned to the one of the lodges.

"Come. We will go to my lodge and smoke a pipe and talk. I would know what brings you to our village, Preacher."

"Horse, the same as usual," Preacher said as he jerked a thumb over his shoulder toward the big gray stallion that stood with his reins dangling. A large, wolflike cur sat on his haunches next to the stallion.

"How many horses called Horse and dogs called Dog have you had in your life, Preacher?" Two Bears asked with amusement sparkling in his eyes.

"Too many to count, I reckon," Preacher replied. "But I figure if a name works just fine once, there ain't no reason it won't work again."

"How do you keep finding them?"

"It ain't so much me findin' them as it is them

findin' me. Somehow they just show up. I'd call it fate, if I believed in such a thing."

"You do not believe in fate?"

"I believe in hot lead and cold steel," Preacher said. "Anything beyond that's just a guess."

Preacher didn't have any goal in visiting the Assiniboine village other than visiting an old friend. He had been drifting around the frontier for more than fifty years now, most of the time without any plan other than seeing what was on the far side of the hill.

When he had first set out from his folks' farm as a boy, the West had been a huge, relatively empty place, populated only by scattered bands of Indians and a handful of white fur trappers. At that time less than ten years had gone by since Lewis and Clark returned from their epic, history-changing journey up the Missouri River to the Pacific.

During the decades since then, Preacher had seen the West's population grow tremendously. Rail lines criss-crossed the country, and there were cities, towns, and settlements almost everywhere. Civilization had come to the frontier.

Much of the time, Preacher wasn't a hundred percent sure if that was a good thing or not.

But there was no taking it back, no returning things to the way they used to be, and besides, if not for the great westward expansion that had fundamentally changed the face of the nation, he never would have met the two fine young men he had come to consider his sons: Smoke and Matt Jensen.

It had been a while since Preacher had seen Smoke and Matt. He assumed that Smoke was down in Colorado, on his ranch called the Sugarloaf near the town of Big Rock. Once wrongly branded an outlaw, Smoke Jensen was perhaps the fastest man with a gun to ever walk the West. Most of the time he didn't go looking for trouble, but it seemed to find him anyway, despite all his best intentions to live a peaceful life on his ranch with his beautiful, spirited wife, Sally.

There was no telling where Matt was. He could be anywhere from the Rio Grande to the Canadian border. He and Smoke weren't brothers by blood. The bond between them was actually deeper than that. Matt had been born Matt Cavanaugh, but he had taken the name Jensen as a young man to honor Smoke, who had helped out an orphaned boy and molded him into a fine man.

Since Matt had set out on his own, he had been a drifter, scouting for the army, working as a stagecoach guard, pinning on a badge a few times as a lawman. . . . As long as it kept him on the move and held a promise of possible adventure, that was all it took to keep Matt interested in a job, at least for a while. But he never stayed in one place for very long, and at this point in his life he had no interest in putting down roots, as Smoke had done.

Because of that, Matt actually had more in common with Preacher than Smoke did, but all three of them were close. The problem was, whenever they got together trouble seemed to follow, and it usually wasn't long before the air had the smell of gunsmoke in it.

Right now the only smoke in Two Bears's lodge came from the small fire in the center of it and the pipe that Preacher and the Assiniboine chief passed back and forth. The two men were silent, their friendship not needing words all the time.

Two women were in the lodge as well, preparing a meal. They were Two Bears's wives, the former wives of his brothers he had taken in when the women were widowed, as a good brother was expected to do. The smells coming from the pot they had on the fire were mighty appetizing, Preacher thought. The stew was bound to be good.

A swift rataplan of hoofbeats came from outside and made both Preacher and Two Bears raise their heads. Neither man seemed alarmed. As seasoned veterans of the frontier, they had too much experience for that. But they also knew that whenever someone was moving fast, there was a chance it was because of trouble.

The sudden babble of voices that followed the abrupt halt of the hoofbeats seemed to indicate the same thing.

"You want to go see what that's about?" Preacher asked Two Bears, inclining his head toward the lodge's entrance.

Two Bears took another unhurried puff on the pipe in his hands before he set it aside.

"If my people wish to see me, they know where I am to be found," he said.

Preacher couldn't argue with that. But the sounds had gotten his curiosity stirred up, so he was glad when someone thrust aside the buffalo hide flap over the lodge's entrance. A broad-shouldered, powerful-looking warrior strode into the lodge, then stopped short at the sight of a white man sitting there cross-legged beside the fire with the chief.

"Two Bears, I must speak with you," the new-comer said.

"This is Standing Rock," Two Bears said to Preacher. "He is married to my daughter Wildflower."

That would make him the father of the little fella Preacher had seen with Wildflower earlier. He nodded and said, "Howdy, Standing Rock."

The warrior just looked annoyed, like he wasn't interested in introductions right now. He looked at the chief and began, "Two Bears—"

"Is there trouble?"

"Blue Bull has disappeared."

# Chapter Two

Blue Bull, it turned out, wasn't a bull at all, not that Preacher really thought he was. That was the name of one of the Assiniboine warriors who belonged to this band, and he and Standing Rock were good friends.

They had been out hunting in the hills west of the village and had split up when Blue Bull decided to follow the tracks of a small antelope herd while Standing Rock took another path. They had agreed to meet back at the spot where Blue Bull had taken up the antelope trail.

When Standing Rock returned there later, he saw no sign of Blue Bull. A couple of hours passed, and Blue Bull still didn't show up. Growing worried that something might have happened to his friend, Standing Rock went to look for him.

This part of the country was peaceful for the most part, but a man alone who ran into a mountain lion or a bear might be in for trouble. Also, ravines cut across the landscape in places, and if a pony shied at the wrong time, its rider could be tossed off and fall into one of those deep, rugged gullies.

"You were unable to find him?" Two Bears asked when his son-in-law paused in the story.

"The antelope tracks led into a narrow canyon, and so did Blue Bull's," Standing Rock replied. "The ground was rocky, and I lost the trail."

The young warrior wore a surly expression. Preacher figured that he didn't like admitting failure. Standing Rock was a proud man. You could tell that just by looking at him.

But he was genuinely worried about his friend, too. He proved that by saying, "I came back to get more men, so we can search for him. He may be hurt."

Two Bears nodded and got to his feet.

"Gather a dozen men," he ordered crisply. "We will ride in search of Blue Bull while there is still light."

Preacher stood up, too, and said, "I'll come with you."

"This is a matter for the Assiniboine," Standing Rock said, his voice stiff with dislike. Preacher didn't understand it, but the young fella definitely hadn't taken a shine to him. Just the opposite, in fact.

"Preacher is a friend to the Assiniboine and has been for more years than you have been walking this earth, Standing Rock," Two Bears snapped. "I would not ask him to involve himself in our trouble, but if he wishes to, I will not deny him."

"I just want to lend a hand if I can," Preacher said as he looked at Standing Rock. He didn't really care if the young man liked him or not. His friendship for Two Bears and for Two Bears's people was the only things that really mattered to him here.

Standing Rock didn't say anything else. He just stared back coldly at Preacher for a second, then turned and left the lodge to gather the search party as Two Bears had told him to.

The chief looked at Preacher and said, "The hot blood of young men sometimes overpowers what should be the coolness of their thoughts."

"That's fine with me, old friend. Like I said, I just want to help."

As they left the lodge, Preacher pointed to the big cur that had come with him to the village and went on, "Dog there is about as good a tracker as you're ever gonna find. When we get to the spot where Standin' Rock lost the trail, if you've got something that belonged to Blue Bull we can give Dog the scent and he's liable to lead us right to him."

Two Bears nodded.

"I will speak to Blue Bull's wife and make sure we take something of his with us."

Several of the warriors were getting ready to ride. That didn't take much preparation, considering that all they had to do was throw blankets over their ponies' backs and rig rope halters. Preacher had planned to spend a few days in the Assiniboine village, but he hadn't unsaddled Horse yet so the stallion was ready to go as well.

The news of Blue Bull's disappearance had gotten around the village. A lot of people were standing nearby with worried looks on their faces as the members of the search party mounted up. Two Bears went over to talk to one of the women, who hurried off to a lodge and came back with a buckskin shirt. She was Blue Bull's wife, Preacher figured, and the garment belonged to the missing warrior.

Two Bears swung up onto his pony with the lithe ease of a man considerably younger than he really was. He gave a curt nod, and the search party set out from the village with the chief, Standing Rock, and Preacher in the lead.

Standing Rock pointed out the route for them, and they lost no time in riding into the hills where the two warriors had been hunting. Preacher glanced at the sky and saw that they had about three hours of daylight left. He hoped that would be enough time to find Blue Bull.

Of course, it was possible that nothing bad had happened to Blue Bull at all, Preacher reflected. The warrior could have gotten carried away in pursuit of the antelope and lost track of the time. They might even run into him on his way back to the village. If that happened, Preacher would be glad that everything had turned out well.

Something was stirring in his guts, though, some instinctive warning that told him they might not be so lucky. Over the years Preacher had learned to trust those hunches. At this point, he wasn't going to say anything to Two Bears, Standing Rock, or the other Assiniboine, but he had a bad feeling about this search for Blue Bull.

Standing Rock pointed out the tracks of the antelope herd when the search party reached them.

"You can see they lead higher into the hills," he

said. "Blue Bull followed them while I went to the north. He wanted to bring one of the antelope back to the village."

"Why did you not go with him?" Two Bears asked. "Why did you go north?"

Standing Rock looked sullen again as he replied, "I know a valley up there where the antelope like to graze. I thought they might circle back to it."

Two Bears just nodded, but Preacher knew that his old friend was just as aware as he was of what had really happened here. Standing Rock had thought he could beat Blue Bull to the antelope by going a different way. Such rivalry was not uncommon among friends.

"Did you see the antelope?" Two Bears asked.

Standing Rock shook his head.

"No. My thought proved to be wrong."

Two Bears's silence in response was as meaningful and damning as anything he could have said. Standing Rock angrily jerked his pony into motion and trotted away, following the same path as the antelope had earlier.

Preacher, Two Bears, and the rest of the search party went the same way at a slower pace. Quietly, Two Bears said, "If anything happened to Blue Bull, Standing Rock will believe that it was his fault for not going with his friend."

"He wants to impress you, don't he?" Preacher said. "Must not be easy, bein' married to the chief's daughter."

"He is a good warrior, but he does not always know that."

Preacher nodded in understanding. He had always possessed confidence in himself and his abilities, and he had learned not to second-guess the decisions he made. But he had seen doubts consume other men from the inside until there was nothing left of them but empty shells.

Eventually Standing Rock settled down a little and slowed enough for the rest of the search party to catch up to him. The antelope herd had followed a twisting path into the hills, and so had Blue Bull as he trailed them. Preacher had no trouble picking out the unshod hoofprints of the warrior's pony.

The slopes became steeper, the landscape more rugged. In the distance, the snow-capped peaks of the Rocky Mountains loomed, starkly beautiful in the light from the lowering sun. They were dozens of miles away, even though they looked almost close enough to reach out and touch. Preacher knew that Blue Bull's trail wouldn't lead that far.

The tracks brought them to a long, jagged ridge that was split by a canyon cutting through it. Standing Rock reined his pony to a halt and pointed to the opening.

"That is where Blue Bull went," he said. "The tracks vanished on the rocks inside the canyon."

"Did you follow it to the other end?" Two Bears asked.

"I did. But the tracks of Blue Bull's pony did not come out."

"A man cannot go into a place and not come out of it, one way or another."

Standing Rock looked a little offended at Two

Bears for pointing that out, thought Preacher, but
he wasn't going to say anything. For one thing,
Two Bears was the chief, and for another, he was
Standing Rock's father-in-law.

"Let's have a look," Preacher suggested. "We can
give Dog a whiff of Blue Bull's shirt. He ought to be
able to tell us where the fella went."

The big cur had bounded along happily beside
Preacher and Horse during the search. He still had
the exuberance of youth, dashing off several times
to chase after small animals.

They rode on to the canyon entrance, where they
stopped to peer at the ground. The surface had
already gotten quite rocky, so the tracks weren't as
easy to see as they had been. But Preacher noticed
something immediately.

"Some of those antelope tracks are headed back
out of the canyon," he said to Two Bears. "The crit-
ters went in there, then turned around and came
out. They were in a hurry, too. Something must've
spooked 'em."

Standing Rock said, "There are many antelope
in these hills. Perhaps the tracks going the other
direction were made at another time."

Preacher swung down from the saddle and knelt
to take a closer look at the hoofprints. After a
moment of study, he shook his head.

"They look the same to me," he said. "I think they
were all made today, comin' and goin'."

He knew that wasn't going to make Standing
Rock like him any better, but he was going to tell
things the way he saw them to Two Bears. He had

always been honest with his old friend and saw n
need to change that policy now.

"What about the tracks of Blue Bull's pony?" Tw
Bears asked.

"He went on into the canyon," Preacher saic
"Can't see that he came back out, so I agree wit
Standin' Rock on that. The way it looks to me, Blu
Bull followed those antelope here and rode up i
time to see 'em come boltin' back out. He wa
curious and wanted to see what stampeded 'em lik
that. So he rode in to find out."

"It must have been a bear," Standing Rock saic
"Blue Bull would not have been so foolish."

"Blue Bull has always been curious," Two Bea
said. "I can imagine him doing as Preacher has said
He looked at the mountain man. "As you would sa
old friend, there is one way to find out."

"Yep," Preacher agreed. "Let Dog have Blue Bull'
scent. If there's anybody who can lead us right t
him, it's that big, shaggy varmint."

# THE EAGLES SERIES BY
# WILLIAM W. JOHNSTONE